"The perils in Arngrim should ... Maddoc said. "While they think we are helping them, they will, in fact, be helping us. They need never know our true purpose."

"And if the girl Nearra were to die during this new test?" asked Oddvar.

"Then," Maddoc said, "your life expectancy would be greatly reduced."

The wizard sat down again in his carved chair and leaned back. "With luck," he said, "the events we set in motion may cause Nearra to see things as they truly are." He smiled, his pearl-white teeth shining from beneath his salt-and-pepper beard. Maddoc's grin was every bit as wicked as Oddvar's.

Within the mirror, Oddvar bowed low and said, "As you wish, master."

THE NEW ADVENTURES

THE NEW
ADVENTURES
VOLUME
2

THE
DYING KINGDOM

STEPHEN D. SULLIVAN

COVER & INTERIOR ART
Vinod Rams

**MIRROR
STONE**

THE DYING KINGDOM
©2004 Wizards of the Coast, Inc.

Distributed in the United States by Holtzbrinck Publishing. Distributed in Canada by Fenn Ltd.

Distributed to the hobby, toy, and comic trade in the United States and Canada by regional distributors.

Distributed worldwide by Wizards of the Coast, Inc. and regional distributors.

Printed in the U.S.A.

Cover art by Vinod Rams
Cartography by Dennis Kauth
First Printing: July 2004
Library of Congress Catalog Card Number: 2004101146

9 8 7 6 5 4 3 2 1

US ISBN: 0-7869-3324-0
UK ISBN: 0-7869-3325-9
620-96596-001-EN

U.S., CANADA,
ASIA, PACIFIC, & LATIN AMERICA
Wizards of the Coast, Inc.
P.O. Box 707
Renton, WA 98057-0707
+1-800-324-6496

EUROPEAN HEADQUARTERS
Wizards of the Coast, Belgium
T Hofveld 6d
1702 Groot-Bijgaarden
Belgium
+322 457 3350

Visit our website at **www.mirrorstonebooks.com**

To Ed Henderson, the dear friend whom I've never actually met—for years of friendship, sage advice, wonders from exotic lands, and tireless manuscript reading. Here's one you haven't seen before publication. My undying thanks.

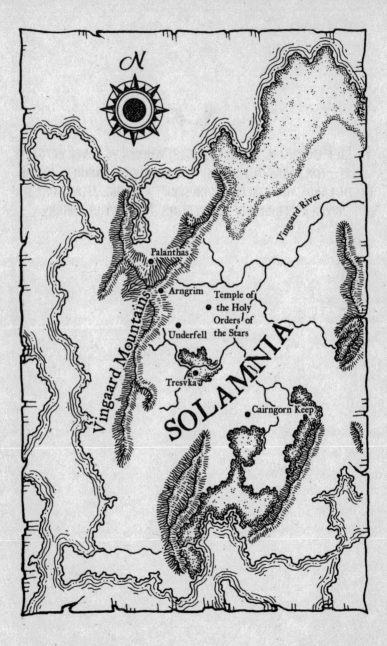

Contents

1   FOG AND THUNDER

"Are we lost?" Sindri Suncatcher asked. "I think we're lost."

"We're not lost," Davyn said, shooting the kender a nasty glance. The young ranger pulled himself atop a moss-covered boulder and looked about. Cold, clinging mist surrounded them, filling the valleys of the Vingaard Mountains. Davyn saw no sign of the path they were searching for.

"Not that I mind being lost," Sindri continued, scrambling up the rock. "My aunt Moonbeam was lost for the better part of thirty years once . . . "

"Why don't you do us all a favor and follow her example?" Elidor called up after the kender. Because the elf always spoke in light, pleasant tones, it was difficult to tell whether or not he was joking. He sat down on the trunk of a fallen pine tree and began cleaning his fingernails with his knife.

Catriona brushed some condensation from her hand-me-down armor. She lifted her head and peered up at the dark gray sky. "There's a storm brewing." She turned to Elidor. "Instead of needling Sindri, you might try contributing for a change. After all, you are supposed to be our guide."

Elidor shrugged. "I pretended to be your guide once. And, of course, I most sincerely regret the deception." He smiled and bobbed his head apologetically. "I knew just enough to stay one step ahead of the rest of you. Now that we're actually in the mountains . . ." He shrugged again. "Sorry."

"Don't worry," Nearra said. "I'm sure Davyn can keep us on track." The thin, pale teenager pushed a strand of blond hair out of her eyes. Then she sat down next to Elidor and adjusted the dagger at her waist. It was a weapon she'd borrowed from Catriona after losing her own, and she still didn't seem quite comfortable with it.

"Of course I can keep us on track," Davyn snapped. His words came out more harshly than he intended. In truth, the fog had him confused. He had expected they'd make it to Arngrim by now. He knew it lay in a hidden valley over the first ridges of the Vingaard Mountains. He knew they were close. But with the blasted fog, he couldn't tell just how close.

Ahead, the Vingaard peaks thrust through the clouds like a towering granite curtain. Tall evergreens clung to the lower slopes; snow reached white fingers down from the heights. Davyn and his four companions stood in the rocky zone along the mountain's midsection—caught between hostile worlds of forest and ice.

The ranger glanced down at the others. He smiled weakly.

Sindri clapped his hands. "We're lost! I knew it! What a great adventure!"

"We're not lost," Davyn repeated firmly. "Let me glance at that map for a moment, and I'll tell you exactly where we are."

Sindri reached into one of the many pockets in his purple cape and pulled out a battered roll of parchment.

Davyn snatched the scroll out of Sindri's hand. He didn't really need the parchment; he'd memorized it the first time he saw it. He was stalling for time, both to get his bearings and to decide what to do next. The world he knew well ended considerably to the east of here. In these wild lands, he had only his instincts and Sindri's tattered map to guide them.

"I heard somewhere that Arngrim is tricky to find," Sindri said. He poked his head around Davyn's waist, trying to catch a glimpse at the map. "Some scholars consider the kingdom to be entirely mythical. Others say Arngrim's just too small to mention on most maps."

Nearra said, "There are many tiny out-of-the-way fiefdoms in Ansalon." A chill ran down Davyn's spine. He lowered the parchment and stared down at her.

"Do you know something about Arngrim, Nearra?" Catriona asked. "Are your memories starting to return?"

Nearra's memory was almost a complete blank. She knew practical things: how to walk and talk and the names of places and things. She knew the country they were in was Solamnia and the continent they lived on was Ansalon. But her entire past remained a mystery.

To Nearra, life had begun just a short time ago when Davyn and the wizard Maddoc rescued her from a terrifying green dragon. Nearra didn't know who she was or what the dragon wanted from her but she was determined to find out. Davyn offered to help Nearra in her quest. Together, they met Catriona, Elidor, and Sindri. The warrior, the elf, and the kender had agreed to help, too.

But trouble dogged their journey. Maddoc proved to be an enemy disguised as a friend. The wizard had sent an ogre, a dark dwarf, goblins, and the green dragon to attack Nearra and her companions.

The friends had survived those trials, but it seemed no one could help the amnesiac girl. Then Sindri found the map scroll. The scroll's legend said that Nearra's cure might lie in the hands of the Scarlet Brethren, a secretive group of wizards who lived in Arngrim.

"Well . . . ?" Davyn asked, fearing Nearra's answer. "Do you remember something?"

The pretty teen clenched her eyes shut, and ran her fingers

through her damp hair. She concentrated for a few moments, then slowly shook her head.

"No," she sighed. "There's nothing. I don't know why I said that." She drew her cloak tighter around her slender body and shuddered. "Why is it so cold here?" she asked. "What happened to summer?"

"The mountains are always cooler than the countryside surrounding them," Elidor said. "The higher you go, the colder they get."

"That's true," Davyn said, hopping down from the boulder. "But Nearra's right. It should be warmer at this time of year." He pulled his own cloak up over his shoulders.

Catriona gazed into the fogbound distance. "The mountains have hemmed in this chilly mist and trapped us as well." She turned and looked sternly at Davyn.

He knew that she didn't trust him. And could he blame her?

"We're not trapped," Davyn said sharply. "We're just getting our bearings." But it was a lie.

Davyn still hadn't told his friends the truth about his own identity. And though he had broken away from his father, he had not entirely escaped Maddoc's grasp. Davyn knew something none of the others knew: Maddoc had planted the map they followed. Why did the wizard want them to head for Arngrim? Was it part of Maddoc's plot to trigger the Emergence in Nearra? Davyn had no idea.

He longed to tell his friends what he knew of Maddoc's plans. But he knew he couldn't reveal his father's plot without betraying his part in it. His only hope was to protect them as best he could. Catriona had been right; they were trapped. At least he was.

Sindri closed his eyes and turned in a circle, pointing as he went. The silver ring on the middle finger of his right hand glinted dimly in the fading light. For a moment, it looked as though the magician might topple off the cliff face and fall down the mountainside.

"My magic tells me that we are very close to the city of Arngrim now," he announced. "I'll be able to tell us exactly which way to go shortly." He kept spinning.

"Quit it, Sindri," Catriona said.

"But my magic. . . " the kender began.

Davyn felt another stab of guilt. The kender was a magician only in his own mind. What magic he possessed—the ability to move objects telekinetically—came from a ring that once belonged to Davyn. Maddoc had given Davyn the ring. But when Davyn decided to defy his father, he had discarded it where Sindri would easily discover it. The kender had been performing spells ever since.

Catriona locked eyes with Davyn. "If you're unsure of the way," she said, "perhaps I should lead for a while."

Elidor stood and stretched. "I suppose it's too late to turn back?" he said.

Nearra looked at him, crestfallen.

"Yes," the elf grumbled. "I suppose it is."

"Look," Davyn snapped, "that storm isn't going to wait forever. If you'd all just stop babbling, maybe I can figure this out."

Davyn pretended to consult the map scroll, all the while trying to pick landmarks out of the fog. The mist parted slightly, and the ranger spotted the prominence he'd been looking for.

"There," he announced, trying not to sound too relieved. "We'll pass through that narrow gorge and, if Sindri's map is right, a trail on the other side should lead us to Arngrim."

Catriona looked at Davyn, skeptically. "Well, if our ranger's sure that's the way," she said. "Let's go before the storm catches us." She shouldered her traveler's pack and headed for the pass, as thunder rumbled behind her. The rest of them followed.

Davyn watched Catriona as she forged ahead. He wished he shared her will and sense of purpose. Catriona had vowed to protect Sindri and Nearra, and she'd stuck steadfastly to her promises. She never wavered, never complained. Despite her incomplete Solamnic training, she seemed the perfect knight.

As they passed through the gorge, it began to rain. The cold droplets inched their way through the companions' clothing and onto their skin. The countryside leveled out on the other side. Low boulders jutted out of the ground at awkward angles. Scrub pine trees clung to the slope like spiny animals. The air reeked of fog and distant lightning.

"Where's the path?" Elidor asked.

"I see it," Catriona called from the front of the group. She nodded at Davyn. "Good work."

"Hey, what about me?" Sindri asked. "It's my map, after all."

"Well, your successes go without saying," Elidor replied. "We just expect them of you."

Sindri grinned, missing the sarcastic twinkle in the elf's eyes.

"The storm's about to hit hard," Catriona said. "We need to find some shelter before this rain freezes us. It'll only get colder once darkness falls."

Davyn looked around, but saw little through the fog. "Let's keep going," he said. "There's nothing for us here—not even a rock over-hang. We'll have to find something along the way."

As darkness crept in around them, driving rain and biting sleet poured down on their heads. Their damp, uncomfortable clothing quickly became sopping wet. Soon, the entire group was shivering. Lightning crashed, casting strange and menacing shadows all around them. The rain did nothing to disperse the clinging fog.

"What's that?" Nearra asked. She left the path and stumbled toward a hulking shape in the mist. They all sprinted after her.

"Thank the gods. It's some kind of building," Nearra said. "But it's a mess."

The structure might once have been a farmhouse, but its best days had long since passed. The timbers supporting the roof were blackened from fire. Holes riddled the walls. The door hung on its hinges, barely clinging to the doorframe.

Davyn put his shoulder to the door, and shoved it open. They all crowded inside the entry hall.

"At least it's dry," Catriona said, casting off her sodden cloak. "I'll light a torch."

Thankfully, Catriona's traveling pack had kept her torches dry. After a few strikes with flint and steel, one blazed to life. Catriona set a second torch alight and handed it to Davyn. "You all stay here," she said, "I'm going to have a look around."

"I'm coming with you," said Davyn, passing the torch to Elidor. Catriona rolled her eyes but she didn't object.

"See if you can find a fireplace," Sindri called after them.

"Right," Elidor said, "we wouldn't want to burn this 'mansion' down when we build a fire."

The building had once been two stories tall, but its second floor had collapsed. Rubble filled the structure's central stairway. Davyn and Catriona exchanged a worried look, then edged around the rubble into the adjoining room.

They entered a large chamber. A wide stone fireplace—big enough to cook a whole pig inside—took up most of one wall. Long, cracked timbers spanned the room's plaster ceiling. Several of these beams had snapped and crashed down to the floor. Others hung half-broken from the ceiling.

The far side of the room had once been a wall of windows, but the wall had collapsed, leaving a tangled jumble of wood and plaster. Mist peeked through the cracks in the rubble.

Next to the wall crouched a shadowy shape. As Davyn and Catriona came closer, the figure turned. The light from Catriona's torch cast long shadows across the thing's lion-like face. Its eyes blazed red in the darkness.

With an incoherent snarl, the beast charged.

2 Battle in the Dark

Davyn stepped back as the beast surged forward. The young ranger tripped over a mound of plaster and his feet went out from under him. He landed with a crash on the rotting floor.

Catriona stood frozen in shock. This monster would be her doom; she could sense it. She'd watched her aunt die, and now she would die, too. Her eyes darted right and left, seeking an avenue of escape.

She considered leaping over Davyn and fleeing the crumbling house. What then, though? Leave the others to their fate at the creature's hands? Isn't that exactly what she'd done when her aunt needed her? Was it better to be a live coward than a dead hero?

The thing barreled across the room, leaving Catriona no time to decide. Though its face looked like a lion's, the creature ran upright, and as quickly as any man. Torchlight gleamed off its strange, metallic skin. Its eyes glittered blood red. In one hand, it clenched a rune-carved long sword. As it closed in, Catriona tossed her torch into the fireplace and drew her sword.

She struck high, but the beast blocked her blow. It slashed at her chest, but Catriona caught its sword against her blade. The darkness and flickering shadows made it nearly impossible for her to see.

Catriona backed into one of the hanging timbers. Her heel caught against the wood, and she stumbled slightly. The beast swung hard, aiming for her head. Catriona ducked at the last instant. Her opponent's rune-carved sword passed over her helmet. The weapon bit into the beam behind her and stuck.

Catriona thrust at the thing's chest. The lion-man twisted sideways, and her sword point traced across its scaly chest with a hollow scraping sound. The cut caused no harm. Her blow had failed to penetrate the creature's metallic hide. The thing stepped away and punched her on the side of the head.

The beast's fist felt like iron. Lights burst behind Catriona's eyes. The creature pulled its sword free of the wooden post.

Catriona staggered away, putting several fallen beams between her and the lion-man—trying to buy time to recover. Fortunately, the monster seemed uninterested in Davyn, who lay stunned near the entryway to the room.

The beast prowled forward. The guttering light from the fireplace danced across its lion-face, making it seem an abomination from the Abyss.

Catriona took a deep breath and shook her head to clear it. The monster lunged again, striking hard with its sword. Catriona blocked him, but the impact sent a shudder through her muscular body. The thing was strong—too strong. Catriona was bone-weary from her long travels. If she couldn't come up with a good counter-attack, the beast would surely overwhelm her.

Across the room, Davyn regained his wits and scrambled toward the fireplace. "I'll get the torch," he called. "Maybe fire will stop it."

"Keep back," Catriona ordered. "I'll handle this beast!" Fear for Davyn's life fought within her against fear for herself.

The creature cackled, its tones coarse and guttural.

It charged again, swinging its sword to cut Catriona's armored skull in half. She stepped behind another beam and the sword missed. She stabbed at the monster again. This time, the point of her sword struck its breast before rebounding with a dull clank. The thing reeled back, but did not fall.

Sweat poured down Catriona's forehead and into her eyes. What did it take to kill this monster? Was its hide completely impervious to her weapon? She glanced at Davyn, standing warily near the door to the room. Could they both escape before it recovered?

As if in answer, the lion-man charged again. Catriona clenched her teeth and raised her sword defiantly.

The beast cut high, then low. The red-haired warrior blocked the blows, her sword shuddering with each impact. She realized that she couldn't survive by defending herself. Her only chance was to go on the offensive.

The next time the monster attacked, she surged forward. She swung with all her might, inching forward with each parry and countercut. Step by step, she forced her attacker back toward the far side of the room. If she could keep it up, perhaps her friends could help her defeat the beast. She called over her shoulder to Davyn, "Get the oth—"

A powerful thrust from the lion-man cut her sentence short. The beast's blade skidded off the chainmail on Catriona's shoulder, barely missing her neck.

Davyn drew his bow.

The lion-man's shimmering black-and-silver hide became nearly invisible in the flickering darkness. The creature seemed to disappear into the shadows, only to reappear moments later, ready to strike.

Catriona kept pushing forward, feeling the ache within her muscles building with each moment. She screamed an anguished war cry, swinging ever more savagely.

The monster merely growled a low chuckle.

"I can't get a clear shot!" Davyn shouted.

"Blast it, Davyn!" Catriona cried. "Get out of here! Get the others to safety!" Sweat poured from her brow. Unbearable weariness filled her body. The lion-man swung for her head. Catriona ducked and leaped forward.

She planted her shoulder into the creature's gut and pushed it back, heading for the crumbling wall.

The monster felt surprisingly light as Catriona tackled it. Though its outsides were metal, its guts must have been made of less stern stuff. Nonetheless, her shoulder still ached from the impact.

Hitting the wall magnified her pain. They crashed into the beams and plaster with a bone-shaking thud. Then the wall gave way and they fell through it into the fogbound darkness beyond.

Catriona hit the cold, muddy ground, and her breath rushed out. The two of them lay tangled in the mire. The thing twisted, trying to slash her with its sword. Catriona punched at its face and her fingers scraped across the lion-man's fangs.

She yelped and jumped to her feet. The creature rose to face her. A long, ebony mane fell in damp strands around the monster's wide shoulders. Its wild eyes glittered. It splashed through the mud and chopped at her once more.

Catriona barely brought up her blade in time. The crash of metal sent a shock down her arm. A fine spray of water flew off the swords and splashed into her eyes. Catriona blinked and backed up, just avoiding a deadly cut aimed at her midsection.

The old fear rose up in her gut. Would this be the day she died? She gritted her teeth and turned a parry into a series of vicious countercuts. The lion-man backpedaled before her assault, but seemed undaunted by the fierceness of the young warrior's attack.

Worse still, the creature didn't appear to be tiring. Catriona's breath heaved out in great clouds, whiter than the clinging fog. Rain drummed against her body, seeping through the cracks of her armor, chilling her muscles and bones. From the creature, she saw nothing—not panting breath, not slowing attacks, not the slightest sign of fear. It was a deadly wraith dancing through the mist. The creature held her life in its hands.

While squiring for her aunt, Catriona had heard tales of knights without fear who lived for the moment of battle. These warriors cared nothing for their own deaths, but worked tirelessly toward their goals. In her dreams, Catriona had aspired to someday be such a knight. Her failure during the fight where her aunt died had dashed such hopes from her mind.

She was a coward. Deep in her soul, Catriona knew that. It was the secret she feared most. Now, as her assault wavered, she felt cold cowardice in the pit of her stomach. The lion-man possessed no such fear.

The beast cut high and her parry came up too late. The lion-man's sword traced a cut across Catriona's left shoulder. Steam leaked from the wound into the sleet-tossed air. Blood dribbled down her arm.

Catriona screamed in pain and anguish. She slashed again and again, using what little strength remained in her.

Images flashed through Catriona's exhausted mind: Elidor, Davyn, Sindri, and Nearra. How could she let them down? They would be no match for this berserker. Elidor's knives would bounce off its iron hide, as would Davyn's arrows. Sindri's magic, erratic at best, would not save the kender's life. And Nearra . . . her memories lost, she was little more than a newborn babe. She could not protect herself, which was why Catriona had promised to protect her.

Was this how she fulfilled her vows, by giving up before an iron-willed monster? By lying down in the mud and letting her friends die? But how could she go on? Already, her sword felt like lead in her hands. If only she could last just a little longer! Catriona prayed to Paladine for the strength to continue fighting.

Catriona's boot slipped in the mire. She toppled backwards. Her weary fingers lost their grip on her sword. The weapon splashed into the mud several yards away. The beast lunged forward, aiming its sword at the hollow of Catriona's neck, between her armor and her chin.

Heart pounding in her chest, she kicked at the monster. Her foot caught its ankles, and it slipped sideways. The creature's sword flew out of its hand, barely missing the side of her head. The weapon skidded across the mud and disappeared into the fog.

Catriona rolled to her right and grabbed the beast as it fell. Her opponent clattered into the mud, its black fur lashing at her face as they tumbled. Its dark eyes burned with hatred.

Catriona lurched forward, slamming her helmet into the thing's forehead with a resounding clank. It blinked, momentarily dazed. A trickle of blood leaked out from near its eye.

The thing roared and lunged at her. Its fangs reached for her eyes. Catriona leaned away from it but kept her grip tight. She squeezed with all her might, trying to keep the thing's arms pinned at its sides.

The mud seeped through her clothes. Her foe bucked and kicked. Catriona felt the last of her strength ebbing away. Mud splashed up in her face and momentarily blinded her.

As she blinked, the lion-man wriggled free.

Its arm snaked around her neck. Catriona grabbed its wrist with both hands, but she couldn't break the beast's grip. Though the rain had washed most of the mud from her eyes, she was still half-blind. She heard the soft hiss of a dagger being drawn from a sheath at the creature's waist.

Lightning flashed and thunder shook the rain-clogged air. Catriona gasped and water sprayed from her lips. Should she beg for mercy? Should she abandon—again—all her high ideals?

No. Better to die silently. Better, still if she had died fighting at her aunt's side, months ago.

The lion-man's guttural voice boomed above the thunder of the storm. "This is the end of you, renegade!"

CHAPTER

3 THE YOUNG PRINCE

Catriona felt the press of the beast's dagger against her throat.

"The touch of your kind will never sully me again!" the lion-man hissed in her ear.

She prepared to die.

"Stop!" cried a voice, cutting through the sound of the crashing rain.

Catriona blinked away the last of the mud and saw Davyn, his bow drawn, standing near the hole in the farmhouse wall. He aimed his weapon at the lion-man. "Stop," Davyn called, "or, by the gods, I'll put this arrow through your eye!"

"And should the ranger miss, rest assured, I won't," Elidor added. The elf appeared out of the fog on the other side of Catriona. In each hand, he held a slender knife, ready to throw.

"I'll never surrender," the lion-man hissed. Catriona prepared to feel its blade slicing her flesh.

Before it could kill her, the dagger flew out of the lion-man's hand.

"I did it!" Sindri cried. "I did it!" The kender jumped up and down enthusiastically, as though he weren't in the middle of a freezing rainstorm.

Heaving with all her remaining strength, Catriona broke the monster's grip and rolled free. Her hand found her sword in the mud. Seizing the weapon, she rose to her feet and leveled it at the creature's metal-scaled throat.

Her foe remained kneeling. Catriona and the others had him surrounded, but she still didn't feel confident that they could defeat him. Her heart pounded in her chest.

The rain washed the beast's dark mane into its eyes. Not glowing red eyes, as Catriona had first perceived, but eyes that looked almost . . . human.

Icy rivulets cascaded down the beast's sleek, silver-and-black coat. Even so close, shadows and fog seemed to surround him. Catriona feared that at any moment it might vanish, appear behind her, and plunge its blade into her back. She felt vaguely sick to her stomach, but she held her sword steady.

"Kill me if you can," the lion-man said in a low, hoarse voice. "The last of the Arngrims won't beg for mercy."

"Arngrim!" Nearra gasped. She stepped out from behind Davyn, holding a sputtering torch in her hand. "Don't kill him! Please! Maybe he can help us."

"We won't kill it," Catriona said, through clenched teeth. "A knight doesn't slay a captured foe, even when that beast has tried to murder her."

"So Kokar's bandits now permit renegade knights among their ranks?" the man asked bitterly. "How far the Solamnics have fallen."

"Excuse me," Sindri said. "But you're mistaken, sir. We're not bandits, in fact, we—"

"Quiet, Sindri," Davyn said coldly. He kept his bowshot aimed between the stranger's dark eyes.

"No, Davyn, Sindri's right," Nearra said. "Can't you see? This knight has mistaken us for someone else."

Knight! The word sent an electric shock through Catriona's nervous system. This was no knight; it was a metal-scaled monster!

How could Nearra make such a mistake? Was the beast controlling her somehow?

Nearra stepped toward the armored creature, holding out the torch to get a better look at it.

"Nearra, stay back!" Catriona warned. A stab of fear—both for her friend's safety and her own—shot through her gut. "That monster almost killed me!"

"Can't you see?" Nearra said. "This is no monster, it's a man—a man who's afraid, just like us." She walked toward the stranger, her blue eyes twinkling in the light of her torch. "We're not your enemies, sir. We're merely lost travelers seeking shelter from the storm. Please, get up."

Catriona was about to bark an order to the contrary, but the cry caught in her throat. The light of Nearra's torch revealed the truth. What Catriona had seen as a metal-scaled beast was, in fact, an armored man. Black hair tumbled, mane-like, from beneath his silver-black helmet. His dark eyes glistened in the torchlight.

"All right," Davyn said. "He can get up. Slowly."

The stranger rose, some of the tension slipping from his armored frame. His shoulders straightened, and he held his head erect. He brushed his long, wet hair out of his eyes. "You don't look like brigands," he said tentatively.

"I told you we're not thieves," Sindri chimed. "Though Elidor has borrowed a few things now and again. Oh, and items have been known to appear in my pockets occasionally but that's just the way my magic works. I'm good at finding things when people need them. I'm Sindri Suncatcher, wizard extraordinaire, by the way." The kender strolled forward and extended his hand to the stranger.

"A kender wizard," the armored man murmured, almost to himself. "I've never heard of such a thing. Of course I haven't seen a kender in so long. I wasn't sure they still existed."

"I assure you I exist," Sindri said. "I haven't perfected any illusions, yet. Though I am working on some."

The man took Sindri's small hand and shook it. "I'm Alric Arngrim," he said. "And I'd very much like to get out of this accursed rain."

Inside they built a roaring blaze in the old fireplace. Then they wrung out their cloaks and sat around the flames, huddling close and trying to regain the warmth the storm had stolen from them. By the light of the crackling fire, Alric Arngrim looked considerably less menacing.

As he removed his lion-headed helmet, Catriona saw now that he was not the savage beast she had mistaken him for. His black-and-silver armor had made Alric seem shadowy and mysterious. The scale mail and animal motifs beaten into the armor's surface added to that illusion.

This man was no monster. His face was careworn, though he did not look old. His dark black hair fell lightly over his wide shoulders. A square, proud chin lay beneath his stubbly beard. Seen clearly, Alric could never be mistaken for even a common ruffian. He moved and carried himself with regal grace.

Catriona silently upbraided herself. She'd been such a fool! She'd been so scared that she hadn't even recognized Alric for a man. She'd been so convinced he was an unstoppable monster. She felt like a complete idiot. She hoped that none of the others could guess her mistake—or the cowardice that had led to it.

Alric gazed back at her, his face world-weary and kind.

"I'm sorry that I nearly killed you," he said. "Desperation brought a savagery to my actions. Had I been thinking more clearly, I would have realized you were not part of Kokar's band. You're all too young and fresh, too inexperienced. War has not destroyed you as it has the renegade chief's people . . ." He took a long, slow breath. "Or mine."

"I . . . I acted rashly as well," Catriona said, turning her eyes toward the floor. "I should have thought first and attacked later."

Alric shook his head. "You were only trying to protect your friends. It was a very brave thing to do."

Catriona nodded, but said nothing. She didn't feel brave inside; she felt like an imposter in knight's armor.

"Who's Kokar?" Sindri asked.

"Kokar is the leader of a band of renegades who roam Arngrim's hinterlands," Alric said. "His bandits have assaulted the borders of our kingdom since the end of the recent war. I believe they are deserters from some regiment of the dragonarmy. They've killed our people, destroyed our homes, and looted every outlying settlement they could find. Arngrim's borders are no longer safe, I'm afraid."

"Arngrim's borders?" Nearra asked. "I thought Arngrim was a city." She leaned her elbows on her knees and looked at Alric with rapt attention. Beside her, Davyn folded his arms skeptically.

"A city kingdom," Alric corrected. "Our holdings are small. And, with Kokar on the loose, they're growing smaller by the day. That's why I rode from the castle to the borderlands—in an attempt to lead the peasants living high in the mountains to safety."

"You rode here alone?" Elidor asked. He arched one blond eyebrow. "That's a funny thing for a young knight to do."

Alric took a deep breath and looked at each companion in turn, as though trying to see into their souls. "As prince," he said, "it is my duty to protect the kingdom and its people."

Prince! The word echoed in Catriona's mind. She'd been so frightened, she'd attacked the prince of the very land they were trying to reach! What a fool she'd been!

"So, you protect this kingdom by yourself?" Davyn asked, pressing Elidor's question.

Alric gazed out from beneath his dark brows at the young ranger. "At first, I was not alone," the prince replied. "A small group of retainers rode with me. Kokar took us unaware and killed my companions. I was lucky to escape. For days I've fled across the mountain wastes. When the storm came, I took shelter here. I thought I was safe, but then I heard you and . . . "

"You mistook us for Kokar's men, as we mistook you for a monster," Catriona said, sympathetically.

Alric nodded. "Yes, I can hardly blame you," he said. "Many times, recently, I've felt like a monster on the run."

Catriona nodded, biting the inside of her own lip to keep her composure. Clearly, beneath Alric's steel armor beat the heart of a caring man. Given her own experience, she could imagine the pain Alric felt at the loss of his comrades.

"Well, that lion armor looked pretty menacing in dark," Sindri said.

"I'll try not to scare you again, little one," Alric said. The corners of his thin lips tugged into a subtle smile.

"Oh, I didn't think you were scary," Sindri said, "just menacing. Something can menace a person without scaring him. At least, I think that's how it must be. I've been menaced several times, but I don't remember ever being scared. Once, in Solanthus, the purse of Olgor the Large materialized in my pocket. Olgor was a merchant as big as—"

"Kender lack both a sense of fear," Elidor said, "and a sense of when to shut up." The elf smiled at Sindri.

The kender shrugged. "I guess I'll finish that story later."

Nearra put her hands close to the fireplace and wiggled her slender fingers. "Well, whether Sindri was scared or not, the rest of us were plenty frightened," she said. "At least I was. I was more scared that Catriona might get hurt than frightened of you, Alric."

"It's a brave person who puts defending her comrades above fear for her own safety," Alric said. He looked pointedly at Catriona.

Catriona felt her face redden and she turned away.

"We're fortunate we found you," Nearra continued. "We came

over this spur of the mountains looking for Arngrim. But we weren't sure exactly where to find it."

"Oh, *I* knew where to find it," Sindri chimed. "It's right here on the map—" Davyn elbowed him in the gut and the kender paused long enough to catch his breath.

"We were having some difficulty in the fog," Elidor explained.

"You were looking for Arngrim?" Alric asked. "Why?"

"Nearra has lost most of her memory," Davyn said. "We were told that a sect of rogue wizards who live in Arngrim might be able to help."

"They're called the Scarlet Brethren," Nearra added.

"Actually," Sindri said, "we don't even know if they exist for sure. I've done a lot of reading on wizards, but I've never come across any mention of this group."

"Oh, they exist," Alric said.

"They do?" Nearra said, her soaring heart plainly visible on her face.

Alric nodded and gazed into the fire. "Yes. They've served my family for many years. They're the court wizards of the Arngrim family."

"That's great news," Sindri blurted. "Do you think they'll be able to help? I've tried to restore Nearra's memory, of course, but my magic is much better suited to finding stuff or moving things with my mind."

"So I noticed," Alric said, resting his hand on the pommel of his sheathed dagger. Sindri smiled and Alric continued. "The Brethren are quite powerful. But they haven't been able to end the . . . troubles plaguing our kingdom. Perhaps they could assist you though, Nearra."

Nearra stood, her blond hair shimmering in the firelight. "Let's go, then. Let's leave right now."

"Are you out of your mind?" Davyn snapped. Then realizing he'd chosen his words poorly, he added, "Sorry, Nearra. That's not what I meant. It's just the rain and the fog and . . . Well, it would be dangerous to go back out into the storm. And we're all tired, to boot."

"Your friend is right, Nearra," Alric said. "Arngrim is a good distance away. It's much too far to travel in this kind of weather, especially at night. Kokar and his renegades are still lurking in the area. If they caught us in the darkness, we'd stand no chance at all."

Nearra bowed her head and sat back down. "I'm sorry," she said. "I get carried away sometimes. None of you can know how difficult it is to live with so many years missing from your life."

They all sat silently around the fire for a moment before Davyn finally spoke.

"You're right," he said, looking almost unbearably sad. "None of us can really understand what you're going through."

Catriona nodded, while secretly wishing there were some parts of her life that she could forget.

"We should get some sleep," Alric suggested. "It's late, and dawn comes early during the summer—even in the mountains."

"Even if the weather hardly seems like summer," Elidor added.

"Indeed," Alric said. "Some day all this strife will end, and summer will return to Arngrim."

They chose three rooms to sleep in, one for the men, one for the women, and one for Alric, who didn't seem comfortable sleeping with the rest. It was just as well. Despite his kind words and gentle demeanor, Catriona and the others didn't quite trust him yet.

Catriona felt slightly guilty about her suspicions. He's the knight I should have been, she thought. The warrior turned on her side, away from Nearra, and pulled her bedroll up to her cheeks. She didn't want anyone to see her cry.

Davyn watched as a black falcon soared above him. He heard the ebony bird calling him, insisting Davyn betray his friends once again.

Davyn opened his eyes with a start. Sweat covered his body, soaking through his clothes. Despite his discomfort, Davyn didn't move. Instead, he looked cautiously around the darkened room with his eyes. He scanned the fallen timbers, the decaying plaster, and the flicker of firelight from the nearby room where Nearra and Catriona slept. On the far side of the room lay two bundles of blankets—the larger, Elidor, the smaller, Sindri.

He let out a long breath. Just a nightmare, he thought.

Davyn lay back down and tried to settle in. But he couldn't stop the thoughts racing through his head.

Was their meeting with Alric as coincidental as it appeared? It seemed a stroke of good chance to run into a prince from the very city they were seeking.

Had it been fortune that brought them to this crumbling building—or was it something more sinister? Davyn suspected the meeting had less to do with fate than with Maddoc's schemes.

The young ranger had seen no sign of the wizard's flunkies, or of Maddoc's black falcon, except in his nightmare. That didn't mean that Maddoc was out of the picture, though. Davyn knew that his father could be subtle in his machinations. Maddoc was surely watching them even now.

Perhaps, he hoped to lure Davyn back into his cadre of spies. Davyn, of course, had no intention of doing his father's bidding any longer. He didn't trust Maddoc. He knew the wizard would stop at nothing to bring about the Emergence in Nearra.

So far, Maddoc's plan had been a failure. But Davyn knew the wizard would never give up until he had reached his goal. His father appeared to have no concern that his plans might injure or kill anyone else.

Many times on their journey, Davyn had nearly confessed his part in Maddoc's schemes and shared his worries with his friends.

But every time he thought he might blurt out the truth, he imagined how his friends would react. Nearra, Sindri, Elidor, Catriona: they were the only friends he'd ever known. If he told them that Maddoc was his father, that friendship would shatter. They would never be able to trust him again. Would they even believe that he'd thrown off Maddoc's influence? No. They would hate him.

Davyn thought of the genuine warmth in the way that Nearra smiled at him. He felt like a traitor. How could he tell her—or any of the rest—the truth? After all the wizard had put them through, it was best that none of them should ever know his secret. He would still honor Maddoc, as a son should, but he would not take further part in the wizard's schemes.

The young ranger turned over and squeezed his eyes shut.

A faint noise drifted to him through the darkness.

What was that sound?

Was he dreaming again?

The sound came again: footfalls moving stealthily through the dilapidated house. They were quiet, but Davyn still detected the faint scrabbling among the wreckage.

Someone was in the house.

4 THE WIZARD'S PAWNS

In a tower very far away from the sleet-battered hovel where his son slept, the wizard Maddoc sat in front of a blazing fire and sipped a glass of the finest Solamnic brandy. Maddoc lounged casually in a chair so large that it almost seemed a throne. The seat was padded with soft, comfortable leather.

He amused himself by gazing at the writhing naked figures decorating the chair's wooden limbs. He wondered what the chair's original owner had thought of the decorations. Maddoc wondered a lot about the previous owner of the chair. Finding out about her was his consuming passion. He obtained his tower because it once belonged to her. The chair had come with the building. Maddoc relished his hand-me-downs from the powerful, long-dead sorceress.

He rubbed his fingers absently over one of the carved figures on the armrest. Seeing him toying with the chair, one might have assumed Maddoc was amused. He wasn't, though—far from it. Tracing the carvings was all that kept him from killing someone. Maddoc didn't want to kill anyone, at least not yet.

The wizard's intense blue eyes glared out from beneath his thick eyebrows as he regarded an image in the mirror next to him.

The face floating on the enchanted surface flickered and wavered, often blurring to indistinctness.

"Concentrate," Maddoc commanded.

"Your forgiveness, master," a voice said. "There are several distractions at this end. Shall I dispose of them?" The face solidified into the waxy visage of Oddvar, Maddoc's dark dwarf servant.

"It's cold," rasped a voice from nearby. "When do we get out of this miserable sleet?"

"I don't know how that bird of Maddoc's stands it," another voice shouted. "Doesn't the fog get under its feathers?"

Maddoc frowned and rolled the stem of the brandy snifter between his fingers. His voice was deep and ruthless when he replied. "If the goblins do not shut up, Oddvar," he said, "you are free to kill them. We'll find others to assist with our tasks."

The chatter within the mirror suddenly went silent. Only the howl of the wind and Oddvar's rasping whisper remained. "Thank you, master," the dark dwarf said. His parchment-colored face wrinkled into a wicked smile. He glanced hungrily at the three goblins standing beside him, before looking at Maddoc once more.

"We have followed your instructions, master," Oddvar said. "We have trailed your son and the other youngsters through the mountains, being careful to stay well out of sight."

"They do not suspect you are watching them?" Maddoc asked.

"Your son?" the Theiwar dwarf asked. "Who knows? Perhaps. The boy is quite perceptive at times. The rest walk around with their eyes blinkered. They're so wrapped in their own petty problems that they have no idea of our presence."

"Keep it that way," Maddoc said. "Revealing our forces at the Temple of the Holy Orders of the Stars was, in retrospect, a mistake. Davyn will be more watchful, even if no one else is. Keep your distance—and see that your friends do as well."

Oddvar flashed his smile again. "It will be my pleasure, master," he replied.

"Don't kill your underlings unnecessarily, though," Maddoc said. Sometimes, the Theiwar's bloodlust could get the better of his judgment. "A trail of bodies could tip our hand just as easily as a false move."

"Don't worry," Oddvar said. "There won't be any bodies." A small yelp came from beyond the image in the mirror.

"What about the youngsters?" Oddvar asked. "Shall we pick one or two of them off if the opportunity arises?"

"No," Maddoc said. "Let us see how this plays out. Perhaps Nearra's concern for her friends' lives may spur on the Emergence. It's not as direct as threatening her alone, but . . . " He paused and rearranged the folds of his black robe where it draped over his chair.

"Perhaps just one, then," Oddvar suggested, "to gauge the girl's reaction."

"No," Maddoc commanded. "Slaying this band of whelps too soon would be a waste. In time, Nearra will grow more attached to them. As she does, she will worry more for their safety. The more worried she becomes, the more tempted she will be to succumb to the power of the Emergence. Subtle threats may be as good as overt ones in this case, and indirect menaces as useful as action against Nearra herself. We will bide our time and see how things go . . . for the time being. Now, tell me the situation."

"The five of them are camped in a ruined house, sheltering from the rainstorm," Oddvar said. He wiped the water off his face, as if to make the point, but did not look discomforted. "When they entered, they met a young knight. They fought him—or, at least the red-head did. We could not get too close without revealing our presence. The brawl began in the house and then spilled outside. Nearra did not involve herself much. In the end, the whole group reached some kind of a truce. Then all six went back into the hovel together. They have not come out since."

"The knight wore armor in the shape of a lion," one of the goblins said.

Maddoc raised his bushy eyebrows. "Really?"

"Yes," Oddvar said. "Firelight flickers from within the home's broken windows. I could send one of the goblins to spy through the wall's cracks if you like."

Maddoc rose from his chair and paced in front of the broad hearth. "No," he said. "Keep your distance unless you suspect the Emergence is in progress. I hadn't expected Davyn and his friends to meet this knight so soon, but it could play nicely into our hands. The troubles they encounter in his presence should be a good test for Nearra." The wizard rubbed his long-fingered hands together. "Oddvar, I have a new mission for you."

"What about these three?" the dwarf asked.

"Have them trail the youngsters while you are away," Maddoc replied. "After that, send them to Tezrat Junction. While you are busy with the lost city, they can make ready the next stages of my plan—should those stages become necessary."

Oddvar turned his head from side to side, looking at the goblins out of Maddoc's view on either side of the magical mirror. "You hear that, scum?" he asked. "You get a little 'holiday' after this assignment—assuming you live through this simple surveillance. Do you think you will live?"

The Theiwar spun suddenly, and the crack of a whip resounded through the magical glass.

The goblins yelped and then chorused, "Yes, Oddvar!"

Oddvar chuckled—a sound like dry leaves crumbling. "Yes," he said, "you will live . . . unless you fail." Then, turning back toward the mirror, he said. "What is it you wish me to do, master?"

Maddoc's eyes blazed red in the darkness. "I'm sending you into the kingdom, to prepare the way. There are forces in Arngrim whose objectives could intersect with ours. You will obtain their . . . cooperation in our scheme."

"Am I to tell them of the Emergence?"

"Never," Maddoc hissed. "Under penalty of a lingering, painful death, you are to keep knowledge of the Emergence from them. I will explain their goals to you, and you will make it seem as though we are helping them—a favor to be returned later. They must never suspect our true purpose."

"Which is to spur on the Emergence with their unwitting assistance," Oddvar said.

"Exactly," the wizard replied. "The perils in Arngrim should play right into our hands. While they think we are helping them, they will, in fact, be helping us. They need never know our true purpose."

"And if the girl Nearra were to die during this new test?"

"Then," Maddoc said, "your life expectancy would be greatly reduced."

The wizard sat down again in his carved chair and leaned back. "With luck," he said, "the events we set in motion may cause Nearra to see things as they truly are." He smiled, his pearl-white teeth shining from beneath his salt-and-pepper beard. Maddoc's grin was every bit as wicked as Oddvar's.

Within the mirror, Oddvar bowed low and said, "As you wish, master."

5 LURKERS

For a moment, Davyn lay frozen, uncertain of what to do. Could he be mistaken about the sound? Should he cry out and alert the others? If he did, and the furtive sounds turned out to be nothing. . . .

No. He couldn't wake the rest. Better to investigate on his own.

Almost silently, the young ranger rose from his bedroll. He grabbed his hunting knife and stole toward the doorway.

He peeked into the girls' room, and saw Catriona and Nearra slumbering peacefully beneath their blankets by the fire. Alric lay abed in his own chamber as well.

Davyn carefully picked his way through the rubble toward the sound. The sun hadn't yet crept over the tall mountains, and shadows filled the ruined house. Only foggy predawn light filtered through the cracks in the walls and ceiling. Everything around Davyn seemed surreal and menacing. The noise seemed to be coming from the ruins on the other side of the hallway, near where the companions had entered the house.

He steeled himself, fighting down his fear as he crept across the ruins toward the source of the faint sounds. Davyn pressed himself against what remained of the room's doorjamb and peeked inside.

29

A slender figure in a well-tailored tunic moved quickly and cautiously around the crumbling chamber, probing into nooks and crannies, lifting aside bits of rubble. Davyn immediately recognized the skulker: Elidor.

The young ranger cursed himself silently. Why didn't he check the bedrolls across his room more closely? Clearly, the elf had stuffed his blankets to make it appear that he was sleeping.

As Davyn watched, the elf stopped rummaging and gave a satisfied chuckle. He stuffed something into a pouch at his belt. Then he rose and dusted himself off.

Davyn stepped from the shadows. "What are you doing?" he asked in a whisper.

Elidor turned calmly, as if he'd known Davyn was standing behind him. "Just looking around," the elf replied. "I thought I heard something, but when I came to investigate—" He shrugged. "I guess it must have been mice."

"Or a rat, maybe?" Davyn asked. Anger rose within him, both because he'd caught Elidor sneaking around, and because he'd felt so frightened.

"Could be," Elidor replied. "Sorry if I woke you. I was trying to keep quiet."

"Is that why you stuffed your blankets to make it appear you were sleeping? And what did you just put into that pouch at your waist?"

The elf arched one blond eyebrow. "My pouch?" he asked. "I'm not sure what you mean."

"You're not stealing things again, are you?" Davyn asked angrily.

Elidor scoffed. "Do you see anything to steal here? I'm shocked you would even suggest such a thing. I wouldn't go questioning other people's motives if I were you."

"What do you mean?"

"Nothing," the elf replied. "Go back to sleep. The morning will arrive before we know it." He pushed past Davyn and went back to their makeshift bedroom.

Davyn followed him out.

They found Sindri sitting up and rubbing his eyes as they entered. "What's going on?" the kender asked.

"Nothing," Elidor replied. "Davyn and I just thought we heard something. But we were wrong. Weren't we, Davyn?"

Davyn said nothing, but returned to his bedroll and pulled the covers up over his head.

Catriona woke with the first muted light of dawn. Sleeping on the rotting floor had left her stiff and aching. After first checking to make sure the others were all right, she wandered outside to stretch.

The pelting sleet and rain had ended, but it still remained nearly as foggy as it had been the night before. Catriona looked around, but she could barely tell which way they'd come from, never mind where they might be going. Davyn seemed to have set them on the right track, but she still didn't trust him completely. Of course, having Davyn lead them was much better than relying on Elidor. The elf was a liar and a thief—a charming thief, to be sure—but a thief nonetheless.

Catriona found a pool of clean rainwater on a flagstone nearby. She dipped her hands in the water and gingerly washed her face. She sighed. It seemed the only person she entirely trusted in the group was Nearra—which was ironic, because none of them even knew who Nearra really was. Catriona hoped that at Arngrim, they might find out.

She assumed that Alric could find his way back to his own city, even through the accursed fog. She still didn't completely trust the young prince, though she felt badly for having fought him. Despite Alric forgiving her and his kind words about her, the red-haired warrior remained unsure of herself. A true Solamnic would have handled the situation better, found a way to sort things out before the fighting had gone so far. They were very lucky that no one had been killed.

Catriona squatted down next to the puddle and washed her arms and legs. She hoped they would have good baths in Arngrim. The sorry state of the countryside made her wonder. It had been so long since she'd felt truly clean. A traveler's life was full of such minor inconveniences. Catriona knew a knight shouldn't mind such things, but she did.

She stood and stretched once more, and suddenly discovered Sindri Suncatcher at her elbow. "Anything wrong?" the kender asked.

"No," Catriona replied. "Just cleaning up a little."

Sindri yawned and thrust his arms out to either side. "I didn't sleep very well last night. The floor wasn't at all comfortable, though it was a unique experience." He smiled.

"Kender can find the silver lining in any cloud," Catriona said wistfully. "Are the others up yet?"

"No," Sindri replied. "They didn't sleep much, either, I guess. Davyn and Elidor were prowling around during the night."

"Oh?" Catriona asked. She tried to sound nonchalant, but the fine hairs on the back of her neck prickled.

"They said they heard something," Sindri continued. "I didn't hear anything though, except the two of them bumping around in the dark."

"I'm sure they were only being cautious," Catriona said. But she wondered if perhaps the elf and the ranger were up to something. Both had joined the expedition under false pretenses. Could they be cooking up some scheme together?

Catriona upbraided herself for being unduly suspicious. There was no reason to believe they were part of any conspiracy. Both had proven themselves in the battle of the Temple of the Holy Orders of the Stars. She pushed the dark thoughts aside and fixed up a long red lock that had strayed out from under her helmet.

"Lovely morning," Sindri said. "If you like fog."

"Come on," Catriona said. "Let's roust up some breakfast."

Everyone save Alric was still asleep when they returned. Catriona prepared a simple meal for the group from the provisions they'd brought with them. The smell of cooking sausage soon roused Nearra, Davyn, and Elidor.

Alric seemed anxious to get going, so the companions ate hurriedly. "No sense wasting daylight," he said. "If we push hard, we can make Arngrim before nightfall."

Catriona walked at Alric's side as they followed the rutted path. Sindri kept watching the fog-bound skies and wishing aloud that Raedon, the copper dragon, would visit them. Alric raised an eyebrow at this, and the group explained about their previous adventure at the Temple of the Holy Orders of the Stars.

The storytelling made time pass more quickly, though Catriona found it difficult to judge their progress from the surrounding countryside. The fog severely limited the companions' vision. Occasionally, a slight breeze would part the mist, and they would catch a glimpse of some far-off mountainside or a distant forest. Mostly, they saw only things close at hand: mud, rocks, shriveled grass, and withered trees. Even the weeds in Arngrim seemed unhealthy.

"My kingdom was not always like this," Alric explained. "Once Arngrim was green and fertile. Farms dotted the hillsides, and the sounds of happy people echoed through the valleys."

"I haven't seen any people," Sindri said, "laughing or otherwise." He peered into the fog, as if a happy peasant might pop out and greet him at any moment.

"There is not much to laugh about now," Alric said. "Since the war, things have grown steadily worse. Winter never seems to leave us. Harvests are blighted and small. And now we are besieged by renegades."

"Are they stragglers from the War of the Lance?" Elidor asked.

Alric nodded, and a drop of mist rolled down the metal face of his lion's head helmet, as if the lion wept. He, like Catriona, insisted on wearing his armor as they walked. "Kokar's band retreated over the mountains, driven out by the forces of good," he said. "They found our kingdom weak and ill-prepared. We fight them where we can, but . . . " He shook his head. "They are many, and there are too few of us left to kill them all. Some of the raiders are very strong."

"Like Kokar?" Nearra suggested.

The young prince took a deep breath. "Yes, like Kokar. I was lucky to escape him the other day. The full body of his forces was too much for my tiny band. If he and I were to meet alone, though . . . "

They fell into silence after that, walking carefully along the mountainside. Just before midday they came to a steep-walled chasm. It was too wide to jump across, and the stone bridge spanning it stood in ruins.

"This used to be one of the most beautiful bridges in the kingdom," Alric said.

The companions gazed at the broken balustrades and moss-covered masonry. "The dragons and their armies have much to answer for," Catriona said.

"We'll have to go around," Davyn said, consulting Sindri's map.

"There's a trail down the cliff face a bit further on," Alric replied. "It's steep but manageable."

On the other side of the gorge, they found a series of small, shabby farmhouses. One farmer stood tending his field of brown-husked corn, as the companions passed. The peasant greeted Alric respectfully, but he seemed wary of the others.

"We do not get many visitors in Arngrim any more," Alric noted.

"That's probably because your kingdom isn't on any of the usual maps," Sindri said. "It's a wonder anybody finds this place at all—nestled in the middle of the mountains the way it is. And, no offense, but I'm not even sure why the raiders are bothering with your kingdom. There doesn't seem to be a lot to loot."

Alric bristled, like a real lion, and focused his gray eyes on the kender. "Things will change for us," he said. "Our people are hard-working and industrious. In my darkest moments I fear that it will all come to naught, but if we work together . . ." He sighed. "The troubles that plague our kingdom cannot last forever."

"Even the wickedest of dragons dies eventually," Elidor said, paraphrasing an ancient elf saying.

"Yes," the prince replied. "The Scarlet Brethren have prophesied that Arngrim's troubles will soon end. Our kingdom will be reborn, and we shall be a power in Ansalon once more."

"I admire your determination," Catriona said. "Your discipline reminds me of the Knights of Solamnia. Did you train with the Order?"

Alric chuckled and shook his head. "I never studied with the Solamnics. I've trained in the methods of my family, handed down from generations gone by. The Solamnic way is not the only path to knighthood. Knighthood is in the heart, Catriona, not in oaths and measures."

Catriona nodded and managed a weak smile. The words stung, though; she had been brought up under Solamnic rules. To have the strictures of the knighthood so lightly dismissed!

Yet, at the same time, Alric's words gave her hope. If there were other paths to knighthood, perhaps she could leave her failures behind. Maybe she would never be a true Solamnic knight, but she could aspire to be something just as good.

Alric seemed to read her conflicting emotions. "You have great promise, Catriona," he said. "Don't let past mistakes weigh you down. Look to the future." He smiled at her. Then a shadow passed over his eyes and he looked away.

"What's the matter?" she asked.

He smiled as he stared into the distance. "I should heed my own advice more often," he said.

They traveled downhill into a valley for several more hours. As they went, they passed small farms, brown fields, shallow ponds, and slow-moving peat-stained streams. The fog cleared a bit, allowing visibility to several hundred yards ahead. The landscape in front of them looked uniformly bleak, gray, and rocky. Arngrim lay hidden in one of these misty valleys, but only Alric knew exactly where. According to their map, more mountains lay on the other side of the hidden city.

As the trail rose again, a mixed forest of pines and hardwoods grew up around them. None of the trees looked very healthy: the trunks were twisted and deformed. Grayish needles and withered leaves covered the few branches that weren't completely bare. Even the tallest trees seemed rotten.

"It's a wonder the trees grow at all in this miserable fog," Nearra said as they followed the path through the forest.

"How much farther?" Davyn asked. He had been checking their map constantly during the journey, but still looked puzzled. Catriona knew that he would never admit not knowing their location. Another reason not to trust him. There was definitely something secretive about the ranger.

"We're almost there," Alric replied. "The city is beyond the hills on the other side of this forest. We should arrive by nightfall." He smiled at Catriona, and she smiled back.

"That's great," Sindri said. "I hope they have supper waiting for us when we arrive. Your people will be glad to see you, won't they Alric? You're not one of those outcast princes who never spoke to his parents after a terrible argument, are you? Though it would be really interesting if you were. I could write a history about it."

A writing charcoal and parchment "magically" appeared in the kender's hands. Catriona resisted the urge to chuckle. She knew

STEPHEN D. SULLIVAN

Sindri had really only retrieved the items from secret pockets within his purple cloak.

As the kender began taking notes, a hissing sound cut the air, followed by a soft ripping noise.

Sindri looked down. A black-fletched arrow protruded from the parchment in his hand. The shaft passed through the paper and poked out of the far side of the kender's satin sleeve.

The small wizard scratched his head. "Where did this arrow come from?" He didn't seem concerned that the shot had barely missed his arm. "I don't remember materializing this," he said. He plucked the shaft from his sleeve and looked at it, slightly annoyed.

"Get down!" Catriona cried. "We're under attack!"

Black-fletched arrows filled the air over their heads as the group dived for cover. One shaft bounced off the back of Alric's armor. He and Catriona both rolled to the western side of the path and landed with their backs up against some low boulders.

Sindri, Davyn, and Nearra dived for the trees on the east. Elidor was nowhere to be seen.

"Is it Kokar, do you think?" Catriona whispered to Alric as they both drew their swords.

"Likely," the lion-armored prince replied. "Though it's strange to find his band this close to the city."

"Unless they were hoping to ambush you on your return," she noted.

Alric nodded grimly.

"Where are they?" Davyn called to Catriona and the rest. He looked around, trying to spot their enemies as he quickly nocked an arrow. "Can you see them?"

"There, I think," Nearra said. She rose slightly from her crouch, and pointed off the path to the west. For a moment, it seemed as though light flashed from within her blue eyes.

"Nearra, look out!" Catriona called. As she spoke, an arrow streaked past the boulders toward the blond girl.

Sindri thrust out his hands to exert his magical powers. His brow knitted with concentration, but the arrow kept coming, straight for Nearra's throat. At the last second, the shaft changed course just slightly. Instead of impaling Nearra in the neck, it caught her above the collarbone, close to her left shoulder.

Nearra gasped and looked at the arrow lodged in her flesh. A shocked expression spread over her pretty face, and her skin went deathly pale. The light within her eyes disappeared as her eyeballs rolled back in her head. Her knees gave way and she fell into the underbrush beside the trees.

6   SHADOWS OF WAR

"B astards!" Davyn cried, leaping to his feet. He fired a quick return volley of three arrows in the direction of the shot.

"Take care of Nearra," Alric called to him. "Catriona and I will hold them off." With a nod to the warrior, he rushed out and sprinted in the direction of the arrow fire. Not wanting the prince to see her fear, Catriona swallowed hard and ran after him.

A hail of arrows greeted them as they rounded the sheltering boulder. Alric batted two shots out of the air, and three more bounced harmlessly off his silver-and-black armor.

Catriona howled a Solamnic war cry, fighting down the terror in her gut, trying to be the knight Alric believed her to be. The chainmail atop her tunic turned one arrow aside. She charged the man who had fired it.

The bowman was a short, tattooed barbarian, with a shaved head and wild eyes. He drew a rusty sword as the young warrior came at him. She chopped at his head but he parried. Catriona had been expecting that, though, and twisted her blade as the two weapons met. She slid her sword down, got under his guard, and felled him with one swift cut.

39

Her stomach knotted slightly. Killing never felt good, even though she was glad that the bowman had died, instead of her. Two more renegades rushed out of the forest to take their comrade's place.

Catriona glanced at Alric. He was already fighting off another three renegades. Catriona knew she would have to deal with these two by herself. She saw more men running toward them through the misty woods. If she and Alric couldn't dispatch this first group quickly, the newcomers would surely surround them.

A woman with feathers in her hair tried to skewer Catriona on a spear. The young warrior batted the weapon aside but, as she did, the second raider nearly chopped her with his axe. Catriona barely dodged his blow in time. The tattooed axe man howled wildly and twirled his stone-bladed weapon readying another cut.

Catriona backed out of the way of his swings. The axe wielder kept coming, spit flying from his cracked lips, bloodlust burning in his eyes. The spearwoman circled around, trying to pin Catriona between the two of them. Catriona wove through the trees, using the trunks to protect her flanks and disrupt the renegades' attempts to surround her.

The spearwoman thrust at the young warrior between a forked trunk. The spear point caught in the chainmail of Catriona's vest, but didn't penetrate. Catriona chopped her sword down on the spear's haft, cleaving it in two. Weaponless, the spearwoman turned and fled, leaving her companion to fight alone.

While Catriona had been disarming the spearwoman, the axe man had circled around to get a clear shot at the warrior's head. She ducked out of the way and his axe bit into the tree behind her. Catriona thrust her sword at the man's chest. The tattooed warrior's axe wasn't stuck, though. He swung backward as Catriona tried to skewer him.

The blunt back edge of his axe smashed into Catriona's sword hand. Her fingers opened reflexively and her sword sailed through the air, clattering amid the trees several yards away. The axe man smiled.

Panic fluttered in Catriona's heart. She dropped to her knees as the axe man aimed a deadly blow at her helmet. Scooping up the broken spearpoint she'd severed moments earlier, Catriona lunged forward under his cut. She drove the spear blade up, deep into the tattooed man's unarmored chest.

The man gasped in surprise. The axe slipped from his hands and his body slumped onto Catriona's shoulder. She heaved him off and got to her feet. Spotting her lost sword, she dashed through the trees to retrieve it.

As she ran, something crashed into her from behind. Catriona pitched forward, skidding headlong into the pine needles, her back throbbing with pain. She felt as though she'd been hit with a battering ram. Spots flashed before her eyes. She glanced sideways and saw a thick, black-fletched arrow lying on the ground beside her.

A longbow. She'd been hit by a longbow shot. She reached around and felt her back. Her mail was badly scarred, but the arrowhead hadn't penetrated her skin. She'd been lucky.

Fear tried to pin her to the ground, but the voice of her Solamnic training—a voice which sounded very much like Catriona's dead aunt—barked at her to get up. Catriona rolled over, grabbed her sword, and quickly scrambled to her feet.

She spotted the bowman, a hundred yards away, standing atop a boulder. He had a clear shot at her; there were no trees close enough to provide Catriona cover. The bowman took careful aim. The warrior brought her sword up, knowing she had virtually no chance to stop the incoming arrow. She'd seen Alric bat two arrows from the air at the start of the fight, but it was something she'd never even attempted herself.

Alric himself was too far away to help and fighting for his own life besides.

Catriona forced herself to concentrate, waiting for just the right moment.

The bowman pulled the string to his ear.

Catriona held her breath and clenched her teeth. She knew the wound would be terrible, probably fatal. Her chainmail wouldn't protect her this time.

The bowstring twanged. Catriona waited for the impact.

The bowman jerked suddenly and his longbow slipped from his fingers. Blood burbled from his mouth and he toppled from the rock, an arrow protruding from his back.

The renegade's shot whisked by Catriona's left shoulder, just off the mark. Catriona breathed a sigh of relief and called to the youthful figure dashing through the woods toward her. "Thanks, Davyn!"

"Don't mention it," he said, skidding to a stop at her side. "It looked like you needed some help."

"Long-range combat is not my specialty," Catriona said. "Is Nearra—" She stopped, afraid to finish the question.

"Her wound didn't look too bad. I bandaged it. I think she'll be all right. I left her with Sindri. Heads up!"

Catriona turned and swung her sword as a blue-painted barbarian leaped off a boulder toward them. Her blade met him in midair, and he hit the ground in two pieces. He didn't get up.

"Thanks for the warning," Catriona said.

Davyn nodded and fired two shots, felling an axe-wielding woman running at them. "Alric seems to be holding his own," the ranger said.

Catriona looked and saw the prince battling three men in a clearing a short distance away. As she watched, Alric cut down first one enemy, then another. In seconds, only one renegade remained facing the lion-armored prince.

"I wouldn't want to be on the wrong end of his long sword," Davyn noted.

"It was no fun," Catriona admitted. "Are the others safe?" she asked, glancing back the way they'd come.

"I think so," Davyn said. "Except for Elidor. I don't know where he is. I wouldn't worry about him too much. These renegades seem a lot more interested in Alric than in the rest of us." He glanced fleetingly up the road in the direction they had been traveling. No renegades blocked their passage in that direction.

"You're not suggesting that we leave Alric to fight on his own?" Catriona asked, shocked.

Davyn scowled. "Of course not. I was just saying."

"Let's help him, then," she said. Davyn nodded, and the two of them ran after the prince.

Alric stood quite a distance through the forest away from them. A long trail of renegade bodies lay in the young prince's wake. As Alric cut down another of his enemies, a man riding a dun horse and wearing a battered dragonarmy helmet and polished chainmail charged forward.

"Look out!" Catriona yelled, only then realizing that she and Davyn had sprinted between two lines of advancing raiders.

Alric turned and hissed, "Kokar!" as the horseman galloped toward him.

"We meet again, you gray pestilence," Kokar called back. He was huge, easily twice Alric's size. In his left hand he brandished a golden scimitar. The curved sword's blade glistened brightly in the fogbound forest. "This time, we will have our revenge. Your accursed kinsmen will not save you."

"But who will save you, braggart?" Alric asked.

Kokar slashed at his head, but Alric dived under the blow. As Kokar rode past, the prince rolled to his feet and aimed a cut at the renegade leader's flank. Kokar twisted in the saddle, parried, and kept going. He wheeled his horse in the forest thirty yards away, turned and charged Alric again.

"Davyn, duck!" Catriona cried. She parried a mace aimed at

her head as she called to her friend. Davyn ducked and Catriona smashed her other fist into the face of the man trying to sneak up behind the young ranger. The attacker stumbled back, bleeding from his nose. Before he could rise again, Davyn finished him off with a strong right cross.

Protecting Davyn left Catriona off balance. She turned to block the mace-wielder once more, but the weapon sneaked under her guard. Catriona grunted as the mace connected with her ribs. She sidestepped the follow-up blow and stabbed at the mace's owner, a wiry young woman with a green painted face.

Painted-Face swung for Catriona's bruised side again. Catriona lunged forward and turned slightly as the blow came in. She caught the mace-wielder's arm under her own, pinning it to her side. At the same time, she slashed sideways with her short sword. But Painted-Face used the same trick. She pushed nose-to-nose with Catriona, and grabbed the young warrior's sword arm with her free hand. The two of them struggled a deadly dance, neither one relinquishing her grip on the other's weapon.

Davyn put an arrow through the leg of a man charging him, and another through the wrist of a renegade taking aim at Catriona's back. Suddenly, Davyn's right knee buckled and his face twisted in pain. He spun, nearly toppling over from the effort. Ten paces away, a woman with a sling took aim at him once more. From behind her, a man with a long spear charged toward Davyn as well.

Catriona saw the spearman coming but, tangled with Painted-Face, she could do nothing to help her friend. Sweat beaded on Catriona's pale forehead and worry knotted her stomach.

Kokar charged Alric again. The renegade's dun stallion snorted, and his hooves kicked up great clods of soggy earth. Hatred burned in the eyes of both horse and rider.

"You'll soon be as dead as the land you cherish," Kokar barked. He cut at Alric with his golden scimitar, but Prince Alric stepped behind a nearby tree. Kokar's sword bit clean through four inches of wood, felling the sapling. Alric stepped out of the way of the falling tree, missing an opportunity to counterattack.

The lion-armored prince spun to face his enemy as Kokar wheeled for another run at him.

Davyn aimed his bow at the woman with the sling. As he let fly, her second stone crashed into his side. Davyn winced and fell to his knees, but his shot grazed the woman's forehead. She, too, fell reeling. The spearman smiled and ran full-speed at the wounded ranger.

Catriona struggled to break the grip of the mace-wielder grappling with her. Painted-Face was smaller than Catriona, but wiry—and considerably less tired.

Catriona spotted the spearman running toward Davyn, and her heart sank. She would not be able to break free in time to save him.

Her stomach clenched in horror as the ranger drew his hunting knife and struggled to get to his feet. The spearman laughed and aimed at Davyn's chest.

With a final, triumphant cry, the renegade thrust the lance at Davyn. But the spear twisted in his hands, and he tripped over the handle. The spearman stumbled forward, and the weapon flew out of his grip. The lance twisted through the air and hit its owner on the back of his head. The man went down like a sack of potatoes.

Sindri Suncatcher stepped out from behind a tree and smiled at his friends. Sweat beaded on the kender's forehead and he looked tired as he concentrated on his telekinesis. The spear flew through the air and cracked itself over the skull of the sling woman, who was starting to get up. The woman fell face first into the leaves.

Catriona's heart soared at the sudden reversal of fortune. She snapped her head forward against the face of the mace-wielder. Her metal helmet crashed into Painted-Face's forehead. The female raider staggered back. Stunned, she lost her grip on Catriona's arm and sank to the ground. Catriona slumped against a nearby tree, gasping to regain her breath.

Sindri helped Davyn to his feet. "I'm okay," Davyn said, nursing his wounded knee. "What about Nearra? Why did you leave her?" Deep concern marked the young ranger's face.

"I put a spell of protection over her," the kender said cheerily.

"You what?" Davyn shouted. "You little fool! Don't you understand the danger she's in?"

"Don't worry, Davyn," Sindri said. "I used my strongest magic. Nearra will be fine." Then his small face darkened slightly. "I'm sorry she got wounded. I tried to stop the arrow that hit her, but my spell didn't work very well."

"Deflecting that arrow may have saved her life," Catriona panted.

"Do you think?" Sindri asked, beaming.

"We'll have to talk about it later," Davyn said. He winced as he stooped and retrieved his bow. "In case you hadn't noticed, we're surrounded."

Catriona glanced up to discover eight more renegades closing in on them from all corners. She looked for Alric, hoping he might help.

The young prince of Arngrim ducked out of the way of another deadly slice from Kokar. Alric countered, and his sword traced a thin cut beneath Kokar's polished chainmail. The wound wasn't very deep, though, and Alric's payment came in the form of a vicious kick from Kokar's steed.

Alric flew through the air and crashed into a medium sized tree. As the prince lay on the ground, Kokar charged again.

Catriona, Davyn, and Sindri stood in a rough circle, surrounded by more than twice their number in renegades.

The kender's telekinesis tripped one of their foes, but his concentration wavered, and three others got through. Davyn put an arrow through one's eye, and Catriona hamstrung another. The third pressed in on Catriona, swinging wildly with a rusty scimitar. She fended off his attack, but her arms felt like lead.

She dared a glance at Sindri, hoping for some help. Sweat poured down the kender's tanned face and his breath came in short gasps. He was concentrating hard, but nothing seemed to be happening.

Davyn drew his hunting knife and blocked another raider's spear. Sindri threw himself at the knees of Catriona's foe, and she was finally able to run him through. Davyn's opponent backed away, keeping just out of the ranger's reach.

A cold shiver ran down Catriona's spine. The renegades had gotten smart. They massed in a circle around the three companions, hemming them in, waiting for the right moment to attack.

The kender's legs wobbled, as if barely able to hold him up. He seemed to be trying to use his telekinesis, but it wasn't working. Catriona didn't feel any better than the kender, and Davyn didn't look so good, either. Kokar's renegades laughed.

A terrible thought flashed through Catriona's mind: she would die here, in the fogbound forest, unable to fulfill her promise to protect Sindri and Nearra.

I will not run, she vowed silently. Not this time. Better to die than to flee and let my friends perish.

The renegades surrounding the friends smiled and raised their weapons for the kill.

"Take as many with you as you can," Davyn hissed.

Catriona nodded; she couldn't find her voice to reply. Sindri, leaning against her leg, said nothing. The renegades rushed forward.

Suddenly, a gray-clad figure materialized out of the fog. Two throwing knives appeared in his hands, as if by magic. The daggers flashed through the air, and two of the renegades fell dead.

"Elidor!" Sindri cried.

The elf stooped and picked up a long knife from one of the dead raiders. As the surprised renegades turned toward him, Elidor drew his blade across the throat of one. Another rushed him, but

Elidor stepped out of the way and stabbed the man in the back. The elf moved swiftly and with deadly grace. He turned to face another renegade.

Catriona and Davyn charged with all their remaining strength. They pushed their enemies back, breaking the enemy line. Sindri weakly waved his hands in magical passes—though his spells seemed to have little effect.

"Where have you been?" Davyn asked Elidor angrily.

"Waiting for the right moment to act," Elidor replied. "No sense getting killed in the preliminaries." He smiled and parried a sword cut aiming to decapitate him.

Catriona smirked in reply, though she was too tired to manage a snappy rejoinder. They weren't out of the woods yet, either.

The four of them had cut the raiders' numbers, but the odds were still against them, five to four. Sindri—who looked completely exhausted—was no help at all.

Five to three, then, Catriona thought.

She parried one sword thrust and kicked out in the opposite direction. Her kick broke the kneecap of a man trying to skewer the kender. Sindri grabbed up a broken spear and cracked it over the man's head. "Thanks, Catriona," the kender said.

Catriona nodded. She wasn't thinking about Sindri, though. Out of the corner of her eye, she could just make out Alric, as he rolled out of the way of Kokar's charge.

The young prince of Arngrim rose and ducked around a tree as Kokar rode in on him. Alric turned and ran, dashing through the trunks and across the back of a wide, flat boulder. The rock angled up, ten feet above the forest floor. Alric leaped over the precipice and sprinted down the slope beyond. But three of Kokar's men lay in wait there. They rushed upslope toward Alric as Kokar and his horse barreled down behind.

Kokar and his steed hurtled over the edge of the precipice. The renegade leader miscalculated the jump, though. On the way down, a tree limb caught him full across the chest. The raider toppled from the saddle and crashed heavily onto the leaf-covered ground; his horse kept going.

Alric turned and charged. Kokar, stunned, tried to get to his feet. Two of Kokar's men raced to their chief's aid as a third tried to corral Kokar's runaway horse.

One of the men got in the prince's way, and Alric slew him with a single sword cut. Kokar rose, leaning heavily on the second man. Alric charged up the hill and stabbed at the renegade chief's chest.

Kokar twisted, thrusting his companion in front of the prince's blade. Alric ran the man through, but his sword caught in the bandit's ribs. Kokar kicked the impaled man in the back, and he fell atop the startled prince. Both the dead man and Alric tumbled down the hill.

Kokar laughed and reclaimed his steed from his last remaining retainer. He pushed the man away and, climbing groggily into the saddle, rode off into the forest.

"He's fleeing!" Catriona called. "Kokar's fleeing!"

Elidor laughed, Sindri whooped, and even Davyn managed a slight smile.

The sight of their leader heading for the hills broke the renegades' morale. Those remaining alive turned and fled. Those fighting Catriona and the others retreated just as quickly. The four exhausted companions took a few half-hearted final cuts at the bandits opposing them.

"Let them go," Davyn said.

Catriona nodded wearily. "They'll not bother us again."

"Good thing, too," Elidor replied. He wiped the sweat from his brow with one hand.

Alric, though, had not given up the fight. He chased after the band retreating into the forest.

"Alric, no!" Catriona cried. "Come back!"

The prince didn't respond. He ran into the fogbound woods, shouting curses and waving his rune-carved sword.

"I wonder what he hopes to accomplish?" Elidor said, shaking his head.

"If he's not careful, he'll get himself killed," Catriona replied. She took a deep breath and turned to go after him.

"Never mind Alric. He can take care of himself," Davyn snapped. "It's Nearra we should be worried about. Sindri left her alone, remember?"

Catriona paused, torn between her concern for Alric and her vow to protect Nearra. "You're right, Davyn," she finally said. "We're all too tired to go after Alric. I just pray that he turns back, before the renegades realize how badly they have him outnumbered."

"Maybe he'll finish off Kokar," Sindri said. "That would be lucky. I bet those raiders wouldn't bother Alric's kingdom anymore, then."

"I'd be happy if they just wouldn't bother *us*," Davyn replied. He walked back toward the bushes where they'd left Nearra. As he went, he glanced up through the trees, as though looking for something in the sky overhead.

Catriona looked up, but didn't see anything.

"Nearra should be fine," Sindri said. "My spell would have kept her safe." He smiled.

Davyn stopped several yards away from the bushes. His body stiffened and his face turned very pale. The others halted next to him. Catriona gasped, reflexively putting a hand over her mouth.

Nearra lay under the bushes where they'd left her. The bandage on her shoulder looked fresh, barely a spot of blood stained it. The front of her dress, though, was soaked red from waist to neck.

Nearra wasn't moving.

7

THE PRICE OF BATTLE

Davyn rounded on the kender and picked him up by the front of his satin shirt. "How could you leave her?" he screamed. "Your spells are worthless! Don't you know it's all a sham!"

"My spells are not worthless!" Sindri cried. "They saved all of us when Slean attacked us! They saved you just now."

Davyn's face turned almost purple with rage. He shook the kender and threw him roughly to the ground. Then he turned away, fell to his knees, and buried his face in his hands.

"Let's not get hysterical here," Elidor said.

"Not get hysterical!" Catriona replied, her voice cracking. "Nearra is dead, and we did nothing to save her!"

"She's not, you know," Elidor said calmly.

"Not what?" Sindri asked, biting his lower lip.

"Not dead," Elidor replied. He walked over and knelt down next to Nearra.

"That's impossible," Davyn said, still huddled by himself. "You saw the blood! No one can lose that much blood and live."

"That's true," Elidor said. He felt for the pulse in Nearra's neck. "But you're assuming the blood belongs to her—rather than to that chap in the bushes over there." He pointed to where a pair 51 of scuffed-up boots protruded from a nearby shrub.

Catriona looked from Nearra's blood-soaked dress, to the bushes Elidor indicated. Sure enough, a man lay on his back in the brush, nearly obscured from view. A look of shock and horror masked the renegade's dead face. A dagger protruded from his neck—the knife Nearra had borrowed from Catriona.

"Thank the gods!" Catriona said rushing to Nearra's side. She cradled her friend's blond head in her lap and checked for signs of further wounds. "Elidor's right," she said. "She doesn't seem to be hurt, aside from the arrow wound."

"See?" Sindri said. "My spells do work." He shot an angry glance in Davyn's direction before joining the others at Nearra's side.

Slowly, Nearra's eyes flickered open. "Am I dead?" she asked. "I remember being shot, and then that horrible man standing over me, about to slit my throat, and then . . . "

"No," Catriona said, blinking back tears, "you're not dead."

Nearra looked confused. "Did I lose my memory again?"

"I doubt it," Elidor replied. "People often drift in and out of consciousness when they're wounded. It appears that you woke just long enough to stick your dagger into the neck of the man attacking you."

Nearra's eyes widened, and she tried to sit up. She only made it part way before pain made her slump back down. She moaned and looked sick to her stomach. "Did I kill him?" she asked, her voice barely more than a whisper.

"Yes, thank the gods," Davyn replied. He knelt over the dead scoundrel and pulled out Nearra's dagger. He wiped the weapon clean on the bushes. Then crossing to the blood soaked blond girl, he offered her knife back.

Nearra shook her head. "Oh, no," she said. "I couldn't. Not after . . ." She closed her eyes and shook, as though fighting some inner struggle.

"Take it," Catriona said. "You never know when you might need it again."

Nearra nodded and Davyn knelt beside her, tucking the dagger into her belt. "Are you all right?" he asked tenderly.

"No," she said. "But I will be. I just need to rest." She closed her eyes again.

Davyn gazed at her a moment, worried, then motioned the others to stand, and move away from their wounded friend. Catriona gently set the girl's head down, then joined the rest.

"We need to get away from here," Davyn whispered to his friends.

"But Nearra said she needed rest," Sindri countered.

"Davyn's right," Elidor said. "There's no rest for us here. We need to move on, get to Arngrim if we can. We should be safe there."

"I'll go find Alric," Catriona said. "The rest of you wait here and protect Nearra."

"We shouldn't wait," Davyn said. "We should go *now*."

"We can find our way to Arngrim without him," Sindri added. "I can find the city using my map."

Catriona felt her face flush. "I'm sure you can," she said, trying to keep her temper under control. "And I imagine we'd get quite a reception in Arngrim after leaving its prince to be slaughtered by renegades."

"You're right," Davyn said. "Go find him as quickly as you can. If those renegades return, though . . ."

"If they do," Catriona said, "don't wait for us."

Catriona's stomach fluttered with butterflies as she ran, alone, through the misty forest. The fear of encountering Kokar's stragglers tingled along her spine. Catriona chided herself for being so self-centered.

She should be worrying about Alric's fate. Without him, they might never get to Arngrim. Or, if they did get there, they might be spurned by the city's rulers.

Catriona hoped Alric hadn't been hurt, or worse. She hadn't known the young prince very long, but already she admired his steadfastness and determination. If only he hadn't run off!

"Alric!" she called. "Alric!"

No answer came. Catriona wasn't an expert tracker like Davyn. She probably wasn't even as good as Sindri or Elidor—elves and kender had an affinity for the woods that humans lacked. Kokar's raiders had left a wide swath of tracks through the forest, though, and the chief's horse left prints that even Catriona's untrained eyes could follow.

She passed several bodies as she ran. The renegades' dead eyes stared blankly, seemingly surprised at their own deaths. The bandits looked ragged, emaciated, almost starved. Perhaps that is why they've attacked Arngrim, she thought. Their bellies are empty and they know no other way. A sliver of sympathy crept up in her, but she fought it down. Whether the raiders were hungry or not, no one had a right to slaughter innocents. These people had attacked her friends without cause. Alric was right to kill them.

She found the prince a short distance ahead, stooping over another body. Blood dripped from Alric's hands and his rune-carved sword. He spun, eyes blazing, when he saw her. Then the face behind the lion-masked helmet softened. "I thought you were . . . one of them," he said.

"Are you all right?" Catriona asked.

"Winded," he replied. "Not used to . . . running . . . so much."

"You seemed unstoppable in battle," she said, smiling. "I didn't think anything could slow you down."

He laughed hoarsely and shook his head. "No. I'm just a . . . man." He stood up and straightened his back.

"Did you get Kokar?"

"No, curse him," Alric replied. He paused a moment and caught his breath. "I put the fear of Arngrim into him, though." He eyed the trail back the way they'd come. "After what we've done today, it'll be ages before he can raise another army to vex my kingdom. If, indeed, he ever can. We've finished them."

"I . . . I didn't do much," Catriona said. "My friends and I are lucky we escaped with our lives."

"Nonsense," said Alric. "All of you fought very bravely—you especially, Catriona." He walked back toward the road. "Did everyone else survive?"

Catriona nodded as she fell in beside him. "Nearra was wounded, but the rest of us are fine."

He removed his glove and brushed one slender hand across the cut on her cheek. "And this?" he asked.

She lowered her eyes and fought down a blush. "It's nothing. No more worth mentioning than your cuts and bruises. I'm fine."

He paused, his hand lingering on her cheek. His fingers felt soft and cool. "It's a shame to mar such a pretty face."

There was no fighting the blush this time. Catriona turned away and said, "Let's get back. The others are waiting." She walked determinedly ahead.

Alric quickly caught up to her. "You are very brave, Catriona," he said. "You're something special."

"No," she said. "No, I'm not. We were lucky. That's all. Lucky to escape with our lives." Unbidden, a memory of the ambush that killed her aunt sprang to her mind. She felt glad that neither Alric nor her friends could see the fear inside her, glad that none of them really knew what a coward she was.

Alric tried to say something, but she kept pushing forward.

By the time Catriona and the prince returned, Nearra and the others were ready to go. Night would be falling soon, and—though Kokar's men had been beaten and scattered—there was still no guarantee that the raiders would not return. Lingering in the forest could prove fatal. They took turns helping Nearra walk as they trudged up the long slope through the woods, and over the rolling hills beyond.

"It won't be long now," Alric assured them.

Davyn's brown eyes lingered on the darkening sky. "Let's hope not," he said.

Catriona caught Alric's attention. "In the woods, earlier, the renegades said they wanted revenge on you. What did they mean?" she asked.

"I've slain their kind before," Alric replied stoically. "The enemies of Arngrim cannot be allowed to stand."

"What do they want?" Catriona asked. "The bodies I saw looked almost starved."

"They may be hungry," Alric replied. "I do not know, nor do I care. If they were willing to work for what they want, I might have some sympathy. But they are renegades from the dragonarmy. They despoiled our land during the war, and now they want to ravage what's left. They only know how to take, not give. They murder, and steal, and burn for their own enjoyment. They are a pack of mad dogs. Even their simple comradeship is base and false. They would never search for one of their own who was lost—as you came for me, Catriona."

Catriona turned her eyes away from him, again feeling the falseness of her courage. "I'm not as brave as you make me out to be," she said.

Alric laughed. "You don't give yourself enough credit, Catriona," he said. "Your comrades think very highly of you, I can tell."

"I don't think—"

"I'm sure they do," Alric interjected. He turned to the four companions walking behind them and asked, "Isn't that right, Davyn?"

Davyn didn't reply. He seemed to be concentrating on a black bird, circling lazily in the cloudy sky overhead. Catriona squinted at the bird, trying to determine if it was a crow or something else.

As she looked, the fog swirled in once more, obscuring her view. Davyn turned his eyes back to the road ahead.

"Is there something wrong, Davyn?" Catriona asked

"Nothing," Davyn replied.

Catriona didn't believe him. Some secret lurked inside him—and that made the warrior reluctant to trust him entirely.

"What was it you asked, Alric?" Davyn said.

"I was saying that the rest of you hold Catriona in very high regard."

Davyn looked slightly annoyed. "Of course we do," he replied. "Every one of us contributes something to our group."

Catriona didn't believe that, either. She saw the way Davyn subconsciously glanced toward the kender when he said, "Every one of us contributes something. . . ."

Sindri had scampered ahead of the group while Elidor and Davyn took turns helping Nearra to walk. As the kender topped the next rise, he jumped up and down excitedly. "I see it!" he cried. "I see the city!"

The rest hurried to join him at the crest of the hill.

"Is that it?" Nearra asked wearily. "Is that Arngrim?"

Alric nodded. "Yes," he said. "It seems like an age since I've seen it, but that is my home."

A narrow mist-filled valley stretched into the distance before them. Towering mountains sprang up beyond the vale, thrusting jagged peaks toward the darkening sky.

At the far end of the valley rose the towers of Arngrim. The city's pointed spires looked strong and solid, echoing the mountain range beyond. A grand castle dominated the city's apex. The keep's fortifications rose high above the walled town at its feet. Arngrim's solid stone masonry appeared almost black in the gathering twilight.

Catriona caught her breath. Arngrim resembled the fairytale kingdoms she'd heard tales of during her childhood. She glanced at

Alric standing next to her in his leonine armor. He was tall, proud, and handsome—the very picture of a storybook prince.

As twilight descended, the city lights of Arngrim winked on one by one, like stars appearing in the night sky. Even shrouded by fog, Arngrim looked magnificent.

"We should hurry," Alric said, "before darkness overtakes us."

Eerie silence filled the cavernous chamber.

Oddvar stared at the ceiling far overhead, admiring the natural beauty of the stone in ways that only a dwarf—even a dark dwarf—could. He cataloged the striations and counted the tiny fissures. He calculated just the right place to strike to make the stones break in half, or crumble into tiny pieces. He imagined what minerals might lie buried beneath the surface, waiting to be mined and brought to light.

The Theiwar didn't mine rocks for a living, but his job was similar in many ways. Instead of stone, Oddvar mined people. He wheedled and cajoled them, worked on the fissures in their character and delved for their treasures. He could turn them into works of art or make them crumble into nothing, all at his master's bidding.

The group in the cavern was different, though. They didn't seem the same as the humans Oddvar usually dealt with. Their cares and concerns remained hidden, inscrutable. Even with careful probing, they did not reveal their inner workings to him. Oddvar wished that Maddoc had given him more information to probe with.

Despite his diplomatic training, the dark dwarf grew impatient. He imagined himself flaying these Arngrimites alive, torturing them until they gave him what he wanted. Only then would he let them die. Oddvar liked killing things. Unfortunately, Maddoc didn't let him do it very often.

Maddoc would disapprove if he slew these people now. But the passion within the dwarf was growing. If he waited much longer, he wouldn't be able to resist the impulse. He needed to do something, so he broke the silence.

"I am willing to sit here and watch the stalactites grow for as long as you like," the dark dwarf rasped. "However, my master would like some indication of—"

"Unlike you, dwarf," a member of the group said, "we adhere to neither Maddoc's wishes, nor his timetable."

"We are not pawns of your master," the leader added. His voice echoed eerily in the vast cavern. "We serve a greater purpose—one which does not bow before Maddoc or his petty schemes."

Oddvar's blood rose hotly. He fought down the impulse to murder all the people standing before him. "That doesn't mean," the Theiwar replied, "that your goals and those of my master are not—in this case—similar."

"Perhaps," hissed a woman whom even Oddvar's eyes could not pick out from the cavern's blackness.

Oddvar stood and gestured theatrically. "You seek a certain power, and here it marches into Arngrim, under your very noses. My master knows of your difficulties, and sends a present—a token of his high esteem for Arngrim."

"He lies," rumbled an echoing voice. "Anything Maddoc does, he does for his own ends."

"In this instance," the dark dwarf replied, "your aims and those of my master run along the same course. The five who enter your kingdom may be of aid to you. In return, my master asks very little."

"How little?" asked a voice from a direction Oddvar couldn't determine.

"Maddoc needs strong servants," Oddvar said. "The weak are useless to him. The process of weeding out the worthy from the ineffectual takes time. My master hopes that you might test these children, so he can see what they are made of."

"And why should we do this?"

"Because," Oddvar replied, "my master has foreseen that one of this band may be useful in resolving your predicament." Oddvar smiled inwardly. He had baited the hook. Now they had only to take it.

"Which one?"

"*That* Maddoc has not foreseen," Oddvar said.

"And if we were to take them all? If all were weeded out?"

Oddvar smiled, outwardly this time. "If you were to take them all, then none of them will have proven worthy and my master will begin again." The dwarf realized this was untrue, but the conspirators in the cave didn't need to know about the wizard's special plans for Nearra. Nor did they need to know what was likely to happen to them if they did spur on the Emergence—as Maddoc hoped they would. "My master is a patient human being. All of you are, as well. Perhaps, though, you have waited long enough?"

The group lurking in the shadows on the other side of the cavern spoke together in hoarse whispers.

Oddvar fought the urge to laugh. They had taken the bait. Whether they knew it or not, this group now did Maddoc's bidding just as surely as the dark dwarf did.

"Yes," the leader finally said. "We have waited long enough."

"That does not mean that we will do as Maddoc requires," said the shadowed woman.

"We will pursue our own ends," added a third. "If those ends are the same as your master's, then so be it."

Oddvar bowed low. "That is all my master asks," he said. Not wanting to overstay his welcome, the Theiwar turned and quickly left the chamber.

Oddvar chuckled to himself as he exited the maze of underground passages and returned to the countryside of Arngrim once more. He couldn't help himself. Another job well done! This would raise him even higher in Maddoc's estimation. And, of course, the wizard's opinion was the only one that counted.

It didn't matter that Maddoc's methods were nearly opposite to the ones the Theiwar favored. Oddvar didn't care for all this intrigue and manipulation. If it had been up to him, he would have hired someone to slay all of Nearra's simpering companions. Then they could force Nearra's Emergence—or simply kill the girl and start again.

If the death of her newfound friends and her own mortal peril would not bring out the qualities Maddoc desired in the girl, then Oddvar didn't see what would. Better to get it all over quickly, one way or the other.

Maddoc, though, thought differently. He seemed to believe that the Emergence was a tricky thing, to be subtly manipulated until reaching the desired effect. Perhaps he was right. Maddoc was a wizard, after all, and knew more about such things than Oddvar did.

Also, the bloodlust that ran savagely through the dark dwarf's soul did not taint Maddoc. Perhaps that was why the wizard did not think in the same way. Oddvar would have been happy to see Nearra, Davyn, and the rest hanging from gibbets. Very happy indeed. Slaying the weak and dominating the strong, *that* appealed to Oddvar.

Each night, before he fell asleep, the dwarf's thoughts lingered on fascinating ways that the group of teens might be killed. He had unique and interesting deaths mapped out for each and every one.

All he needed was Maddoc's authorization to set his deadly plans in motion.

Oddvar doubted that permission would ever come.

The thwarting of his secret ambitions did not bother the dwarf. Maddoc was the master; he merely the servant of the magician's will. Disobeying Maddoc would bring swift and terrible retribution.

Oddvar didn't like to think about that. His own destruction—
that was the only death Oddvar did not like contemplating.

So, he played his part and waited.

The dark dwarf hoped that when the Emergence came, it would
cause more bloodshed than even he could ever imagine.

8   The Sleeping City

I'm tired," Sindri said. "Will there be a nice
place for us to sleep tonight? Oh! Wait. Will
we be staying in that castle? Is that where your family lives? It's
okay if we're not staying in the palace. I'm used to roughing it. All
of us are."

Prince Alric smiled down benevolently at the kender. "Yes," he
said, "my family does live in that castle. And yes, you will be staying
there tonight as my guests, all of you. Assuming that you want to."

Sindri clapped. "Oh, good!"

"We would all be honored to stay as your guests tonight, Prince
Alric," Elidor said. He bowed politely.

Catriona's heart soared. Staying in the castle! Though she'd trained
with Solamnic knights and traveled with her aunt, she'd never been
any place nearly so grand. And now, to be lodging in a palace as guests
of a young prince! The thought sent thrills through her.

The journey down from the hills took longer than any of them
had anticipated. As they traveled, night descended across the valley.
The fog thickened with the darkness. Even though they were close
to the city, they might have lost their way without Alric leading
them. Eventually, they left the withered hills behind, and now
approached the great entryway to the city.

The gates of Arngrim towered above their heads, three stories tall. Iron bindings with rivets the size of a man's fist held the massive timbers together, forming a great set of double doors. The huge portal stood shut, with no guards standing outside it.

"The gates are closed at sundown," Alric explained.

"Was it always that way?" Nearra asked. As she spoke, she seemed half asleep. She leaned heavily on Davyn and Catriona for support. Though Nearra's wound had stopped bleeding, she still looked very pale and weak.

Alric shook his head. "Not always. Only since the war."

"Because of the renegades?" Sindri asked.

"Yes," Alric replied. "The renegades." He looked to a heavily armored guard standing atop the wall and cried. "Ho! It is I, Alric. I have returned! Open the gates!"

The guard didn't reply, but moved away out of their sight. A moment later, a rumble like thunder shook the roadway as the great gates creaked open.

Alric and the companions walked inside and the huge doors swung shut behind them.

Dim light leaked from the houses on either side of the city street, painting the cobblestones in long black shadows. The homes themselves were tall and slender, cramped close together, as if to use every available inch within Arngrim's walls. Many of the buildings were made of the same gray stones as the streets. Some had timber-framed upper stories above rock foundations. Slate tiles crowned many of the roofs. Others were made of thatch.

The street the companions walked was wide enough for three horse carts. Numerous smaller side streets and back alleys wound off the main road to either side. Sindri peered down every avenue that they passed. Elidor did as well, though he was more circumspect about it.

They saw few people on the streets, but the sounds of quiet conversation and low music drifted out from inside the taverns and houses they passed. The few citizens they met bowed courteously to Alric, then scurried off.

Catriona noted that all the people looked thin and worn, which was not surprising given the long war and Arngrim's difficulties with the renegades.

The wide street snaked through the city, past several community wells and a fountain square before leading to the castle itself. The palace towered over the buildings surrounding it, and even the great wall ringing the city. Its pointed spires seemed ready to tear open the misty sky, revealing the stars hidden behind the clouds.

Two guards stood before the huge iron portcullis barring the main entryway through the palace's outer wall. Burnished black-and-silver armor, similar to Alric's, covered the sentries from head to toe. Visored helmets concealed their faces. They held long poleaxes, tipped with spear points, erect at their sides. The guards said nothing as Alric approached the portal. They merely nodded a respectful bow, and the great metal grillwork slid up into the gatehouse.

Sindri paused to look at the guards as they passed through the gateway. "Their armor has lion designs," the kender said, "just like yours."

"Not exactly like mine," Alric replied. "But they are similar."

"As befits the sentries of a prince," Catriona noted.

Sindri stood next to one of the knights, studying the armor, until Davyn tugged on the little wizard's cape. The kender shrugged at him and followed the rest of the companions through the gatehouse. Beyond the portcullis lay a courtyard lined with ornate stone barracks and stables. No lights issued from the buildings, though torches burned on either side of the doors to the main keep itself.

Catriona noted the tidy, immaculate appearance of the courtyard. One would never have guessed that the buildings surrounding it housed companies of men and horses. She would expect nothing less from knights under Alric's command.

Two more sentries, armored in the same lion motifs as those outside the gatehouse, stood guard on either side of the castle's main doors. The doors themselves were similar to the gates of the city, made of wide, iron-bound timbers. The timbers' large rivets were shaped like lion heads. Two great lion-faced door knockers glared out at the visitors.

Alric walked past the guards and knocked. Echoes like thunder boomed within the huge building. A moment later, two guards swung the doors open from inside.

"Thanks for waiting up for us," Sindri said brightly as they passed into the castle proper. The guards did not reply, or even acknowledge the kender's existence. Sindri frowned and noted, "Well, that's a bit rude."

Alric, walking at the head of the group, glanced back at the kender. "The guards of Arngrim are trained in complete obedience," Alric said. "They live only to serve and protect the royal family and never speak while on duty."

"They never speak?" Elidor asked. "How would they raise the alarm, then—if an alarm became necessary?"

"Alarm bells are placed throughout the castle," Alric said. "They are rung if the need arises. They have not sounded in many years. Despite the renegades, the city of Arngrim remains a bastion of safety. So long as you shelter with us, your sleep will be untroubled by war or strife."

Davyn nodded. "We could use some restful sleep." He looked at Nearra, who was still leaning on him. She walked automatically, her eyes half closed.

"I will introduce you to my parents," Alric said. "And then we'll find you quarters."

"The Brethren . . ." Nearra said sleepily. "We need to find out about the Scarlet Brethren."

"All in good time," Alric replied.

He led them through vast, candle-lit halls, past ancient tapestries, glowering portraits of Arngrim ancestors, mounted hunting trophies, and polished coats of arms.

"It's more like a museum than a castle," Davyn whispered to the rest.

"Yes," Elidor replied. He rubbed his chin and smiled slightly.

"That's not entirely fair," Catriona said. "If you had a family home like this, you'd want to cherish and display its history."

"My aunt has a trunk full of 'memories,'" Sindri said. "It's not as big as a castle, but . . ."

Two sentries opened an ornate double doorway at the end of a long hall. They stood to either side of the portal as Alric and the companions passed through.

The room beyond was the most brightly lit area that the travelers had seen in all of Arngrim. Rows of torches lined the walls, and three huge chandeliers, each blazing with candles, dangled overhead. Brightly-colored tapestries hung from the walls, and beautiful carpets lined the stone floor.

At the far end of the room, four silver thrones sat atop a tiered platform. Two large seats perched in the middle of the dais on the topmost level. Two smaller thrones sat one step down, on either side of the central riser. All four had blue velvet backs and were carved with lion motifs.

In the left-hand chair on the top platform sat a woman in a flowing silver and gray dress. A silver circlet set with rubies rested upon her wrinkled brow. Her long, iron gray hair had been rolled into a braid and fastened to the back of her head. She gazed at Alric and the companions with piercing blue-gray eyes. She smiled and rose as the lion-armored prince approached the throne.

"My son," she said, extending her arms.

"Mother," Alric replied, mounting the steps and gently embracing her.

"How good it is to feel your touch once more," the queen said. Her eyes sparkled with delight.

"Yes," Alric replied. "At times during my journey, I feared that I would never see you again. Where is Father?"

"Already abed," said Queen Arngrim. "Your return was foretold, though, and he knew you were safe before sleep took him."

Alric turned to his companions. "The sentries must have spotted our approach long before we entered the city."

His mother sat back in her throne. "I am Queen Valaria Arngrim. I welcome you to our home and city. My husband and I thank you for the safe return of our only son. After the war and our long isolation, we welcome the addition of new blood to our ranks of friends and allies."

She gazed beneficently at the travelers, her blue-gray eyes beaming.

Catriona found herself kneeling, almost without knowing that she'd decided to do it. When she looked up, she saw that all her friends—even Sindri—had knelt as well.

"We know you are weary after a long and difficult journey," the queen said. "Rooms have been prepared for you. You may stay in Arngrim as long as you like."

Rousing slightly, Nearra stumbled to her feet. "We . . ." she began, "that is, I . . . I've come to ask . . ." Davyn rose to support her, but before he could help, her eyes rolled back into her head, and she fainted.

The queen looked gravely concerned. "Does she require a physician?"

"She's been wounded," Davyn said, kneeling to tend his friend, "but not badly. I think she just needs some rest."

"I will send a medic to her chamber," the queen replied, "just in case."

"The rest of you must be exhausted as well," the queen replied sympathetically. "There will be plenty of time to speak on the morrow. Tonight, rest within the confines of Castle Arngrim, knowing that you are safe from renegades and all other menaces. After you have slept and recovered, we will meet again. My husband and I will be happy to discuss why you have come to Arngrim then.

"Our physicians will attend the rest of you as well." The queen turned to Alric, looking concerned. "What of you, my son? Are you all right?"

Alric shook his head. "My complaints are minor," he said. "See to my friends' injuries first."

"Very well," said the queen, turning back to the travelers. "A guard will show you to your chambers."

"Mother," Alric said, interrupting, "if I may, I would like to show my friends the way to the guest quarters."

He caught Catriona's eye and smiled slightly. Catriona fought down the urge to blush.

Queen Arngrim looked at her son, then nodded slowly. "Very well," she said. "If you have nothing of pressing importance to tell me—"

"Nothing that can't wait until later," Alric replied.

"See to your friends, then," the queen said. "We will speak with you afterward." She nodded again, giving her son permission to leave.

Alric turned and motioned for the companions to follow him. The others stood and headed for the doors. Davyn and Catriona helped Nearra, who had revived just a little. As they helped her from the room, the blond girl's eyes lingered on the queen.

"What happened?" she asked sleepily as the doors closed behind them. "What did she say about the Scarlet Brethren? Will they help us?"

"Your fainting kind of put an end to that line of questioning," Elidor replied.

Nearra's eyes widened. She opened her mouth to speak, but her knees gave way again. Davyn and Catriona caught her before she fell.

"Nearra," Davyn said, "you're in no condition to speak to royalty or anyone else right now. You need rest, sleep."

"And the attentions of Arngrim's physicians," Catriona added.

"Yes, perhaps," Nearra admitted. She had a faraway look in her eyes, as though she weren't seeing the castle corridor around them at all.

"I'll see that the physicians are sent to your chambers as soon as they arrive," Alric assured them. "This way, please."

He led them down a series of long, dimly lit stone corridors into another part of the castle. They passed numerous guards along the way, but saw no signs of any other people. "Your rooms have the best views of the city," Alric said, "though it is sometimes difficult to see through the mist."

"Is Arngrim always this foggy?" Sindri asked.

"Not always," Alric said. "More often since . . . the war."

Elidor raised one eyebrow. "Why would that be?"

Alric shrugged and his lion-blazoned armor rattled. "No one knows."

"Perhaps the Scarlet Brethren could find out," Sindri suggested.

"Perhaps," the young prince replied. "They have more pressing duties than tending the weather, though." He smiled. "Ah, here we are already."

He stopped before a short, brightly lit corridor with white-painted plaster walls. Light blue candles illuminated sconces on either side of the hallway. The white wooden doors set into the walls featured silver handles, hinges, and decorative trim. Two silent guards stood watch at the hallway's far end.

"You all have separate but adjoining rooms," Alric said. He pointed to five sets of identical doors on the right-hand side of the corridor. "You can open the doors between them if you like, or keep them closed for privacy. Each room has its own bath, and water has already been drawn."

"How is all this possible?" Davyn asked suspiciously. "We've barely even arrived."

"After the sentries spotted us outside the city, word was sent ahead to make ready," Alric replied. "As you were unknown to those watching, and you were traveling with me, it was assumed that you were to be my guests."

"That's very efficient," Catriona noted.

"Running a castle is largely a matter of anticipation and protocol, or so my mother tells me," Alric said.

"Those four silver thrones," Elidor began, "two were obviously for the king and queen. Who were the others for? Advisors?"

"You might say so," Alric replied. "I sit to my father's right during court affairs. My bride, when I take one, will sit to my mother's left." His gaze came to rest on Catriona.

Catriona felt her face redden, and she turned away, pretending to attend to Nearra, whom she was still supporting.

"So, which room is mine?" Sindri asked.

"Choose as you like, master kender," Alric said. "As I said before, they are all alike." Then he pointed to a pair of white doors set on the other side of the hall. "The double doors across from your rooms are a common area, with books, reading lamps, and comfortable chairs."

"Comfortable enough to sleep in?" Sindri asked.

"I think you'd prefer the bed, master kender," Alric said. "You'll find our accommodations . . . princely." His gray eyes twinkled, and a smile tugged up the corners of his mouth.

"I'll take the room next to Elidor's then," Sindri said, "because I'm sure that Davyn and Catriona will want to be next to Nearra, to protect her. Oh, I could be next to Catriona, too—unless you want to be, Elidor. Catriona didn't promise to protect you, though, like she did me."

"A room on the end will be fine with me," the elf said. "I'll take the one on this side, if no one objects." He glanced toward the guards at the far end of the corridor.

"Yeah, that's good," Davyn said. He caught Catriona's eye. "Let's get Nearra into bed. The sooner those physicians come, the better."

"I . . . I'm fine. Really," Nearra protested. She let go of Catriona and leaned heavily against Davyn.

Davyn looked down at her, concern written on his face.

"Our best physicians will be here shortly," Alric assured them. "Good night to you all. Pull the bell cords in your rooms if you need anything. A servant will attend you."

"Thank you, Alric," Catriona said, offering him her hand in friendship.

Rather than shaking it, the young prince took Catriona's fingers and pressed them to his lips. "Until tomorrow," he said.

Catriona's skin tingled and, for a moment, she couldn't find the voice to reply. "Tomorrow," she finally said.

Ten minutes later, Alric Arngrim paced the ornately furnished antechamber outside the private quarters of his royal parents. Worry creased the young prince's brow.

Queen Valaria sat in an overstuffed chair by the hearth. The fire cast dancing shadows across her face. She looked very calm and alert. "Be patient, my son," she said. "We have waited a long time to end our people's suffering. Another few nights will not make a difference. For now, it is enough that you have returned home safely."

"Why didn't you tell me that Father was away when I arrived?" Alric asked.

The queen smiled indulgently. "You did not arrive alone, my son," she said. "Rather, you brought with you strangers—people we have never seen before. People who could, perhaps, be spies sent by our enemies. Would you have me betray to them that your king is not at home?"

"You don't know these people," Alric said.

"Nor do you," the queen replied. "You met them little more than a day ago."

"They decimated Kokar and his renegades with me," Alric countered.

"They did, but that could be a ruse as well. Many times an enemy will plant an agent who at first will seem to be a friend. Only when confidence is gained does the traitor show his true colors. You tell me they are interested in our royal wizards. Perhaps their motives are not what they claim them to be. Perhaps they have been sent here to destroy us."

Alric shook his head. "Nearra is amnesiac, just as they say."

"Others have pretended to be Arngrim's allies, only to turn out to be our enemies."

"But not these teenagers," Alric protested. "They may be the ones!"

"They may be," Queen Valaria replied. "Time will tell."

"But we have so little time left!" the prince said.

"Time enough," his mother replied. "Rest now. Whether these travelers are friend or foe, we need you refreshed and ready to deal with them. Your future—the future of all Arngrim—depends on it."

9 CASTLE ARNGRIM

When Catriona woke, she could not remember where she was. A cloudy blue satin canopy floated overhead. Everything around her felt soft and warm, comforting—so different from the hard life on the road she had become accustomed to. It seemed as though she must have died and gone to Paradise.

She closed her eyes and luxuriated in the feeling a few moments longer. As she raised her arms over her head, her fingertips brushed against her cheek and felt the bandage clinging there. Then it occurred to her: I'm in the castle—Castle Arngrim—Alric's castle.

Last night, the physicians had come quickly and tended to Nearra and the rest of the companions. They'd cleaned and dressed the Nearra's wound, then given her a draught to help her sleep. As Nearra settled in, the healers had bandaged the others. They'd taken special care with Catriona's cheek. "By Prince Alric's orders, no scar shall mar your pretty face," the chief doctor had said. The words made her blush, but Catriona very much appreciated the effort.

Then the healers left, and Catriona and her friends had fallen into a deep, well-earned slumber. Even now, Catriona felt that she could hardly be awake. Everything seemed like a wonderful dream.

She sat up in bed and gazed around the luxurious room. Everything was tidy and well-kept, from the lush rugs covering the flagstone floor to the carved mantelpiece over the room's fireplace. On a low table near the fire sat a silver teapot and a covered plate.

Catriona wrapped herself in a blanket and tiptoed across the room to the table. On the covered platter she found some rolls, raspberry jam, and butter. She poured herself some tea and ate. Both the tea and the rolls were somewhat cold, but Catriona didn't feel like complaining; she'd had far worse during her long travels.

How late have I slept? she wondered.

It was difficult to tell. Pearly light drifted in through the room's only window. It mingled with the warm glow from the fireplace, filling the room with a hazy illumination.

Fog. Again, Catriona thought and sighed. She finished her food, scampered to the window, and looked out. The city of Arngrim rose out of the mist like jagged rocks jutting from an endless gray sea. The peaks of the buildings moved in and out of view, as the fog ebbed and swayed. Though the shapes of the homes were ordinary enough, everything looked mysterious and unreal.

Sounds drifted up to her from beyond the castle walls; merchants calling to buyers, children playing, the hoof beats of animals on the stone city streets. How wonderful to be alive and in Arngrim! With Alric on their side, obtaining the help of the Scarlet Brethren should not be difficult.

And with Nearra cured, Catriona might move on to other things in her life: other quests, or—perhaps—something else entirely. She gazed out the window at the foggy city, and dared to imagine herself living here.

Why not?

She could learn much from Alric. He was a finer knight than she, and seemed willing to teach her. She could complete her training—if not precisely in the Solamnic way—and then venture out into the world once more.

Or perhaps she could stay. An empty throne sat beside Queen Arngrim—a place for the future princess, Alric's bride. The two of them could rule and fight side by side, banishing all misery from the kingdom, making Arngrim great once more. Catriona sighed, wrapped in the romance of the notion.

A knock sounded on the door to her chamber.

"Just a minute!" Catriona called out. "I'm not decent!"

While traveling, Catriona made a point to sleep in her armor—a practice common among knights. Here, with faithful sentries all around, she'd dared—for once—to take off her metal shell and relax. Lifting the weight of her chainmail from her shoulders had felt so good. Now, though, it left her in an awkward position. Even wearing the silky nightgown she'd found laid out on her bed last night, she felt exposed. She couldn't let anyone see her like this.

Catriona hurried to the room's tall oak wardrobe and flung it open. Inside the wardrobe hung a range of beautiful dresses—nothing like the warrior's garb Catriona was used to. For a moment, the range of choices made her head swim.

Then she grabbed a simple cream-colored dress from the closet, threw it over her head, and wriggled into it. "Almost there!" she called, adjusting the fit. "Just a minute longer."

"Take your time," Elidor replied from the other side of the door. "You've missed breakfast, but there's still lunch in the common room. Join us when you can."

Catriona finished dressing and went across the hall to the common room. The room was large, more than four times as large as her bedroom—and had carpeted floors. Silver chandeliers hung from the ceiling, and enormous paintings decorated the white-plastered walls. Dark oak trim capped the chamber's corners, and wound around the ceiling and baseboards.

She found her friends sitting around the fireplace, eating from silver plates. They dined on brown-shelled eggs, seasoned highland mutton, and fresh-baked potato bread with sweet butter and raspberry jam. It all looked and smelled wonderful.

The others looked up as she entered the room. Catriona froze in the doorway, feeling self-conscious; her friends had never seen her in a dress before.

Davyn smiled. "Catriona, you look . . . " he began.

"Almost ladylike," Elidor finished. He laughed warmly.

Catriona blushed. "It's all I had time to throw on. I'll change into my armor later."

"Don't let them bother you," Nearra said. She was lounging nearby, draped across an upholstered couch. She wore a clean blue dress, similar to the one Catriona had found in her own wardrobe. Nearra's blond hair was tied up in a blue bow. The bandage on her shoulder had been freshly changed and, though she still looked pale and weary, she seemed in far better health than she had the night before. "They're just jealous that we have new clothing and they don't."

"Actually, there's a whole closet full of clothes in my room," Sindri said. "It's all very nice. I spent the morning trying things on. But, the wardrobe didn't really match my status as a wizard. It was all much more suited to the kender you usually meet."

"There were clothes for me, too," Davyn said. "But I don't feel right accepting gifts from people we hardly know."

"For once," Elidor added, "Davyn and I are in agreement." He bowed slightly to the ranger, who scowled back at him.

Nearra shook her head. "You'd think those two liked sleeping on the ground and sheltering in burned-out buildings!" she said. She smiled, then winced.

"Are you all right?" Catriona asked, moving to her side.

"I'm fine," Nearra replied. "I just can't seem to shake this headache. It's been with me since we came to the castle."

Davyn looked concerned.

"Do you need a physician again?" Catriona asked.

"No," Nearra said. She lay back on the couch and sighed. "I could probably use a cleric, though."

"I guess true clerics haven't returned to this part of the world yet," Sindri said. "You can hardly blame them. It was hard getting this far into the mountains."

"Probably true clerics have more important places to be than out-of-the-way city-kingdoms," Davyn said. He crossed to the window and looked out, as if watching for something.

"Or maybe clerics don't trust this place," Sindri said. "My magic indicates there is some kind of enchantment on this land."

Catriona rolled her eyes. But Sindri ignored her.

"It's all kind of weird, isn't it?" he continued. "I mean, with the fog, and everything being so old, and the silent guards, and all those staring portraits, and . . . "

Elidor shook his head. "Kender have no sense of tradition."

"That's not true," Sindri replied. "It's a tradition in my family to slide down Crackbone Tor on New Year's Day. That way, if your luck is going to fail you during that year, you find out right away."

All the others chuckled—even Davyn.

"Does anyone know what time it is?" Catriona asked. "I can't believe I slept so late."

"It's well past midday," Elidor replied. "Nearly teatime—as the people of Palanthas call it. I, too, slept in."

"We all did," Sindri interjected. "I guess we must have been exhausted. It's strange. I really never sleep late. Well, there was this one time—"

"Alric stopped by while you were sleeping, Catriona," Nearra said, gently interrupting the kender. The blond teenager didn't open her eyes as she spoke, but lay quietly on the couch. "We're to have an audience with his parents when we feel up to it."

"I don't know if that's such a good idea, for you, Nearra," Davyn said. He left the window and stood next to her, behind the couch. "You're still weak. The rest of us can talk to the king and queen for you. We can ask for the help of the Scarlet Brethren."

"No," Nearra said, sitting up suddenly. She winced and blinked hard, holding onto the couch back for support. "This is *my* problem. It's because of me that you're all here. I appreciate all that you've done for me—the dangers you've faced—and I appreciate that you're still willing to do things on my behalf. But I need to know whether the Scarlet Brethren can help me or not. I can't just lie back and wait for you to bring me the news."

"We understand," Catriona said, laying her hand sympathetically on Nearra's arm. "We'll make sure that you can attend the audience."

Nearra smiled. "I'm not quite that infirm," she said. With some effort, she rose from the couch and walked, hesitatingly, to the mantelpiece. "Thank you for the offer, Catriona, but I'm quite sure I can make it to the throne room on my own."

"I tried to find the throne room, but I couldn't," Sindri said. "Those armored guards kept getting in my way."

"Really?" Catriona asked.

Sindri nodded. "Yep. Every time I left this corridor, one of them followed me. Then, just when I would get someplace that looked a little interesting, another would step from the shadows and block my way. I think there must be a lot of secret passageways in this castle, because I never saw them coming."

"Did they say why they stopped you?" Nearra asked.

"Ha! Did they need to?" Davyn replied.

The kender frowned at the ranger. "They never said anything," Sindri said. "They just got in my way and lowered their weapons. They weren't really unfriendly, just creepy and . . . determined."

"I, too, was followed when I tried to take my morning—or in this case, early afternoon—constitutional," Elidor said.

Davyn looked suspiciously at the elf, but said nothing.

"Well, that's not really surprising," Catriona replied. "Even though we're guests here, they don't actually know us yet."

"They seem to know some of us well enough," Davyn said. Elidor frowned slightly; Sindri merely smiled.

Nearra rose from the couch, a determined look on her pale face. "Well, the sooner we talk to the king and queen, the sooner we can see the Scarlet Brethren, and the sooner we can get out of here and away from Alric's creepy watchdog guards."

Catriona opened her mouth to speak, then closed it again. She wasn't in any hurry to leave Castle Arngrim, though she could see why Nearra and the others might be. Instead of saying anything, she went to the corner and pulled the bell rope to summon a servant.

Half an hour later, all five companions seated themselves in a row of high-backed chairs set in the audience chamber next to the throne room.

Alric, the queen, and the king sat on a small dais across the room. The royals' chairs resembled miniature replicas of the thrones the travelers had seen the day before. The tall seats were covered with silver inlay and far more elaborate than the carved wooden chairs the companions used.

Queen Valaria seated herself on the right. There was an empty spot next to her, reserved, Catriona supposed, for Alric's future bride. King Conar Arngrim sat on the left, with Alric in the seat on his right.

Conar wore purple robes and a crown of jeweled silver. Silver bracers—wide armbands extending from his wrist nearly to his elbow—carved with lion motifs, adorned his aging arms. His hair was iron gray, like the queen's. It would have fallen to his shoulders, but he kept it tied back, behind his ears. His steel blue stare was every bit as piercing as the gaze of his wife. Across his lap lay a silver scepter, which Catriona judged would make a decent mace if the king needed to suddenly protect himself.

Attacking the royals would have been folly, of course. Four of their silent guardsmen flanked the dais on which the royal family sat. Six more stood by the three exits to the room. One door led to the corridor through which the companions had entered. The second led into the throne room, or so Catriona assumed from its placement. She guessed the third probably emerged into passages leading to the royal chambers.

Searching out exits had been part of Catriona's Solamnic training. She did it automatically whenever she entered an unknown area. In this case, she felt somewhat guilty about it. She and her friends had come as guests of the royal family. It would be unseemly if the king and queen knew she was divining escape routes from their audience chamber. Catriona felt glad that neither Alric nor his parents could read her mind.

King Conar smiled benevolently at his guests. "So, Alric," he said, "these are the young people your mother has told me about." The king's utterance was deep, but dry, as though long years of speaking had taken their toll on his voice.

"Yes," Alric replied formally. "May I present Davyn, Nearra, Elidor of the elves, Sindri of the kender, and the knight Catriona."

"Knight-in-training," Catriona said softly. She had no right to claim herself a true knight yet, no matter how much she wanted Alric and his family to think well of her.

"A pleasure to meet Your Majesty," Elidor said, rising from his seat and kneeling. Catriona and the others did the same.

They remained kneeling until the king said, "Sit, sit. You are our guests, not our servants or subjects."

The companions got up and seated themselves once more.

"We are pleased that you have come to our city," the king said. "And we understand that you have rendered some service to our son."

"Indeed, Father," Alric said. "Together, we vanquished Kokar and his band. My entire retinue had been killed by the renegade and his followers. I was lucky enough to escape. If I had not found Catriona and her friends, I might not have survived."

"Alric helped us as much as we helped him," Catriona added, fighting down embarrassment. "Without him, we would never have made it to Arngrim."

"I would have made it," Sindri said. "I am a great wizard, you know."

"Indeed?" the king said, raising a long-whiskered eyebrow.

"Catriona is being modest," Alric added. "I really did very little to help them. She and her companions defeated twice their number in Kokar's men with no assistance from me. With his army devastated, Kokar will not trouble Arngrim for many years. These five have struck a mighty blow in the defense of our king-dom—though not without cost." He indicated the fresh bandage on Nearra's shoulder.

"As we have seen," Queen Valaria said. Addressing the pretty blond girl, she asked, "How are you this day, my dear? Did the physicians treat you well? You still look a little bloodless."

"I will recover, ma'am, I mean, Your Majesty," Nearra said. "Thank you."

She rose to her feet and some of the color came back to her face. Nearra's eyes flashed, reflecting the candles that lit the windowless room. "If we could please talk about why we've come. I have lost much of my memory. We have reason to believe that the wizards known as the Scarlet Brethren may be able to help me. Alric told us that they worked for your court. Could we speak with them, please? Could you get them to help us—to help *me*?" She kneeled before the royal dais, though her gaze remained fixed on the king and queen.

"The Scarlet Brethren are, indeed, the royal wizards of Arngrim," the king said. "They are very powerful, and might be able to help with your plight. However, I regret to inform you that they are currently occupied with other matters."

Nearra's expression wavered between confusion and anger.

"Do not lose hope, girl," Queen Valaria interjected. "We will still aid you if we can. Unfortunately, the Brethren are not here. They are on a pilgrimage away from the city. They are traveling to a sacred location, many leagues from our castle, to perform a ceremony which may help end the misfortune plaguing our kingdom."

"Though their mission is of the most vital importance," King Conar continued, "we will send word for them to hasten back to Arngrim as soon as they are able. Once their duties are done, we will see to it that the Brethren give you the help you crave."

"How long?" Nearra asked, tears budding at the corners of her eyes.

"We are not wizards," the king replied. "We have no way of knowing how long it may take to complete their mission."

"Rest assured, though," the queen said, "you are welcome to stay in Castle Arngrim as our guests for however long it may be. We will do what we can to aid you and to ease your discomforts. When the wizards return, they will find you ready for whatever trials the cure to your malady may force you to endure."

A look of anger flashed across Nearra's face. For a moment, Catriona feared that her friend might lash out at the king and queen. Then the anger passed, and Nearra bowed again. "Thank you," she said quietly. She rose and returned to her seat.

"We understand your impatience," the queen said sympathetically. "Know that we will do everything we can to end your suffering just as soon as possible."

Nearra seemed unable to answer, so Davyn spoke for her. "Thank you, Your Majesty."

"Alric is right," the king commented to his wife. "These youngsters are brave and strong."

The queen sighed. "If only you were grown warriors, perhaps you could bolster our army. With more like you, our city might be saved."

"Pardon me for saying," Sindri said, "but it seems to me that you've got plenty of warriors here already. We can't go any place in the castle without bumping into them. I almost feel like I'm in a museum dedicated to suits of armor." He grinned.

"Why can't your knights rout renegades like Kokar and any others who invade your land?" Davyn asked.

"It is true," the queen said. "Our royal guard is powerful and well trained."

"They are, in fact, perfect servants," the king continued, "loyal, obedient, and unswerving. Unfortunately, there are far too few of them to drive our enemies from the land. Those who protect the castle and city are all we have left of a once mighty force."

"You should recruit more, then," Catriona said.

"Alas, that is not as easy as you might hope," the queen replied. "The blood of Arngrim has grown thin over the years. The lines of our great warriors have waned almost to non-existence."

The king looked very sad. "Every year, more of our people die than are born. If one of our knights perishes, there are none to replace him or her. Our kingdom has long been separate from the world outside."

"If the miseries that plague our land could be banished," the queen said, "if trade with other nations could be reestablished, then Arngrim would grow strong once more. Sadly, the long war has isolated us. If our troubles do not end soon, we will vanish into the fog of history."

"That is why the Scarlet Brethren have left the city," the king concluded. "That is why they work so diligently to break this . . . this curse that hangs over Arngrim. Something must be done—and soon. We fear that the recent war may have sounded a death knell for our kingdom. The loss of our people, both peasants and knights, could be more than the nation can bear. Though driven off, Kokar may have been the final nail in our coffin lid. Within a generation, Arngrim may be no more than memory."

"I can see how that might happen," Sindri said. "Your kingdom is already hard to find—even if you have a map. It's almost like Arngrim doesn't *want* to be found—with the fog and all. No wonder you don't get many travelers."

For a moment, Catriona feared that the king and queen might take offense at Sindri's words, but Conar and Valaria merely smiled at the kender.

The king leaned back in his chair and sighed. The crown resting on his head suddenly looked very heavy to Catriona. "You youngsters shouldn't worry about such things," he said. "You have enough troubles of your own, I'm sure—especially the beautiful Nearra." He fixed his eyes on the girl and she blushed slightly.

"Because of your bravery, and the aid you gave our son, we offer you sanctuary here until the Scarlet Brethren return," the queen said. "You have the run of the castle and the city. Go where you wish and enjoy the hospitality of Arngrim."

"Does this mean your weird knights won't follow us around any more?" Sindri asked.

The king and queen laughed. "They will guard certain sections of the castle that are forbidden to outsiders—such as the royal chambers," the king said. "On the whole, though, you may explore our realm unhindered."

"Great!" Sindri piped. A slight smile flickered at the corner of Elidor's lips as well.

"Go now. Regain your strength," Queen Valaria said. "Dinner will be brought when you call for it."

"Dinner?" Davyn said. "But we just got up. We barely had lunch."

"You slumbered for most of the day," Alric explained. "Time can pass quickly in Arngrim."

"So, the place *is* enchanted or something!" Sindri chirped. "I knew it! I knew there was a reason we couldn't find it more easily."

Alric laughed indulgently at the kender. "The fog that suffuses our valley makes it difficult to count the passage of hours."

"Especially in this windowless chamber," the king added. "Tradition is all that keeps me from remodeling it."

The companions all laughed, too, then wished their hosts good day. When the five friends exited the audience chamber, they were only slightly surprised to note that—as the king and queen had said—the sun was already setting beyond the fog-shrouded windows.

As they walked back through the winding corridors toward their chambers, Nearra leaned heavily against Davyn.

"Are you all right?" Catriona asked her.

"Just that headache," Nearra replied. "It won't seem to go away." She stopped suddenly in front of one of the portraits on the wall. It was an ancient painting, showing a tall, pinch-faced man in flowing red robes.

"What is it?" Davyn asked, concerned.

"I . . ." Nearra began, "I feel like I've seen this picture before."

"Ooh! A vision!" Sindri said. "More evidence of enchantment! This place is turning out to be so interesting!"

"More likely Nearra read a history of the Arngrims," Elidor suggested.

Nearra shook her head. "I don't think so," she said. "I should go back to my chambers. Rest some more."

"A wound like yours can take a lot out of a person," Catriona noted.

"I'm sure she'll be fine," Davyn replied protectively. He took Nearra's arm and led her away from the painting. Elidor helped support her on the other side.

Catriona gazed at the knights, wizards, princes, and ladies

in the portraits and tapestries as the companions walked down the candlelit halls. She didn't know what Nearra had seen in the pictures, but she knew what she saw: chivalry and a tradition of knightly nobility. Clearly, the Arngrims held the same goals she aspired to.

Despite the kingdom's troubles, Alric and his family were living the life Catriona wanted to lead. They were fighting the good fight to save the things they cherished.

As the five friends neared their quarters, footsteps echoed down the hall behind them. The companions wheeled, their reflexes still keen from the dangers of the journey. Davyn reached for his knife, though he and the rest had left their weapons in their rooms.

Alric, dressed in an informal blue and gray tunic, skidded around the corner behind them. At the sight of him, all the companions relaxed.

"Catriona," Alric said, coming to a halt, "I'd be happy to give you a tour of the castle if you like." As Catriona started to blush, the prince hastily added, "And your friends as well, of course."

Catriona glanced at the others, secretly hoping that they'd refuse Alric's offer.

"No thanks," Davyn replied. "Nearra really needs to rest."

"That's all right, Davyn," Nearra said. "You can go."

Davyn shook his head. "No, really. I'd rather not. I'm tired myself." He yawned and tried to look sleepy, though Catriona thought he wasn't doing a very good job of faking it.

"I'd love to see the castle," Sindri chimed. Elidor glanced from Catriona to the prince and elbowed the kender. "Ow! What did you do that for?" Sindri asked.

Elidor sighed and shrugged at Catriona.

"Since three's a crowd and four's a party, I, too, would be delighted to take a *guided* tour," Elidor said. His violet eyes gleamed. Catriona noticed that Davyn frowned at the elf. Clearly, despite all they'd been through, the two still did not trust each other. Catriona couldn't blame either one; she didn't completely trust Davyn and Elidor, either.

"What about you, Catriona?" Alric asked.

She smiled. "I'd be honored."

"That's great," Sindri said, beaming. "Make sure you show us all the weird, magical, off-limits-to-strangers stuff. It's not often that I get a chance to tour an enchanted castle, and I don't want to miss anything."

10 NIGHT WALKERS

"Davyn! Davyn!"

The cry woke the boy immediately. It wasn't very loud, but it came from Nearra's chambers.

He sprinted to the connecting door, but found it locked. She'd locked it before he left her, he remembered. Cursing, he ran out his door and through the main door from the corridor into Nearra's room.

He found her standing next to her bed, dressed in a pale blue nightgown. Her body was drenched with sweat and her blond hair hung in tangles over her shoulders. Her eyes looked wild.

"What is it?" he asked.

"This place!" she said. "I can't stay here!"

"You have to stay here," Davyn said. "We have to stay here. The Scarlet Brethren are coming. They may be able to restore your memories."

"No," she said, shaking her head. "Something terrible is going to happen. I know it!" Her eyes remained fixed and staring, as though she were looking past the room's four walls and into some other place. "Do you see them? Do you see them staring at me?" She pointed to a portrait on the wall of her room. It was yellow with age, and showed a young woman in Arngrimite lion armor. The portrait didn't move. It didn't look sinister in any way.

89

Davyn put his hand on her forehead. "You're feverish," he said. "Try to lie down. I'll get you something to drink." He took a pitcher of water from the table by her bed, poured her a glass, and held it to her lips.

Nearra swallowed a bit, and then blinked. "Davyn?" she asked. "What are you doing in my room?"

"You had a nightmare," he replied. "You called me. It's all right now." He set the glass of water down by her bedside and helped her back into bed. "I think you're running a fever. It would probably be best if you didn't get up again."

Worry played across her pale face. "I don't remember getting up at all."

"I think you were sleepwalking. It's all right now. It's all over." He paused and held his breath. "Are you remembering anything?"

Nearra shook her head. "I have flashes, but nothing recognizable. Maybe Sindri's right. This place does make me feel kind of . . . creepy. I'm not sure why. If only I didn't have this blazing headache." She closed her eyes and rubbed her temples.

"Do you want me to ring for the doctors?"

"No," she replied. "I just need sleep." She smiled at him again and then looked meaningfully toward the door. "Please, don't nursemaid me so, Davyn. I may not have my memory, but I'm not a baby."

Davyn sighed. "All right," he said. "Call if you need me."

"I will. Don't worry. But . . ."

"But what?"

"What if I go sleepwalking?" Despite her protests, she looked worried.

"The doors are locked," Davyn said. "The window is too small to climb through, and the locks are very sturdy."

She nodded. "Yes. You're right. With the doors locked, where could I go?"

Davyn smiled reassuringly, but the truth was, he had no idea where she might go—even with the door locked. He didn't know enough about either Castle Arngrim or the Emergence to know what kind of danger might confront Nearra. He felt certain that his father had sent them to Arngrim. But to what purpose? Was Nearra's sleepwalking part of the Emergence?

Silently, he cursed himself for ever becoming involved. If only he'd seen the danger in his father's schemes. If only he had been able to convince Maddoc to leave Nearra alone.

Until a few weeks ago, defying his father had been completely unthinkable. Even now, Davyn felt some guilt about going against the wizard's plans.

Maddoc was old and wise. What if he did know what was best? What if Nearra and the others, and even Davyn himself, needed to be sacrificed for the greater good?

Davyn wished he could share his worries with someone, if not his actual involvement with Maddoc's schemes. Nearra was closest to him, and he couldn't tell her. Especially not her. He'd kept his distance, emotionally, from the others so far. At this moment, though, he longed for a friend.

Nearra smiled weakly at him. "Go on," she said. "I'll be fine." She tried to make it convincing, but her eyes looked glassy, and her hands trembled.

"I'll lock the adjoining door from my side," Davyn said.

"Just make sure you don't lose the key," she said, forcing a laugh.

"I won't."

He left through the corridor door, taking her key with him. He locked the outer door, and then went to his own room. As he slipped inside, though, he heard a faint creaking sound out in the corridor.

Davyn shut his door all but a crack—just enough to peer out into the hallway. For a moment, he feared that Nearra had somehow discovered a way to open her door.

Because everyone in the castle was sleeping, only a few candles remained burning in the hallway. The light from the thin tapers left large portions of the corridor in shadow. Straining to see through the darkness, Davyn spotted a shadowy figure stealing quickly down the corridor.

Davyn's heart leaped in his chest. He went out and checked, but Nearra's door remained locked tight. Who had been lurking in the corridor? Could it be one of Maddoc's spies? Davyn had to find out.

He quickly locked the interior, adjoining door to Nearra's room. Then he dashed down the hall after the shadow. Nearra's initial cry had awoken him. He'd been in bed, not wearing his boots. The stone floor felt cold through the stockings on his feet, but at least that gave him the chance to catch up to the intruder without making a racket.

The intruder was well ahead of him, and made little noise. Davyn ran in the direction he'd last seen the shape, racing past the glowering portraits on the shadowed walls. The corridor ended in a T-shaped intersection.

Which way had the spy gone? Davyn thought that the royal chambers lay to the right. Maddoc's agent probably wouldn't go that way. That part of the castle would be more heavily guarded by the silent knights.

Davyn raced to the left and turned another corner just in time to hear the creak of a door ahead. The young ranger skidded to a stop and listened. His sharp senses quickly located the source of the sound. He padded almost silently down the corridor to the doorway.

The door had not been latched, so he pushed it ajar, just slightly. A pale blue light filtered out from inside. The room appeared to be a study. Bookcases lined its walls, and an ornate desk sat in the middle. Neither the fireplace nor the room's many candelabra were lit.

A shadowy shape moved through the chamber, searching. A pale blue glow, the room's only illumination, came from something cupped in the intruder's hand.

A chill shot down Davyn's spine as he realized he did, indeed, know this prowler.

11   The Hand of a Friend

Elidor moved around the darkened study quickly and deliberately. He picked up the candlesticks, then replaced them. He checked behind the paintings lining the walls. He examined a lion-head bust on the mantelpiece, weighed it in his hands, and put it back down. Finally, he moved to the desk. Finding it locked, he stooped and began working on one of the drawers.

Davyn realized what was going on: Elidor didn't care a whit about Nearra or any of the rest of them. He didn't care if they were kicked out of the castle before the Scarlet Brethren helped Nearra. The elf didn't care about his so-called friends. He intended to rob the Arngrims!

Elidor crouched behind the desk, his back to the door. The sound of soft clicking, like a key turning in a lock, echoed through the room.

Davyn slipped silently into the chamber and crept up behind the elf.

Elidor turned at the last instant, daggers appearing in both his hands. Then he stopped and a crooked grin spread over his face. "Oh, Davyn," he said. "It's you."

"It would serve you right if it wasn't!" Davyn whispered. "It would serve you right if I'd been one of Alric's sentries!"

"The guards are nowhere near here," Elidor said. "I took note of their locations during my tour earlier. The king and queen were right when they said they had too few knights." He smiled, his eyes glistening in the pale blue light. "Far too few to guard all this palace's treasures."

Davyn saw that the elf's illumination came from a small stone set in the abdomen of a metal cricket attached to a chain at Elidor's wrist. The glowing bug cast only as much light as the stars on a clear night—more than enough for an elf to see by. Davyn wondered a moment why Elidor risked using it, then he noticed the insect's back legs. They were twined together, and looked very much like a key. Before he could look further, Elidor tapped the bug's back and its legs straightened. To all appearances, it was now nothing more than a dimly glowing charm.

Fury built up within Davyn's gut. "Are you out of your mind?" he asked. "What are you doing here?"

"Just checking out a few things," Elidor said. He turned away from Davyn and began rummaging through the desk drawers.

"Are you trying to find something to steal? I can't believe you're doing this!"

Elidor laughed quietly. "I'm a thief. It's what I do. Oh, here's something nice." He held up a small silver pin in the shape of a lion's head, then quickly stuck it into a pocket.

"Stop that!" Davyn said, grabbing the elf's right wrist. "What if you get caught? You could get us all expelled from the castle."

"I'm not going to *get* caught."

"Ha!" Davyn said. "I've caught you already."

Elidor smiled again, and this time there was something sinister about it. "Yes, but you're not going to tell anyone, Davyn," he said.

"The Abyss I'm not!" Davyn shot back. "Do you think I'm going to jeopardize getting Nearra help? Have you forgotten the promise we all made to her?"

"I haven't forgotten," Elidor said. "I don't see that this has anything to do with it."

"Doesn't have anything to do with it?" Davyn sputtered. "If you get caught, it'll mess things up good. That's why I'm going to call the guards and tell the Arngrims what you've been up to."

"But telling anyone about my activities would surely jeopardize Nearra's meeting with the Scarlet Brethren," Elidor said smoothly. "By reporting on my . . . proclivities, you'd be bringing about exactly the result you fear. I don't think you're that foolish, Davyn."

"The Arngrims will know that the rest of us aren't in this with you," Davyn countered. "My turning you in will be proof we're not involved. When they search your things, they'll find whatever it is that you took from the burned-out house as well. They'll know you're just a renegade looter, like that bandit Kokar."

For a moment, anger flashed in Elidor's violet eyes. Then he mastered himself, and smiled once more. He gently removed his wrist from Davyn's hand.

"Ah," Elidor purred, "but if you tell the royal family about my, shall we say, 'personal' activities, I'll have to reveal yours as well. You're not as pure as driven snow, either, Davyn."

A chill ran down Davyn's spine. "What do you mean?" he asked.

"I'd have to tell them about the company you keep when no one's looking," Elidor said. "Company like goblins, black-plumed birds, and a certain dark dwarf. Oddvar, I believe his name was?"

The chill settled, rocklike, in the bottom of Davyn's stomach. "How . . . ?" was all he could manage to say.

"You're not the only one who can spy on people, ranger," Eldior said. "Some of us, in fact, are much better at such pursuits than others."

Davyn felt the urge to seize the elf by the shirt and shake the truth out of him. Then he remembered Elidor's daggers—no longer evident, but never more than a quick gesture away from the elf's fingertips.

"What do you know?" Davyn asked, his voice hoarse and dry.

"You're not as innocent as you pretend," Elidor said. "I know that the wizard you purport to have nothing to do with is, in fact, guiding your every movement. I know that the creatures that attacked Nearra during our journey were doing the wizard Maddoc's bidding—just like you."

Davyn felt as though he were twisting on a gibbet, swaying in a harsh wind while above an icy sea. Short of Elidor revealing himself to be another of Maddoc's agents, Davyn couldn't imagine how things might be worse.

"Why are you so worried about me when you're the one leading Nearra and the rest into yet another trap?" the elf said sarcastically. "Tell me, Davyn, is everything going according to plan?"

The young ranger's tongue sat frozen in his mouth.

"The wizard has you in his pocket, boy," the elf said coolly, "and now I have you as well."

Anger boiled away the chill from Davyn's soul. He balled his fists up and tensed his arms. He considered beating the daylights out of the elf. "What do you want?" he asked through clenched teeth.

"Want?" Elidor said with a laugh. "I don't want anything from you. Not yet, anyway. I merely wish to be left alone to pursue my hobbies in peace. If you leave me alone, I'll leave you alone. Then you and Maddoc can get on with whatever you're up to."

"We're not up to anything," Davyn insisted. "I don't work for him anymore."

"And a lynx can change its spots."

"It's true," Davyn said, his voice rising. "I'm helping Nearra now. That's all I want. That's why I came to stop you stealing."

Elidor shrugged. "If you insist. But, please, keep your voice down, or you'll have the guards on both of us. Now. . . If you would be so kind as to leave, I have things to look after."

"You're going with me," Davyn said.

"I'm not."

"You are," Davyn insisted, "or I'll turn us both in. So help me."

Elidor smiled again, an expression that Davyn was rapidly coming to hate. "You're angry enough that I think you might actually do it," the elf said. "Very well. There's nothing more of value here anyway. Let's go."

He shut the drawers of the desk and went to the door. Just before opening it, he turned. "From now on, Davyn, you keep out of my way."

Davyn didn't reply. What could he say? Elidor had him, and he knew it.

They walked in silence back to the guestroom hallway. There, Elidor bowed once before ducking into his room. Davyn waited for the elf's door to close before retiring to his own chambers.

The young ranger sat down on his bed, his body quaking with a mixture of anger and fear. How had his life become so messed up? He ran his fingers through his sweat-drenched hair and took a deep breath. He needed to get out of this trap he'd gotten himself into, but he couldn't see how to do it.

No. That wasn't true.

There was one way.

He could tell the truth—the whole truth—to Nearra and the others. Then Elidor would have no hold over him, and neither would Maddoc.

The others would hate him if he did it, though. He had seen their betrayed looks when he told them just part of the truth. After the battle in the temple, he'd said that he had met Maddoc in the forest before finding Nearra. Even that lie had been a blow to Nearra's trust in him. How much worse would it be if she discovered that Maddoc was his father?

No. He couldn't tell her, or the others. Not now.

Maybe once Nearra had her memory back. Then all his lies wouldn't seem so important. Then, they'd know that Davyn had done everything he could to help—despite his association with the wizard.

Davyn pushed the sopping wet hair back out of his face, and dried the tears he hadn't even noticed from his cheeks.

A bath would feel so good right now. It was late, but Alric had said they should ring if they needed anything. After all, what were servants for?

Yes. He'd take a hot bath and forget all about tonight's unpleasantness with Elidor.

First, though, he needed to check on Nearra and make sure she was okay.

Davyn rose from his bed, went to the door connecting the two rooms, and turned the key. He opened the door and peered inside.

Blankets lay scattered on the floor. Nearra's bed was empty. Davyn looked around frantically. She was not in the room.

Nearra was gone.

CHAPTER

12   Dark Shadows

Davyn ran through the darkened halls. He didn't dare call out her name. He didn't want to alert anyone—not his friends, not the royal family, not the guards.

Only *he* had any comprehension of what Nearra might be going through. The lock on her door had been charred and twisted, shattered beyond repair. Had Nearra done that somehow? Had it been part of the Emergence?

And where was she now? When he found her, would he even recognize her, or would she have become Maddoc's *creature*?

Davyn didn't know precisely what his father had planned for the girl but, as time went on, he feared it more and more. What good could come of these nightmares Nearra was forced to endure? What good could come of the deadly tests that Maddoc had arranged for her? Would anyone benefit from this Emergence save Maddoc himself?

Certainly, Nearra would not.

Davyn cursed himself for being a fool. How could he have ever thought his father was a good man, when Maddoc consorted with goblins and dark dwarves? The wizard had lied to Davyn, sending a dragon to kill the companions after he promised to let them be. Clearly, Maddoc was willing to sacrifice the others to achieve his goal. Perhaps he intended to sacrifice Davyn as well. If the wizard would let his son die, who could tell what terrible fate Maddoc might have in store for Nearra?

Just considering it made Davyn feel sick to his stomach.

Perhaps the worst had already happened. Perhaps there was nothing left of the sweet, blond-haired girl that Davyn knew and cared for.

The lock on the outer door had shattered easily under Nearra's grasp. She remained unsure how that had happened. She barely even remembered getting out of bed.

The castle's corridors were very dark, a vast winding maze of history. The flagstones of the floor felt very cold beneath her bare feet. Nearra hardly noticed it.

She had no clear idea of where she was going; no real idea of where she'd been, either. Everything seemed one long, waking dream. Except for the headaches; those were a nightmare.

Images flashed through her fevered brain: standing in the rain, the wind lashing her dark cloak to her slender body; soaring above the mountains, like a great hawk, looking down on the fertile valley below; a dark underground chasm, filled with fire and murder; fog, wrapping itself around her like gray death.

The eyes of the portraits she passed stared at her, accusingly.

Her blood rushed in her ears, her heartbeat a booming drum.

She leaned against a cold stone wall and clutched her hands to her head, trying to make the pain go away.

It didn't.

She remembered the portrait of the pinched-faced wizard. His painted eyes came alive; his stare bored into her brain. Other portraits she'd seen came to life, too, whispering behind her back, cursing her. Though alone in the darkened corridor, she felt surrounded by enemies.

Why was this all so familiar to her? Lightning seemed to flash within Nearra's head.

She saw a king and queen, sitting atop silver thrones. They were kind, benevolent people; they treated their subjects fairly. They loved their subjects almost as much as they loved their handsome young son.

Suddenly, a shadow entered the throne room. The king and queen clutched at their throats. They fell to the floor, gasping for breath, maybe dying. Their attendants and courtiers fell with them. The whole court writhed on the flagstones. The darkness merely laughed.

"Alric!" the queen cried.

The corridors of the castle flew by, a blur of motion. Nearra glanced to her left and caught a fleeting glimpse of a mirror. In the mirror, she saw not herself, but a dark-haired woman in a green dress. The woman winked at her and smiled wickedly.

The portraits on the walls hissed at Nearra as she ran. The voices rose in pitch and volume, assaulting her ears, making her head throb worse.

"Cursed for all time . . . !"

"You're mad . . . insane . . ."

"Rue the day . . ."

The cold, mocking laughter of the darkness rose above them all. The sound howled like the wind. It ripped at her body even as it tore through her mind.

No! Stop! Nearra thought.

"Too late!" the darkness whispered back.

Images of death swirled all around her: people she didn't know—thousands of them, a line of the dead stretching back over the mountains.

Ahead of her, rising out of the fog, came her friends: Elidor, Sindri, Catriona . . . and then Davyn. Nearra lifted her bloodstained hand, and black lightning flashed. Davyn and the others screamed.

Moments later, they rose again as hideous specters. Their pale flesh hung in tatters from bleached bones. Each one pointed at her accusingly.

Nearra tried to cover her eyes, to block out the terrible phantoms. But her hands had become transparent. She could see right through them.

Then, she was back in the castle once more. At the far end of the corridor, a sentry burned—a pillar of flame. He stood silent and still, as if unaware of the fire consuming him.

Nearra turned away and dashed down a side corridor. The serpent of her nightmares followed after her, hissing and laughing, waiting to pounce and devour her whole.

The sound inside her skull built to a deafening cacophony.

This wasn't like before—not like the voice she'd heard in her head at the temple, this was a thousand times worse. A thousand dead voices screaming in her head.

She crumpled to the floor and clutched her hands over her ears.

A sound welled up in her head and burst from her mouth.

She screamed.

"LEAVE ME ALONE!"

The piercing wail shook the hallway like thunder.

It was so loud, it almost didn't sound like Nearra's voice.

Davyn dashed around the corner before the echo died away and saw Nearra, huddled in a heap in the middle of the corridor.

Shattered glass fell like razor-sharp raindrops all around her. Everything breakable in the hall lay in ruins: the window panes, a large mirror above a bureau on one wall, several pieces of porcelain statuary, and every bit of pottery. Jagged debris littered the floor. The flagstone directly in front of Nearra smoked, as though a fire had been recently extinguished there. A fist-sized spot in the floor glowed red hot.

Stepping carefully among the shards, Davyn hurried to his friend's side.

"Nearra!" he whispered. "Nearra, are you okay?"

He knelt down beside her. She didn't seem to be hurt, though cold sweat drenched her hair, her nightgown, and her bandages.

"Nearra!" he said, taking her in his arms. She shuddered, and silent sobs wracked her body.

"It's all right," Davyn whispered. "I'm here now. Nothing can hurt you." He stroked her hair tenderly.

She looked up at him, her eyes brimming with tears. "What happened?" she gasped.

"I don't know," Davyn replied, then felt the dagger of a half-truth twisting in his stomach. He opened his mouth as if to explain, then stopped. A faint, clattering sound drifted down the corridors to his ears.

"We have to get out of here," he said. "The guards are coming. We don't want them to find us."

She nodded weakly and he helped her to her feet, being careful not to step on the shattered glass.

"This way," Davyn said. He led her down the corridor the opposite way he'd come.

As they dashed around the corner, he caught a glimpse of two of Arngrim's silent guards entering the hallway from the other end. Davyn didn't wait around to see their reaction to the mess.

The next few minutes passed in a frantic haze. Davyn kept them moving, fearing the guards might be on their heels. They turned left, and then right, and then left again. Davyn's keen sense of direction served him well in the twisting corridors, though he wished he'd taken Alric's tour of the castle.

While they ran, the young ranger kept his eyes and his ears trained for indications of pursuit. But if the knights were following them, Davyn saw no sign.

They slowed only as they neared the guestroom hallway. Davyn brought them to a halt just around the corner from their quarters. "Wait here," he whispered.

Nearra nodded her understanding. Her blue eyes—scared but trusting—remained fixed on Davyn.

A pang of guilt stabbed through his stomach. He looked away from her, forcing himself to concentrate on scouting the corridor ahead.

How could Nearra trust him? He had nearly led her to her doom more than once. If she knew his true background, she would run from him as fast as they were fleeing from the Arngrim sentries.

He would have to tell her. He would confess and the guilt would lift from his shoulders forever. He would explain that he'd broken from Maddoc's schemes. He'd reveal what he knew of the wizard's plans for Nearra. He would tell her of the Emergence and together they could stop it.

But first he would have to earn Nearra's trust—make it clear that, no matter what his lineage, no matter that he'd come to her under false pretenses, he was on her side. Now and forever.

Davyn peered around the corner into the guest hallway beyond. The corridor lay still and empty; the few candles lighting it burned low in their holders.

He turned back to Nearra. "The coast is clear," he said, taking her hand.

They walked around the corner and ran smack into Elidor.

A nightshirt adorned the elf's wiry frame, but he didn't look like he'd been sleeping. "What's all the commotion?" Elidor asked. He smiled and glanced meaningfully at Davyn. "Doing a little 'exploring' of your own, Davyn? Did you find anything interesting?"

Davyn felt as though the elf were laughing at him. He fought down an urge to wipe the smug smile off of Elidor's face.

"Nothing's wrong," Davyn said, a little more loudly than he'd intended. "We just took a little walk. We're going back to bed now—going back to our own rooms."

"Did you hear an alarm when you were out?" the elf asked. "Something woke me from my sleep. I thought it was an alarm bell." He cocked his head as if listening.

Davyn's face reddened. "I don't hear anything," he replied, not really wanting to stop and listen. "We didn't hear any alarms during our walk."

Nearra shook her head. "No," she said, "we didn't."

Catriona, dressed in a nightgown but carrying her sword, appeared in the doorway to her room. "What's going on?" she asked. "Is Nearra all right?"

"I'm fine," Nearra said.

"She's fine," Davyn insisted, a little too forcefully.

Catriona looked as though she didn't believe them. "Well, you should get to your beds," she said. "After our long journey, we still need sleep. We all want to be rested for the Scarlet Brethren when they arrive."

Yawning, Sindri Suncatcher poked his head out his door. "Are you all up, too?" the kender asked. "Do any of you know the way to the pantry? I could really use a midnight snack."

"Ring the bell," Davyn suggested. "One of the servants will bring you food."

"Where's the fun in that?" Sindri asked. Then he paused. "Hmm, if I do, do you think the food will appear magically? That might happen in an enchanted castle. That would be so exciting!"

Davyn ignored him. "C'mon, Nearra. Let's get you back into bed."

"All right," she replied. "I'm exhausted."

As Davyn escorted her to her door, she added, "I just hope I don't have any more bad dreams."

Davyn glanced at the others, trying to gauge how much they knew or guessed. All of them, even Elidor, looked concerned. Davyn smiled weakly at them, then helped Nearra into her room.

"This kind of chaos is intolerable," King Conar Arngrim said. He shifted in the throne-like chair that dominated his personal study. His eyes fell across his desk, the candelabra, the paintings on the wall, before finally coming to rest on the lion's head bust over the mantelpiece. "Look at this mess. One of these outsiders is responsible."

Queen Valaria sat on a stuffed sofa across from her husband. "Yes," she said, "but which one?"

"My guess would be the kender," Alric said. The young prince paced in front of the room's small fireplace. The fire inside burned low; reflections of the red embers danced in Alric's gray eyes. "Sindri's kind are known for such pranks. Often, they do not even intend the trouble they cause."

"The kender should be expelled from the castle," the king said angrily. "It was a mistake for you to bring them here, Alric. You should have been sure first."

"And how much longer would you have our son wait, Conar?" the queen purred. "Surely our kingdom has suffered enough. The arrival of these youngsters is exactly what the omens predicted."

"They didn't predict a kender," the king said grumpily. "We can't be sure that these five, not any of them, are the ones foretold."

"I believe they are," Alric said. "I believe that they can help us end the curse that plagues our country. Do not judge them by their youth, father. I have seen their courage, their valiant deeds. I truly believe that one of them possesses the Lionheart."

"You would say that," the king replied. "Any fool can see the feelings you have for that girl. But just because you're fond of her doesn't make her—or any of her companions—the one we're waiting for."

"But, Father—" Alric began.

The king cut him off. "We've waited too long, Alric, far too long, to make any mistakes now. Know your thoughts well, Son. We've planned meticulously for this opportunity. Even if the gods are with us, we will likely get only one chance. An error in judgment could mean the end of Arngrim . . . the end of you."

"I will not make a mistake, Father," Alric said. He turned and left the chamber, slamming the door behind him.

13

THE RIDE

A thin ray of sunshine crept into Catriona's room the next morning. She dressed quickly, joyful anticipation in her heart. She couldn't say exactly why she felt so exuberant. Perhaps it was seeing the sunshine after so long in the fog. Perhaps it was getting two nights of relatively undisturbed sleep.

Living here, in Castle Arngrim, she felt some of the weight of guarding her friends lifted from her shoulders. She hadn't realized how heavy that burden had become. Now, it seemed a responsibility shared among both her friends and the castle sentries.

True, Nearra had experienced some problems last night, but Davyn had been right there to help her. By the time Catriona arrived on the scene the trouble, whatever it had been, was all but over. Nearra didn't seem much the worse for wear; Davyn had apparently handled things well. Nearra appeared totally confident in him. Catriona wondered if she'd been wrong to mistrust the young ranger. Though he'd come to them under questionable circumstances, he now seemed totally devoted to Nearra's well-being.

Catriona luxuriated in the soft cushions of the bed for a moment, feeling the silken covers caress her skin. Perhaps she should stay **109** in bed for a while longer. It wasn't something a knight would do, but a princess might . . .

She eyed the silver-embossed bellpull hanging near the bed curtains. She could ring it and enjoy breakfast in bed. Then the servants would help her dress in the finest clothes from her wardrobe. Then she would find the prince, and . . .

No. This was no way to be thinking. Her duties were not yet discharged. Perhaps her obligations to Nearra and the others would soon be fulfilled—but they had not been yet. But maybe, soon . . .

The young warrior put on a casual blue dress, then found the others breakfasting in the common room. Everyone seemed stronger and healthier than they'd been since beginning their long journey into the mountains.

Sindri babbled constantly—still hoping to prove the castle enchanted—while wolfing down surprising portions of bacon, eggs, and sticky buns. Catriona wondered why he didn't choke on his food, he talked so much. The kender's brown hair looked shiny and clean, and his satin shirt and purple cape had been newly pressed.

Elidor seemed rested and alert. He was dressed in his usual gray tunic. His violet eyes flickered around the chamber, taking everything in, as though he were cataloging the room.

Davyn wasn't quite so cheerful. Resting in the castle didn't seem to have done him as much good as the others. He and the elf exchanged sidelong glances occasionally. The young ranger sat at Nearra's elbow, talking with her in a low voice. Catriona assumed that Davyn was still concerned about the girl. She wondered, briefly, what the two of them had been up to last night. Just taking a walk—as they'd claimed—didn't seem likely, but nothing going on in the castle that morning indicated that anything more serious had happened.

Nearra looked better than she had in the past few days. She still complained of a headache and rubbed her temples from time to time, but she was far more alert than she had been. Between conversations, Nearra looked around skittishly, like a housecat who has been transplanted to a new home.

Nearra refused Catriona's offers of assistance, and those from other members of the group. She would only let Davyn through her self-imposed walls. This worried Catriona a bit. It didn't seem healthy—especially not given Davyn's dubious background, even if he had been on his best behavior lately.

Still, Nearra and Davyn seemed neither to want nor need her aid. They weren't babies, Catriona reminded herself. They could certainly ask for help if they truly needed it.

Catriona promised herself to keep an eye out for them, just in case. Then she went back to enjoying a sticky bun.

Just as they finished eating, Alric appeared at the chamber door.

"Good morning," he said. "I hope you all slept well." His gaze took in all the companions, then lingered a moment on Catriona.

She smiled and nodded to him. "Very well indeed," she replied.

The others voiced their agreement.

"Good," Alric said. "Very good."

"Tell me," Nearra said, her face looking slightly weary and pained, "is there any word from the Scarlet Brethren?"

Alric shook his head. "I'm afraid not. You'll be the first to know when they return, I assure you."

Nearra nodded. Alric smiled sympathetically at her.

Then he crossed the room to Catriona's seat and gently put his hand on her arm. "Cat . . ." he said, "Catriona, I was wondering if you would do me the honor of riding with me this morning?"

Catriona's heart fluttered and she swallowed hard. The words caught in her throat, but she managed to force a smile. "L-let me fetch my armor," she said.

"Oh, we won't be hunting," Alric replied, "just riding and seeing the kingdom a bit—if you're interested."

"Yes, I'd love to," Catriona heard herself reply before she had even thought about it.

"What about the renegades?" Elidor asked. "We never did catch Kokar."

"We'll take an armed escort with us," Alric replied.

Davyn raised an eyebrow. "Didn't you have an escort with you the last time you ran into Kokar's band?"

Alric frowned at him. "There are far fewer renegades now—thanks to all of you—and we won't be venturing into their territory, in any case," he said. "Still, your point is taken. Catriona, you may certainly ride in your armor if you wish."

Catriona wished that her friends had kept out of this. A moment ago, she'd been going on a nice ride with a young prince. Now she was worried about venturing into battle again.

She was about to say, "No, I don't need any armor," when she spotted the worry on Nearra's face. The blond girl was clearly concerned for Catriona's safety. "It might be best, if you don't mind."

"Not at all," Alric said. "I'll wear my armor as well. That way, you won't feel so conspicuous." He smiled at her, and Catriona found herself smiling back.

"Can I go with you?" Sindri asked.

Before either Catriona or Alric could answer, Nearra said, "Weren't you going to explore the city today, Sindri?" The blond girl turned from the kender and winked at Catriona.

Sindri scratched his brown hair, caught in a quandary of conflicting desires. "That's right," he said. "I was going to explore the city of Arngrim and look for clues about its enchantment—just to prove to you all that I'm right. And Elidor was going to go with me." He smiled.

"Not exactly," Elidor corrected. "You were planning on having a look around Arngrim, and so was I—but we weren't planning to go together."

"Are you sure?" Sindri asked. "I'm sure we'd have a great time.

Maybe together we could figure out why Arngrim is so weird and creepy. No offense, Alric."

Alric laughed, somewhat stiffly. "I assure you, master kender," he said, "there's nothing to discover. Arngrim is merely an isolated kingdom. We've been on our own for a long time, which is why our ways may seem strange to you."

Sindri shrugged. "Well . . . maybe . . . So, what do you think, Elidor?" He looked hopefully at the elf.

Elidor leaned down and put a slender hand on the kender's shoulder. "Sindri, my friend," he said, "I'm sure that your idea of a good time in the city and mine are quite different. Perhaps we could meet up afterward and stop in a tavern."

"That would be great," Sindri said, smiling. "I'm sorry, Catriona and Alric, I'd love to join you for a ride, but I really can't. I forgot I'd made other plans." He made a flourish with his purple cape and bowed.

"That's all right, my young wizard," Alric said, suppressing a smile. "I'm sure there will be some other time."

"Nearra and I will stay here," Davyn declared.

For a moment, Nearra looked surprised. Then she said, "Yes. My wound is still bothering me a bit. It's probably best if I keep to the castle."

Davyn looked relieved.

"Very well, then," Alric said. "I trust the rest of you will enjoy yourselves. Master elf, master kender, I hope our fair city will entertain you. Catriona, if you like, I will wait outside your room while you change before fetching my own armor."

"No," she replied. "You go ahead. I'll meet you at the stables by the castle gate, if that's all right."

Alric bowed courteously. "I shall meet you there." He turned and left the room.

"When do you think Alric will invite the rest of us riding?" Sindri asked.

"When we're all six-foot-tall redheads in chainmail," Davyn replied.

They all laughed but Catriona felt stung by the remark. "Alric and I are simply two warriors with much in common," she said. "I'm sure we'll spend the day discussing knightly pursuits."

"Of course," said Nearra. A smile tugged at the corners of her mouth.

"I don't have time for romance," Catriona insisted.

She frowned. Should she have accepted Alric's offer at all? Going with him meant leaving Sindri and Nearra, both of whom she'd promised to protect, on their own. The two should be safe enough inside Arngrim's stone walls; the place was crawling with loyal guardsman. Still, the young warrior felt a stab of guilt at leaving her friends alone.

"You'd better get going, Catriona," Elidor said. "You don't want to keep the prince waiting." He didn't smile when he said it, but Catriona couldn't help feeling that he, like Davyn, was ribbing her a bit.

"I'll see you all this evening," she said, and hurried back to her room.

Twenty minutes later she stood, armored and ready to go, in the courtyard in front of the castle's main entrance. Her forest green tunic had been freshly cleaned and pressed. In fact, she had difficulty telling which tunic belonged to her, as there were now three nearly identical ones in her wardrobe, along with a nice collection of dresses. Catriona knew that they had all been supplied for her use, but she still felt better riding out in her own things.

Her chainmail and helmet had been polished and cleaned as well, though she couldn't be sure when the castle staff had done it. The servants had wisely left her sword alone. Catriona could tolerate someone cleaning her armor, but a warrior didn't like anyone tinkering with her weapons.

The thought dredged up the painful memory of Catriona's dead aunt. For a moment, Catriona felt unworthy to look so splendid. She didn't deserve to be riding out on a warm morning, touring with a young prince while her aunt—the best knight she'd ever known—lay dead and buried.

Then Alric smiled at her and all Catriona's dark thoughts melted away. He gave her a boost into the saddle of her white mare. Catriona didn't need his help, but she didn't mind it, either. Alric mounted his own dapple gray horse and the two of them rode out the gates of the castle into the city. With them went a retinue of nearly a dozen servants and two armored sentries.

The Arngrimites they passed waved and bowed respectfully to the prince. The peasants whispered to each other as Catriona rode by. Did they think she and Alric were romantically linked, or were they merely curious about this flame-haired visitor to their ancient city? Catriona had seen no redheads since arriving in Arngrim; all the citizens had brown, black, or dun colored hair.

Though a few rays of sunshine peeked through the clouds, fog still clogged the streets of Arngrim. Everything looked hazy and dreamlike, as if she and Alric were riding through a city in the clouds. Catriona half expected to spot a giant peeking at them over Arngrim's pointed rooftops.

Soon they passed through the titanic city gates and into the hilly countryside beyond. Catriona imagined that, in better times, the rolling countryside would have been lush. Long grasses meandered up the rises and down the glens nestled between the sharp mountain peaks. The plants' slender blades were yellow and brown, rather than green. The whole gave the impression of a tangled patchwork, clinging desperately to the ground beneath the swirling mists.

Alric led Catriona and their retinue north, through hidden dells and across rocky stream beds.

"How long have the streams been dry?" Catriona asked.

"Ages, it seems," Alric replied. "Too long. The fog drains all the vitality out of our land. Where once Arngrim grew green, now it lies gray and brown. It will be green again one day. Soon."

"Now that the war's over," Catriona added.

Alric only nodded.

He pointed out local sights as they rode, showing her thorn-tangled battlefields where his ancestors had proved their honor and won freedom for Arngrim. Everywhere the couple went, the clinging mist pressed in around them, making the day cooler and less pleasant than it should have been.

Catriona didn't mind the weather; she'd endured worse. Besides, she enjoyed Alric Arngrim's company immensely. They rode side by side when the terrain permitted it. Their retinue of porters and castle servants brought up the rear. Though the servants looked weary, they never complained.

Alric suddenly pulled his horse to a stop. He put a gray-gloved finger to his lips and said, "Listen."

At first, Catriona didn't hear anything. Then, as the horses calmed, and the servants stopped clattering about, a faint sound drifted to her ears. It was lilting, like distant birdsong, soft like a whisper. For a moment, Catriona couldn't place it. Then she smiled.

"Water," she said. "Running water. But all the watercourses we've seen have been dry."

"Arngrim is not yet a desert," Alric replied. He motioned her forward, around the corner of a tall bluff. Catriona rode ahead with Alric following close behind.

The grass brushed the flanks of their horses. The dry blades parted before them as they rounded the bend and entered into a hidden valley.

Catriona gasped.

Overhead, a gentle breeze wafted the clouds. The afternoon sun burned away the fog, filling the clearing with golden light. Lush grass replaced the dying weeds around them—a sea of emerald blades nestled between the sheltering valley walls. Flowering trees and shrubs lined the banks of a small brook that meandered toward a shimmering pond in the valley's center.

A stream flowed out of the pool toward a picturesque canyon at the back of the valley. There, the hills gave way to tall, multicolored rock formations.

Alric leaned sideways in his saddle, reached down, and plucked a yellow flower from the ground. He handed it to Catriona.

"The chill of our winters does not reach here, not yet," Alric said. "If I have my way, it never will."

Catriona accepted the flower, feeling the color rise in her cheeks. The bloom was lovely, the loveliest thing she'd seen in Arngrim.

She smiled wistfully at him as she wove the flower into the chainmail at her shoulder. "Are you some young god who can halt the progress of the seasons?" she asked playfully.

Alric looked away from her. "Of course not," he replied. "I would if I could, though. Catriona, Arngrim is not the bleak, foggy place that you've experienced. All of my country was once like this valley. When our kingdom is restored, when we are strong again, the clinging mist will burn away, just as it has here. Then springtime will return to our land."

He took a deep breath of the clean, warm air. Catriona noticed a glisten of moisture at the corner of his eyes. They rode forward through the valley, toward the shimmering pond.

"I feel so alive when I'm here," Alric said. "All the rest of my life is gray and dead—bound to the castle, enslaved by the rigors of ruling with my parents. Here, though . . ." He took another deep breath. "Here is the way life is supposed to be."

Catriona felt the sun's warmth on her skin, even through her armor. A gentle breeze tugged at her hair.

Yes. This was the way things should be. If only all of Arngrim could be like this valley, pure and fresh.

"This is the way the land will be when I rule it," Alric said, as though reading her thoughts. "We have toiled long in darkness and shadow. For many years, our country has been as you've seen. Fog shrouds the land; summer never truly comes. We are beset by enemies from beyond our borders. The struggle to survive never ends."

He sighed and looked toward the sun as they rode along the water's edge. "I desire better things, both for myself and for the people who live under my family's protection. Arngrim's peasants deserve more. Their lives should not be ones of suffering and survival. They deserve more."

Catriona looked across the lush valley and wished that Alric's dream were true, that all Arngrim could be like this.

"Arngrim will grow strong again," Alric said, his deep voice almost dreamlike. "I will break the dark grip that holds us. I will drive the last of the renegades from our land. I will rebuild the villages, the castle, the armies. Our nation will be a model of peace and prosperity, once more admired throughout Krynn. The land will be rejuvenated and fertile again." He gazed back, out of the valley, the way they'd come. "All this," he whispered, "I swear."

For a moment, the sun glinted off his burnished leonine armor, and—to Catriona—Alric did look like a young god sitting astride his gray horse.

Catriona wanted to help him accomplish his dreams. She wanted to ride beside him and drive the ravages from his land. She wanted to rout all the dark things the War of the Lance brought to Arngrim, to erase all lingering traces of poverty and strife. She wanted to be a part of the country's revival.

This could be her purpose. This could become her life. She could learn her knightly craft at the prince's side, while serving the same cause he served. Perhaps this was what destiny had in store for her all along.

She opened her mouth to tell Alric, then stopped, remembering her vows.

Sindri must come first; Nearra must come first. If the kender were safe, though, and if Nearra regained her memory, then Catriona would be free to be with Alric. She knew these were big "ifs," but with the Scarlet Brethren on their way, and the kender safe in Arngrim, Catriona's dreams did not—at the moment—seem so unreachable.

Alric noticed her looking at him and smiled.

She fought down a blush and said, "It's a beautiful dream. Perhaps, someday, I . . ." Her voice nearly caught in her throat. "I'd like to help you, someday, if I could."

"I'd like that, too, Catriona," Alric replied. "Very much."

For a moment, her heart thrilled. Then she felt her stomach tighten. She was a liar, not the person Alric thought her to be. She couldn't start their . . . relationship this way. She had to tell him the truth.

"Your Highness," she said, "there's something you should know about me. I . . . I'm not the warrior you think I am. I have failed in my vows. I have been a coward. My aunt . . . I was her squire. She died because I was afraid . . . because I ran. I've tried to make up for it since, but . . . I can't. I never can. I'm so ashamed." She turned her head toward the ground.

Alric put his hand on her chin and lifted up her face. "Catriona," he said quietly, "we've all made mistakes. There are some things we can never atone for—no matter how much we try. But we must keep trying. We must do what's right."

Catriona blinked back tears and nodded, though her heart still felt heavy.

"I don't believe you're a coward," Alric said. "I see in you both strength of character, and beauty."

Goosebumps prickled up Catriona's arms. She couldn't bear to look him in the eyes.

"I know you won't fail your friends," he said, "or me."

The cloud lifted from Catriona's soul. She'd done it! She'd told him the worst and he didn't hate her. He didn't hate her at all. In fact, he nearly seemed to . . .

No, she couldn't think that way. Not yet. Instead, she focused on the landscape once more. "This is really a very beautiful valley."

Alric sighed and his voice became cheery once more. "Let's have lunch near the canyon at the end of the brook," he said. "The servants packed us a picnic."

She caught his eye and laughed. "I'd almost think you'd had this picnic planned all along!" she said.

"Guilty," he replied. "I hoped to bring you here to impress you with the beauty of the country—and the rightness of my cause."

"You have, good sir knight," she said, wiping the last of the tears from her chin.

They found a spot near the far end of the stream and dismounted. The servants laid out a blanket amid the grass, and set down a tray of small game hens, a huge bowl of strawberries, and a basket of dark bread.

Alric turned to the servants. "Thank you. You may leave us now." He turned to Catriona. "They'll be eating their own lunch over there." He motioned to a patch of brush several yards away from the stream. "It will give us a bit of privacy. I'd like to share this beautiful spot with you alone."

Catriona blushed as the servants and the armed sentries hustled out of sight.

Alric removed his lion-faced helmet and stripped off his silver-scaled breastplate to better enjoy the sunshine. His mane of hair fell across his muscular shoulders, making him look noble and handsome. A silver, lion-head pendant with a blue gem for its eye hung from his neck. The lion's eye seemed to twinkle at Catriona.

"That's a lovely medallion," Catriona said.

"I've worn it for as long as I can remember," Alric said. "It once belonged to my father. And his father before him. I suppose you could call it an Arngrim heirloom." He looked at it for a moment then tucked it beneath his shirt.

"Feel free to remove your armor as well. You won't need it here."

Catriona sighed. "All right. But turn your back." Alric obliged. She removed first her helmet and then her stiff chainmail shirt. She took a deep breath, unconstricted by armor, and felt the warmth of the air seep from her lungs into the rest of her body. When Alric turned back to her, she smiled.

Sitting side by side on the blanket, Catriona and Alric looked as though they'd been friends all their lives. They ate through all the food as they talked and laughed. Then they lay back and watched the clouds pass overhead. They closed their eyes and soaked in the warm afternoon sun.

Catriona reached into the stream with both hands and splashed the cool, clear liquid onto her face. For an instant, she felt happier than she ever remembered feeling in her life. As she knelt down, a voice echoed across the water.

"River runs like crooked fate, can it be you've come too late?"

Catriona sat up and looked around. She saw no one but Alric, reclining on the blanket with his eyes closed, a short distance away.

"Alric, did you say something?" she asked.

"No," he replied, cracking open one eye.

"Hourglass clogged with fleeting sand, betrayal lurks at either hand," the voice said. It was soft and supple, like a purr. The friendly tone didn't disguise its malevolence.

Catriona stood, peering over the tall greenery.

As she did, a creature bounded through the shoulder-high grass. The thing was huge, larger than a horse. Bat-like wings adorned the back of its leonine body. A sinister human face peered out from amid its mane. Razor-sharp teeth lined the monster's wicked mouth.

The thing spread its huge wings and leaped into the air, hurtling toward Alric and Catriona.

14 Rough Justice

S urely we can work this out," Elidor said. He
tasted blood in his mouth and his ribs ached
badly. The two ruffians holding him laughed.

"Trying to sell things from the castle!" shouted a third man, a
big, lantern-jawed oaf. "Are you trying to curse us all?" He again
slammed his hamlike fist into the elf's gut.

The town of Arngrim was turning out to be much less "entertain-
ing" than Elidor had hoped. After leaving Sindri in the marketplace
to question the townspeople, Elidor had hurried off to do a little business of his own. But as soon as he'd shown these men his wares, they
turned on him, seizing his arms before he could draw his concealed
daggers. The elf made a mental note to himself: never do business
with strangers in dark alleys, even if they promise a fat payday.

Bert, the lantern-jawed fellow hitting him, smiled showing a
set of crooked yellow teeth. In one of his hands—the one he wasn't
using to punch with—he held the small statuette that Elidor had
found in the burned-out house, along with the lion-head pin the
elf had pilfered from the king's study.

"This statuette you tried to pawn off on me belonged to me
sister," Bert said. "I ain't heard from her in months. Where'd you
get it, scum?"

"I acquired it during my travels, from a wandering salesman," Elidor lied.

In payment, he got another of Bert's fists crashing into his ribs. "Been in my family since before the Cataclysm, that has!" Bert said. "This lion-head pin you offered to throw in, I suppose you got that from a 'salesman,' too?"

Bright white spots danced before Elidor's eyes and gongs rang in his ears. He fought down nausea and tried to wriggle free or reach his knives, but Bert's friends held him too tightly.

"Want another?" Bert asked. "Or do you wanna talk?" He reeled back his fist again.

"All right! All right!" Elidor said. "I'll talk." Blood burbled up in his mouth, and he spat it onto the pavement. "I found the statuette in a burned-out house on the edge of the mountains. I didn't know it belonged to anyone. Keep it if you like."

Bert's yellowish eyes went wide. "Burned-out house . . . ?" he said, as if pondering. Then his face twisted into a mask of rage. "If it were burned, 'twas you that did the burning!"

"No, honestly," Elidor said. As usual, telling the truth had only made things worse. The elf didn't know why he ever resorted to it. He had the distinct feeling that Bert now intended to kill him.

"Ask Prince Alric if you don't believe me!" the elf gasped. Unfortunately, one of his teeth seemed to be loose, which made it more difficult to speak. "Ask the king and queen! I arrived here with their son!"

Bert's eyes narrowed. "Ask the king and queen," he said mockingly. "Maybe we would, if we ever seen 'em. They sit in their towers, lording over us while the land rots. Only justice is, they're trapped in this dying kingdom, same as us!"

"Careful what you say, Bert!" one of his companions cautioned. "They might be listening!" The two men holding Elidor looked around fearfully.

"Well, I can understand how you feel," Elidor said, scrambling for a new tactic. "I feel trapped here myself. Which is why I was looking for a little cash, just to spur me on my way—as it were."

The ruffians laughed, their rough voices echoing between the stone walls of the alley.

"Only the dead leave Arngrim," Bert spat. He hit Elidor in the gut again, just for good measure. "Maybe we should send you on your way."

Elidor changed tactics again, hoping it might save his life. "Killing me would make the king and queen very upset. I'm the only elf in Arngrim, and they're quite fond of me."

"He could be right," one of the men holding him said. "I never seen no elf before."

"Is that why he's tryin' to run away?" the other asked sarcastically.

Elidor backpedaled. "It's just that I'm tired of being 'kept.' I feel more like a pet than a man, and—"

His attackers laughed again. "Welcome to Arngrim!" one said.

Sweating, Elidor kept working his angle. "Because of my . . . unique status, I'm sure the royal family would be very angry if I were harmed in any way."

Bert showed his yellow teeth in a remorseless grin. "Who says they're ever going to find out? There's people in these parts that disappeared and no one seen 'em again. People like me sister." He reached behind his tunic and withdrew a knife nearly the length and breadth of Elidor's forearm.

The elf cursed himself silently for missing the concealed weapon when he'd first met this man: a foolish mistake in a series of bad moves, and one that looked likely to cost him his life.

"Look," Elidor said desperately, "why don't you keep both the statuette and the pin, and we'll just forget this ever happened."

Bert took a step toward the elf, reeling back the knife to plunge it into Elidor's stomach.

As Bert stabbed forward, the weapon suddenly jerked sideways, taking Bert's arm with it. Instinctively, Elidor pulled away from the thrust. The move caught the man holding Elidor's right arm by surprise. As the elf lunged aside, it left his captor in the path of Bert's weapon. The long blade plunged into the man's side.

Wounded, though not fatally, the man loosened his grip on the captive elf. Elidor pulled his arm free and smashed his fist into the face of the other man holding him. That man reeled back, bleeding from the nose. Bert stood in shock, staring at his own knife, protruding from his comrade's side. The statuette and pin fell from Bert's other hand and clattered to the street.

Elidor dropped down and swept Bert's feet out with a spinning kick. Bert crashed to the ground while, at the same time, his wounded friend slumped to his knees. The man gasped, "Bert, ye stabbed me." Then he fell over.

Bert's face turned purple with rage. "Accursed pointy-eared demon! Now I know you're one of them!"

Elidor turned to run. Bert dived forward and caught him by the toes. Elidor sprawled across the narrow street, smashing into a stack of empty barrels.

Bert got to his feet. He and the broken-nosed man came at Elidor, murder in their eyes. Dazed, Elidor reached for his throwing knives, but his fingers fumbled in the sleeves of his tunic. His stomach sank as he realized that he wouldn't make it. The fallen barrels blocking the street in front of him wouldn't buy him enough time. He was about to die.

Just when death seemed inevitable, the barrels scattered in front of Elidor came to life. They rolled across the cobblestones, smashing into the legs of the ruffians. Bert and his friend staggered and fell to the pavement.

Laughter echoed through the alley. The elf scrambled to his feet. His razor-sharp throwing knives sprang quickly into his hands.

Elidor turned and sprinted in the direction of the laughter. As he ran, Sindri Suncatcher stepped out from around the corner.

The kender beamed at Elidor. "I thought you could use some help," the diminutive magician said.

"I never thought I'd be glad to see you," the elf replied. "Don't just stand there, run!"

Sindri paused only long enough to propel the barrels into Bert and Broken-Nose once more. As the ruffians floundered, Sindri laughed and bolted down the narrow street alongside his friend.

"That was fun," Sindri said as they twisted down Arngrim's back alleyways. "What were we fighting about?"

Elidor looked at him. Even after sixty-three years of living, a kender's sense of "fun" never ceased to amaze the elf.

"We had a disagreement over some items I was trying to sell," he said.

"Really?" Sindri said. "I didn't know you were a peddler." They completed another twist in the maze-like alleys and came within sight of the castle. Looking back, they spotted no signs of pursuit.

"Everyone needs a little extra income," Elidor explained. "From time to time, items come into my possession . . . "

"Me, too," Sindri said brightly. "And sometimes, people seem to think that I've stolen them—though of course I never have."

Elidor chuckled. "We are kindred spirits, my friend," he said, "doomed to be misunderstood by those around us."

"So, was it that lion pin and the statuette you were trying to sell?" Sindri asked.

Elidor silently cursed the kender's sharp eyes, but there seemed to be no way out of telling the truth this time. "Yes."

"Too bad we couldn't stop and rescue them," Sindri said. "They looked valuable. Where did you get them from, anyway?"

Elidor paused, wondering whether to lie or not. After a brief analysis, he decided to meet the truth halfway. "I found them in the ruins of that house we stayed in," he said. "Those people in the alley seemed to think they belonged to someone they knew."

"Maybe they did," Sindri suggested. "Maybe the gods put those things in the ruins so that you could return them to their rightful owners. That happens with me a lot. I'm always finding things that other people need, or are supposed to have. Though, of course, my powers are magical in nature, rather than divine."

Elidor smiled wryly. He knew that the kender was no more magical than the elf was divine. Sindri's little "tricks" had certainly come in handy, though. Elidor eyed Sindri's silver ring, recognizing it as the one Davyn had worn previously. He wondered why Davyn had let the ring pass into the kender's keeping. He wondered if the magic of the ring might work for him, as well. But stealing from a kender? That could prove tricky.

Elidor rubbed his ribs and nodded. "Tell me, Sindri," he said, "did you find any sign of that enchantment while touring the city?"

"No, not really," Sindri said. "Just a lot of unhappy people, though not as unhappy as the ones you found. But, I did notice that there doesn't seem to be anything new in Arngrim. Nearly everything is an antique. And I don't think the people get out much, either. How could they never have seen an elf or kender before?"

"Yes," Elidor said. "They seem very insular." Perhaps the little magician was correct; maybe there was something mysterious going on in Arngrim. But what?

Elidor secretly vowed that as soon as his ribs felt better, he'd have a closer look around the castle. If the Arngrims did indeed have secrets, Elidor could only imagine what the royal family might pay to keep them.

15 THE JAWS OF DEATH

The stench of the monster nearly overwhelmed Catriona as it leaped toward her. It stank of rotted meat, musk, animal waste, and blood. Its tawny fur was matted and patched with burrs.

Catriona ducked and rolled to one side. She silently cursed herself for removing her helmet and chainmail vest. What had she been thinking? A knight should never be caught so unprepared. Even here, in the last unspoiled corner of Arngrim, evil still waited to catch the unwary.

Alric dived, too, and the monster passed over their heads and landed on the far side of the little stream. It turned, a smile on its hideous face, and flicked its tail toward them. The tuft at the end of the tail looked like a huge, curled-up porcupine; long, barbed spines covered its entire surface.

Several spikes shot from the tail, flying like bolts from a crossbow. Alric scooped his helmet from the ground and held it before him just in time to turn aside a spine aimed for his chest. Catriona twisted sideways and the second barb barely missed her. The missile tore the front of her tunic, just below the breast. A third spine flew over the brush separating Alric and Cat from where the servants had been eating.

The servants screamed and searched frantically for cover.

The monster laughed.

"Freshest meat is best to eat," it purred.

Catriona retrieved her sword from the ground. She didn't dare try to put on her chainmail. If she did, the creature would pounce on her before she could finish. "What is this thing?" she cried to Alric.

"Manticore!" Alric replied. "Our myths speak of such monsters. I had always thought them merely legend."

"I wish to the gods that were true!" Catriona said.

The manticore leaped again, its leathery wings beating the warm afternoon air. It swiped at Alric as it passed overhead, but the young prince ducked away.

The monster landed on the back of one of the retainers in the clearing beyond the picnic. The woman screamed and both of Alric's sentries rushed to aid her. Alric and Catriona ran, too, dashing through the tall grass, shouting and waving their swords to try and distract the monster's attention.

The armored sentries attacked fearlessly, their swords flashing. The manticore fell back before their onslaught, leaving the wounded woman bleeding on the ground. The monster fired tail spikes at the guardsmen, but the barbs bounced off their silvery armor.

Catriona sprinted forward, while Alric stopped to assist the wounded woman. The other servants ran around aimlessly, fear of the beast overwhelming their good sense. Alric barked orders at them, but none seemed to be listening.

Catriona fought defensively, trying to cover for her ill-timed lack of armor. The monster slashed at her with its claws, raking for her eyes and gut. She fended off the talons with her sword.

The creature kicked one of the Arngrim sentries in the chest. The man flew through the air and crashed down atop some rocks on the far side of the stream. Catriona and the remaining sentry slashed at the manticore with their swords.

Catriona's weapon bit into the monster's right flank. The manticore howled and took to the air. As it rose, it grabbed the other sentry in its paws. To his credit, Alric's knight didn't scream as the monster lifted him off the ground. The manticore circled once, then dropped the knight down onto the same rocks where his comrade had fallen. Both sentries lay limp and unmoving, like broken dolls. Though no blood leaked from their crushed armor, Catriona knew they were dead. Her stomach clenched at the thought of the brave lives lost.

The manticore banked right and headed toward a pack of servants fleeing into the nearby canyon. The men and women ran heedlessly, unaware of the monster diving toward their unprotected backs.

"Not that way, you fools!" Alric called after them.

Catriona wished the servants had not fled away from where Alric and she could protect them. At the same time, it occurred to her that the canyon would limit the manticore's maneuverability, making it the perfect place to battle the monster. She and Alric could take advantage of the narrow confines to slay the beast. But while the canyon might provide opportunity for a trained warrior or prince, it would surely prove a death trap for the frightened peasants.

Catriona dashed after the retainers just as the manticore swooped into the canyon opening. Alric was only a few seconds behind her.

She reached the creature as another peasant fell dead under its onslaught. The manticore turned, whipping its tail in her direction. Catriona met the barbed tuft before the spikes could fire. Her sword smashed into the deadly bolts, breaking off many and rendering them useless.

Howling an ancient war cry, Alric charged the beast. The manticore flicked one of its wings at the young prince, catching him across the eyes. Though Alric's leonine helmet protected him from being blinded, the force of the blow staggered him. He reeled back, fumbling to keep the helmet on his head.

How quickly their fortunes had changed! Minutes ago, romantic notions of chivalry and courtship had swirled through Catriona's head. Now she and Alric were fighting for their lives—while their armor lay discarded next to a babbling brook. It would be horribly ironic, she thought, if this romantic "lark" cost both their lives.

A swipe from one of the monster's claws dashed all frivolous notions from Catriona's head. She blocked the talons, then counter-attacked fiercely, forcing the manticore to turn its attention from the stunned prince.

As Alric rose to his feet, the monster took to the air again. As Catriona had hoped, the canyon walls boxed it in. The beast tried to maneuver, but she leaped up and slashed at its left wing.

Her sword bit into the bat-like membrane, tearing through the leathery skin. The wing sagged, unable to support the creature's weight. The manticore splashed into the stream, a half-dozen yards away. It raised its tail and fired wildly.

Catriona ducked and the deadly barbs sailed over her red hair. The monster staggered and blinked water out of its eyes.

Catriona closed in and raised her sword for the kill.

Someone behind her gasped.

Catriona glanced back and saw Alric standing stock still. A long spike from the manticore's tail protruded from his unarmored chest.

16

THE LIBRARY OF ARNGRIM

"Davyn, I'm not going to collapse in fits," Nearra said. "You needn't hover over me like a mother cat."

"But last night—" Davyn said.

"Last night I was feverish," Nearra replied. "I feel much better today. With a good breakfast in my stomach, it's like I'm a whole different person."

Sitting on the divan in the common room, smiling up at him, Nearra did look better today, more . . . normal. Davyn smiled at her. But worry gnawed at his insides. "A whole different person. . ." Nearra had certainly seemed like that last night—a strange, mad person who had the power to break every shard of glass in the entire hallway. Was this the deep magic that Maddoc sought inside her? Was this part of the Emergence?

Davyn liked Nearra as she was—liked her more and more every day, in fact. Away from Maddoc's influence, she was a cheery, personable teenager. How could his father want her otherwise? How could anything good come from what the wizard had planned?

Nearra rubbed her temples and Davyn knew that, despite her brave words, the girl's headaches had not vanished entirely. "Honestly," she said, as if trying to assuage his dark thoughts, "everything makes much more sense to me today. I almost feel I know this place. I've seen the people in the paintings here before. Everything seems so . . . familiar."

That worried Davyn. He'd hoped to avoid whatever "traps" his father had laid out before them. Hooking up with Alric seemed too complex a plot for even Maddoc to have planned in advance. Davyn felt sure that the young prince could not be another of Maddoc's agents. That didn't mean that all of them weren't still in his father's clutches, though.

Davyn went to the window of the common room and stared out, half expecting to see Maddoc's falcon circling overhead. But though the fog had lessened, the young ranger still saw no sign of the black bird.

". . . and how could I know this kingdom?" Nearra asked.

Davyn realized that he hadn't been paying attention. He'd missed most of whatever she'd said. "Maybe you read about Arngrim in a book," he suggested absently. "Sometimes, when I read about a place in a book, it's almost like I've been there."

Nearra's blue eyes lit up. "Reading!" she said. "Of course!" She seemed overjoyed for a moment, but then winced and rubbed her forehead.

"Are you all right?" Davyn asked.

"Of course," she snapped. Then her face softened. "I'm sorry. I'm still a bit under the weather."

"Maybe you should rest some more."

"Not when you've hit on just the thing!"

"What thing?" Davyn asked, feeling progressively more nervous.

"Reading! The castle must have a library."

Now he felt puzzled. "I suppose it does."

"We can go there and read about Arngrim—perhaps find a clue as to how I know this place," she said enthusiastically. "Reading Arngrim's history might give me some clues to my past. Maybe we could even discover some hint as to who I truly am and where I came from."

"Maybe." The cold dagger in Davyn's stomach returned. Anything they might find in the library could have been planted there by his wizard father.

Nearra rose from the divan and took his hand. "Come on," she said. "Let's go see."

"You should rest."

"I can rest anytime," she said. "Davyn, I know you're trying to look out for me, for my health. But the best thing for me is to find out who I am. If I know that, all my other troubles will disappear."

Davyn doubted it, but he didn't resist as she pulled him out of the door. Instead he decided to keep Nearra from finding the royal library.

"Davyn, are you sure this is the way?" she said after their third wrong turn.

"Pretty sure," Davyn said, wishing he were a better liar.

"Let's ask someone," Nearra replied. She flagged down a servant and quickly got directions.

"Honestly," she said when she returned, "you may have a wonderful sense of direction in the wilderness, but you're completely helpless inside castle walls!"

She laughed and he smiled back, but the dagger in his gut twisted a little more.

"You know," she said as they arrived before an ornately carved pair of oak doors, "I think I could have found this place even without the servants. Do you think I could have visited the castle before?"

Davyn shrugged.

"But if I had visited," she said, "why don't Alric and his parents recognize me? Perhaps I was a peddler or a servant or something. I don't think the king and queen notice their servants very much. The Arngrims seem so aloof, don't you think?"

"Yes," Davyn said. "I'm sure they have a lot on their minds."

"I'm sure they do," Nearra replied. She threw open the library doors; the room beyond was dark and silent. Nearra darted back down the hall and fetched a lit candelabra. Holding it before her, she and Davyn stepped inside.

Beyond the portal lay a hall three times the size of the big common room across from their chambers. The library was tall, nearly twice the height of a normal room. Bookshelves lined its walls from floor to ceiling on all sides save one. A huge unlit fireplace dominated the final wall. Over the fireplace hung a life-size portrait of King Conar, decked out in his best royal robes. He was younger, and looked very handsome and regal. Davyn and Nearra both noticed the king's striking resemblance to his son, Alric.

Several desks and tables stood on the room's carpeted floor. Because the chamber was located deep within the bowels of the castle, there were no windows to provide natural light. Candelabra sat scattered at regular intervals throughout the library. Nearra lit them with a taper from her candleholder as she passed. Soon, bright illumination filled the ancient room.

They noticed now that not all the bookcases were filled with books. A great many shelves lay empty—perhaps reserved for future use. Cobwebs lined the room's corners, and a thick coating of dust covered nearly everything. Clearly, the library didn't see much use.

"Where shall we start?" Nearra asked.

"Um, history, I suppose?" Davyn replied, still feeling nervous about the whole expedition.

"That's a good idea," Nearra said. "Maybe we can find out more about the people in the portraits—discover where I know them from."

"Maybe you'll even find the book you read about them in," Davyn suggested. A worrisome notion gnawed at the back of his mind: maybe Nearra hadn't read about Arngrim in any book. Maybe her "memories" were all part of Maddoc's schemes. Who knew what kind of subtle spells the wizard might have planted in his friend's head?

The two of them browsed the book spines until they found a

likely section flanking the fireplace. They dusted off the cobwebs and pulled down the volumes, one by one.

"This one's very old," Davyn said. "It doesn't have any illustrations—so you couldn't have seen the portraits in a copy of this." The pages of the tome seemed as though they might crumble in his hands, so he gently put it back.

"This one's too old as well," Nearra said, checking another. "We need something more recent." She scanned the bookcase, looking up toward the empty shelves near the top and pouted. "Why did they have to put the new stuff up so high?"

"Maybe they're more familiar with those histories, and need them less," Davyn suggested.

"Fetch me a ladder, would you?" Nearra said. "I want to get some of those down." She pointed to the last occupied shelf in the stack.

Davyn fought down his nervousness. These were just old books. What could they possibly find that would do any harm? He could head off any suggestions or information that seemed to come from Maddoc. At least, he hoped he could. He brought a rolling ladder from one of the other walls. She scrambled up it.

She seemed full of life now. Gone was the weak, confused girl of last night. A manic energy suffused her. Davyn hoped her optimism would last. Perhaps that was the best way to fight Maddoc: to pursue Nearra's memories, wherever they might lead and exorcise the ghosts that haunted her.

Nearra descended the ladder with a handful of old volumes. "Some of these seem new," she said.

Davyn frowned. "I wouldn't exactly say new," he replied. "I doubt any of them were written in our lifetimes. 'More recent' might be a better way to put it."

Nearra cracked open the cover of the first book. "Okay, you're right," she said. "These are from a while ago. But at least they have hand-painted illustrations." She paged through the volume quickly. "Look!" she said, "here are some of the people we saw in the portraits."

Davyn looked over her shoulder. "That makes sense. We figured they were old relatives of the Arngrims."

"Some were their advisors, too," she said. "Here's a picture of the Scarlet Brethren. Ugh. They look like bloodstained monks. I guess that pinch-faced portrait upstairs must be one—though these aren't showing their faces beneath their hoods. Pretty creepy. They should choose better outfits." The men and women in the illustration were dressed head-to-foot in bright red, hooded robes. The wizards' faces remained hidden in shadow.

"Their garb is probably traditional," Davyn said. "A lot of these magical societies have gone on for ages. Some wear the same style of robes for centuries."

Nearra thought a moment. "I guess you're right. This book is pretty old. I wonder if they've changed their fashions since?"

"We'll find out soon, I hope," Davyn said. A chill ran down his spine. Would meeting the Arngrim wizards really do Nearra any good?

"It's funny," Nearra said, "I remember the people in some of these portraits, but I still don't know where from."

"Nothing's coming back to you?"

She shook her head. "Maybe this isn't the book I read." She set that tome aside and grabbed the newest looking volume of the Arngrim family history.

"Here's more," she said, paging past illustrations of portraits they'd seen in the castle. "These are more recent, judging by the styles of clothing."

"Still not modern, though," Davyn said. "Everyone looks like they've stepped out of a pre-Cataclysmic storybook."

Nearra smiled. "Yes, I—" She froze. Her eyes went wide, and her face turned pale.

"What is it?" Davyn asked, fear knotting his insides.

Nearra stared at a portrait of a woman with black hair. The woman stood atop a bluff, which Davyn recognized as one of the hills above the city. The wind whipped the woman's fur-trimmed green dress around her slender form and tugged her long hair into raven streamers. Her face was thin and angular, with a hint of cruelty around the corners of the mouth and eyes. The woman's purple eyes gleamed like opals.

Nearra's jaw dropped. "Davyn, I know this one," she said breathlessly. "This woman is me!"

CHAPTER

17 DREAMS AND NIGHTMARES

The bottom fell out of Davyn's stomach. He had seen the woman in the portrait before, as well. Her likeness hung on a huge tapestry in the study of his father, Maddoc. Davyn knew the woman's name, but little else. She had been some type of sorceress, and—in retrospect—his father had always been very cagey when talking about her.

"What do you mean, she's you?" Davyn asked, his mouth suddenly bone dry.

"I know it makes no sense," Nearra said. "In my dream . . . my nightmare the other night, I looked in a mirror and saw this woman staring back at me."

"Maybe it was a window, not a mirror," he suggested.

Nearra shook her head. "I don't think so," she replied. "I saw a mirror just like it in the castle earlier that day."

"There was a mirror near where I found you," Davyn said," a broken mirror. You just imagined seeing this woman."

"No," Nearra replied. "I've definitely seen this woman somewhere before. Her appearance in the mirror was some kind of memory, I think."

She continued to stare at the illustration. "The text says that her name is Asvoria and that she is—I mean, was—a great sorceress." **139**

Her voice fell to little more than a whisper. "It says that her lust for knowledge knew no bounds. But, rapt in her desires, she lost sight of her humanity. She became so obsessed with magic that nothing else mattered to her. She wandered Krynn seeking new spells and new sources of power. Those who got in her way—"

She stopped reading and looked up at her friend.

"What?" Davyn asked.

"Those who got in her way," Nearra said, "she killed."

Davyn swallowed hard. The description of Asvoria rang too familiar with him. They might have described his own father, Maddoc. Maddoc had been willing to destroy Davyn's companions just to get what he wanted. Was Asvoria everything he hoped to become?

The young ranger felt sick to his stomach. Could the nightmare be trying to warn Nearra about Maddoc's plans? Could the vision of Asvoria somehow represent Maddoc's agents watching her? Nearra was so wrapped up in the history book that she didn't notice that Davyn had started to tremble.

"Apparently this account was written as a report to the royal family," she said.

"A report? Why?" Davyn asked.

Nearra took a deep breath. "Because Asvoria was coming here, to Arngrim."

Davyn's mouth felt almost too dry to speak. The eerie parallels to his life seemed overwhelming. "Why?" he finally asked.

"The Arngrimites had something she wanted, apparently," Nearra said. "The author speculates that it may have something to do with the local wizards."

"The Scarlet Brethren?"

"The author doesn't say," Nearra said. "She recommends that the king refuse Asvoria admission to the kingdom.

'Should Asvoria gain access to Arngrim,' she writes, 'there is no telling the havoc she might wreak. The sorceress is *not* to be trusted.'"

140

Nearra flipped the remaining pages of the book, her brow knitting in frustrated anger. "The rest of the pages are blank."

She slammed the book shut and stood, scanning the many shelves with her blue eyes. "There must be more," she said. "Help me find the history that comes after this one."

Davyn feared what they might discover, but he did as she asked nonetheless. They pored through the stacks for over two hours, paging through moldering books and checking crumbling scrolls. In the end, they had to admit defeat.

"Everything here is as old as the Cataclysm!" Nearra declared.

"I think that book you read from may be the last history ever written about Arngrim," Davyn said. He could understand her frustration but, personally, he felt more than a little relieved.

"The Arngrims are a royal bloodline," Nearra said. "They have to keep family histories. There must be some record of the Arngrims's interactions with Asvoria."

"Perhaps the sorceress turned aside at the last moment," Davyn suggested. "Maybe she didn't come to Arngrim at all."

Nearra didn't seem to hear him. "Maybe they keep the newer books elsewhere," she said. "In the royal chambers, perhaps?"

"If they're there," he replied, "I doubt we have any chance of seeing them."

"We may not," Nearra said, "but I bet Catriona could convince Alric to let us borrow them."

Davyn nodded, hoping that Nearra couldn't sense his ambivalence.

Nearra smiled hopefully. "We'll ask her the first thing when she gets back."

> ⤙⋯

"Catriona. . . !" Alric gasped. A look of shocked surprise washed over the prince's face. He gazed at the manticore's barb for a long moment, as though unable to believe his eyes. Then he slumped face-first to the ground. His body landed with a soft *thud*.

Catriona's heart froze. The monster laughed. It bounded out of the stream toward the warrior.

Fear clenched at Catriona's gut. She fought down the emotion and raised her weapon. The manticore whipped its tail at her, but it didn't fire any spikes; the remaining unbroken barbs looked stunted, or perhaps immature.

Catriona blocked the tail and counterattacked, slashing at the beast's side. The manticore dodged away from her and moved toward Alric, apparently seeing him as easy prey.

As the monster turned, Catriona lunged at it. She stabbed down and caught the manticore in the hindquarters. Her sword traced a long wound into the beast's backside.

The manticore wheeled and batted her aside with a slap from its remaining good wing.

Catriona staggered, stepping awkwardly into the stream. Her ankle twisted, and she went down, landing in the water.

Baring its pointed teeth, the manticore charged.

Catriona thrust herself up, out of the brook. She regained her feet and raised her sword. The manticore proved too quick. Before she could defend herself, the monster swiped at her with its huge paw.

Catriona screamed and twisted away. But she was too slow. The manticore's claws raked across her back, shredding her tunic and the delicate skin beneath. The wounds stung but they weren't deep—nowhere near enough to kill her.

Catriona gritted her teeth and swung back, putting the entire weight of her body behind the blow. Her sword chopped into the manticore's right forearm, severing it just above the paw.

The beast squealed in rage and pain. It reeled back, away from the warrior, its dark blood spraying into the air.

As the manticore reared up, Catriona lunged forward. She stabbed her sword deep into the monster's breast, piercing its black heart. The manticore howled and fell backward. It crashed into the grass and died twitching. The hollow look in the eyes of its nearly human face made Catriona shudder.

Stunned at her victory, the young warrior caught her breath a moment before remembering:

"Alric!"

Catriona raced to the young prince's side. Alric looked pale, almost bloodless. The manticore's spike protruded from his chest, just to the left of his heart. Blood covered the front of his gray tunic.

Catriona's heart withered. Alric couldn't die! Not now! Not like her aunt! She couldn't stand to fail another person she loved.

She loved Alric. Catriona felt surprised at the realization and yet it seemed so right. She knelt down and cradled his pale head in her lap. His eyes were closed, his body, unmoving. His skin was cold, deathly so. She could almost have believed he was sleeping if not for the widening red stain on his chest.

Tears sprang to her eyes. Then something occurred to her.

If the stain on Alric's tunic was widening . . .

His heart must still be beating!

She pressed her head to his chest and listened. Faintly, as if from leagues away, she heard a dull, waning throb.

Just then, the prince drew a ragged, shallow breath.

He wasn't dead yet! She could still save him. She had failed her aunt, but that was in the past. This time, she hadn't run. This time she could do something to save a person she loved. She vowed not to let Alric down.

She would get him back to the city. The best physicians in Arngrim would treat him. The young prince would live. She would *not* lose him! First, though, she needed to stop his bleeding.

Using his own shirt and strips torn from the hem of her tunic, she bandaged Alric quickly and efficiently. Her Solamnic teaching included battlefield medicine, and Catriona thanked the gods for that training now. After she secured Alric's wound, she stood and surveyed the landscape.

"Help!" she called. "The beast is dead and the prince wounded Help! We need to get him back to Castle Arngrim!"

No one emerged from the tall grass. She jogged along the bank of the brook shouting. But she didn't see a living soul. All the servants had run off or been killed by the manticore.

Catriona hung her head and covered her face in her hands. If only she hadn't come here to Arngrim . . . If only she hadn't agreed to go riding . . . None of this would ever have happened.

She took in a deep breath. This was no time for sorrow. She had to do what she could to save Alric.

Thankfully, the horses remained still tethered nearby.

She stripped off the remainder of Alric's armor to make him lighter to transport. Then she stood and lifted him in her arms. He felt amazingly light, no heavier than a child in her arms. Was her strength of conviction so great, or had he wasted away to almost nothing?

Not daring to think about it, she placed Alric gently in the saddle of his horse, then climbed up behind him. "I'll get you home," she said, "even though I don't know the way. I won't fail. I promise."

She gave a final glance around the clearing but saw no one who remained alive. Fighting down the urge to panic, she spurred Alric's horse and swiftly rode back the way they'd come.

Catriona let the horse run as much as she dared. She didn't want to jar the prince and exacerbate his wound any more than necessary, but she also knew they didn't have much time to save Alric's life. She left the spike in place; pulling it out would surely cause him to bleed to death. As they rode, she made sure not to drive the barb deeper into the prince's pale flesh.

The fog returned as soon as they left the green valley. Catriona wished for a guide to speed them home. Though she had an idea of which way they'd come, they had no time to waste in returning.

Additionally, she knew that darkness would soon descend upon them. Finding her way back to a castle in a strange land with a wounded prince wasn't a task she would have chosen for herself—but what choice did she have?

She *would* make it. Alric *would* live. Catriona had not waited this long to find someone, only to lose him now. She would not let death claim her love. She would sooner give up her own life.

WATCHING AND WAITING

As darkness descended on the castle like a cold, gray shroud, a bright fire danced in the fireplace of the common room in the guest quarters.

Nearra paced the perimeter of the room, while Elidor and Sindri played a game of fox and hounds at a board set on a table in one corner. Davyn stood by the window, staring out at the city, worry gnawing at his guts. Lights flickered from within the houses and shops, but they did little to illuminate the fog. Davyn stared hard, trying not to let the tension he felt show in his body.

"How's your headache?" Elidor asked Nearra.

"Almost completely gone," she replied, never stopping her wandering. "I don't think I've felt this alive since I first woke up in the forest."

"That's great," Sindri said. He smiled earnestly at Nearra. "Elidor, I've got your hounds at bay." The elf frowned and moved one of his pieces across the board.

"I really feel like I know this place," Nearra continued, "like I may have been here before. I only wish we'd been able to get into the royal collection—see the books that came after the histories we found."

"We don't even know there *is* a royal collection," Davyn countered, keeping his back to her. "The servants didn't know anything about one, and the royal family denied having any books in their apartments."

"That's absurd," Nearra replied. "What's a kingdom without history?"

"She's right," Elidor said. "All royal families keep track of their lineage and annals. They feel it adds legitimacy to their reign."

"Well, maybe the Arngrims are different," Davyn said. "Maybe they decided to stop keeping the histories during the war. We all know what a tough time they've had."

"Or maybe the histories were destroyed during the war," Sindri suggested. "The castle's kinda ratty in places. There could have been a fire or something. Or maybe the histories were destroyed by the enchantment that looms over this place."

"Enchantment." Davyn scoffed.

"Elidor thinks this is a strange place too, you know," Sindri offered. "Some odd things happened to us this afternoon."

"Oh?" Nearra asked.

"Nothing worth mentioning really," Elidor replied. "The Arngrimites aren't very friendly to strangers, that's all." Something in the elf's tone told Davyn that Elidor was hiding something. The ranger wondered what their resident thief could be plotting now.

"Well, I think some things are worth mentioning," Sindri countered. "Did you know, for instance, that no one has left Arngrim for ages, and that everything from outside the kingdom is old, and that some peasants haven't ever seen the king and queen?"

"We know how busy they are," Davyn said. "We also know they've been cut off since the war. There's nothing unusual about that."

"Believe what you want," Sindri replied, "but Arngrim's a pretty strange place."

Davyn secretly wondered if the kender might be correct. Could this all somehow tie in to Maddoc's plans?

147

"Maybe we can find out more about the history of this place when Alric returns," Nearra's blue eyes flashed with manic intensity. "I'm sure he won't deny us access to any records the royal family might have—especially not if Catriona asks him."

Davyn didn't know quite what to say about that. Nor, apparently, did Sindri or Elidor. They'd all noticed Catriona's attraction to the young prince. How far might that relationship go? Davyn wondered if Catriona would abandon her quest to restore Nearra's memory. Thinking about it, he decided it might be best if all of them abandoned it.

Did Nearra really need what she'd lost? Wouldn't she be better off living a peaceful life, far away from Maddoc and his plans? Davyn thought so. Unfortunately, the only way to get Nearra to see that would be to reveal his connection to the wizard.

Sindri broke the awkward silence. "Are you trying to find the same book you read before?" he asked. "I know you were thinking that maybe your memories of Arngrim came from a book you read."

"I'm not thinking that anymore," Nearra said. Her blue eyes shone intensely. "I know far too much about this place. Everything in it seems familiar. I must have been here before. I'm thinking that maybe I lived in Arngrim, possibly even in the castle, before I lost my memory."

"But wouldn't they recognize you?" Sindri asked.

"Not if I were just a servant or a tradesman—or maybe the child of one of those people," Nearra replied. "I'm sure the royal family can't pay attention to *everyone* who spends time under their roof."

"Arngrim is a long way from where you woke up," Elidor pointed out.

"That's true," she replied, "but who's to say how long I may have wandered before Davyn . . ." Here she paused, probably remembering Davyn's original account of their meeting and trying to reconcile it with what she knew now. Davyn held his breath.

"Before Davyn found me," Nearra finished. "I may have been away from Arngrim for years. Maybe I had my memory all that while, or maybe I lost it and then left the city. That could make sense with what Sindri said about no one leaving in ages. Maybe they didn't know I'd made it out of the mountains alive. Who's to say?"

"Maybe *that's* the enchantment," Sindri suggested. "Maybe once you visit Arngrim, you can't leave without losing your memory. That would explain why no one beyond the mountains has ever heard of the place."

"Well, if you originally came from here," Elidor said, "someone here must know you."

Nearra nodded. "That's what I'm thinking, too. That's why I'm planning to explore the city tomorrow. I intend to talk to the peasants and see what I can find out. With luck, by the end of the day, I'll have discovered who I am—whether the Scarlet Brethren return from their pilgrimage or not."

"Any news about that?" Elidor asked.

Davyn shook his head and went back to looking out the window. "None," he said glumly.

"I hope Catriona gets back soon," Nearra said. "She and the prince have been gone all day. It's dark. Do you think they're all right?"

"Alric should know his way around his own kingdom," Sindri said.

"They took a lot of people and guards with them," Elidor said. "I'm sure they're fine. They probably just lost track of time." Elidor winked at Davyn.

Davyn nodded, but remained at the window. Was Catriona all right? Perhaps she had wandered into some elaborate trap of his father's. Was that the wizard's plan now—to separate them and pick them off one by one?

He wished he had more confidence in the Arngrims—especially Alric—to protect the companions. He wished he knew more about

149

his father's schemes. He wished he knew some surefire way to counter the doom he felt hanging over the whole group.

Elidor yawned. "You win, Sindri," he said, tapping the board once and standing up.

"But my fox hasn't made it to the den!"

Elidor stretched his arms and yawned again. "I think it's time for me to retire. I'll see you all in the morning." He rose and quickly slipped out the door.

"Nearra, would you like to play?" Sindri asked.

"No, thanks, Sindri. I think I'll turn in early tonight, too."

"What about you, Davyn?" Sindri asked.

"Oh, I don't like playing games," Davyn said, never taking his eyes off the window.

Sindri sighed. "I might as well go to bed then, too." Sindri packed up the game and scurried out the door.

Davyn gazed out into the fog. He noticed a shadow moving overhead—just at the limits of his vision.

The fine hairs the back of Davyn's neck stood up. A bird circled over the castle: Maddoc's black falcon!

The wizard was watching them, watching *him*. He could almost hear his father's voice echoing in his mind: *Traitor! False son! Coward!*

Despite the spectral taunts, Davyn would not give in. He would protect Nearra, or die trying.

He wondered if, perhaps, that was exactly what Maddoc had in mind.

19 INSIDE THE ARMOR

Elidor rose silently from his bed and crossed to the door of his chambers. He slowly lifted the latch, making sure to cause as little noise as possible.

Cracking open the door, he peered into the corridor outside the companions' chambers. Empty, as he had anticipated. All but a few candles had already been snuffed for the night.

Everyone was sure to be asleep by now.

Elidor stole silently into the corridor, checked the corners for guards, and then sneaked off into the castle proper. The elf moved quickly, on feet trained to make little sound in either wilderness or city. He passed a long, dimly lit gallery full of portraits, pausing only long enough to wonder how Nearra might know these people.

He turned left at a marble stairway, then right at the statue of a grim old king. Then he came to a crossroads. Uncertain which way to go, he pressed himself against the wall and thought—trying to call to mind the details he needed.

"What are you doing?" a small voice asked.

Elidor nearly jumped out of his skin.

He rounded fiercely on the intruder, a slender knife springing to his dexterous fingers. He stopped the blade just short of the kender's throat.

151

Elidor's violet eyes narrowed. "What I am doing," he hissed, "is none of your business."

"Oh," Sindri said. "I just thought you were going out exploring, in which case, I figured you might want some company. The castle's pretty big and empty. It could get lonely exploring alone. And, besides, you're about to wander into a guard post."

"I am?" Elidor said.

"Yeah," Sindri replied. "They moved stations this evening. I noticed it when I took a walk just before dinner. If we're going to have any chance to discover and break the enchantment hanging over this castle, we'll have to avoid the sentries. Follow me." Sindri turned left and padded off down the deserted hallway, with Elidor trailing behind.

"But I'm not going this way!" the elf hissed. He felt certain that the kender's rambling would get them both caught.

Sindri stopped, nearly skidding into a large, ornamental vase. "Aren't you going to the library?" he asked.

Elidor felt his temper rising. Was he that easy for the kender to read? "Yes," he said, "but you're going the wrong way."

"Well, you can go the other way if you want," Sindri said, "but there are more guards to duck—even if my way's longer. There's a servants' stairway down this direction that nobody uses. The corridor at the bottom of the stair goes almost straight to the library."

"Look," Elidor said, "thank you very much for the directions, but I can find my way on my own, now. If you'll just toddle back to your room . . ."

"Oh, no. I was going to the library anyway. It's no trouble at all. C'mon. This way." The kender smiled so genuinely that Elidor wanted to punch him. The elf could think of no better plan, though, than to follow the annoying little wizard.

After fifteen minutes of adhering to the kender's circuitous route, Elidor hissed, "Do you have any idea where we are?"

"Well," Sindri replied, "there are a few more twists and turns than I remembered."

The elf's temper rose again. "We've come down too far," he said. "The library is above us somewhere. In fact, the whole castle is above us, as far as I can tell."

The kender smiled. "We could be near the dungeons then!" he said. "That's great. Dungeons are a good place to hide secrets—even better than libraries."

"Quiet!"

The sound of marching feet echoing through the halls ahead of them froze both companions in their tracks. Elidor pushed them back against the nearest wall and held his breath.

"Guards, you think?" Sindri whispered.

Elidor shrugged.

"Let's see," the kender said.

Before Elidor could stop him, Sindri crept around the corner into the narrow passageway leading toward the noise. Cursing silently, Elidor followed.

The corridor stretched a short distance before ending in a larger, crossing passage. Candlelight blazed in the hallway ahead, casting long shadows into the narrow byway. Sindri cautiously approached the lit corner, with Elidor right behind.

They pressed themselves up against the wall to take advantage of the shadows, and then peered around the bend.

A stream of red-robed figures carrying scarlet candles marched down the rough-hewn stone hallway ahead of them. They whispered a nearly inaudible chant as they went. Two dozen silver-and-black armored knights escorted the procession. The knights remained silent save for the rhythmic clanking of their armor. The strange pageant wound down the passage and turned at the far corner. As they disappeared, the light receded with them.

"Do you think that was . . . ?" Sindri whispered.

"Possibly," Elidor replied. "It seems likely."

"We should follow them," Sindri said. "I have some questions I'd like to ask."

"For once, I agree with you," Elidor said. The thought of seeing where the Scarlet Brethren were headed intrigued the elf. The castle itself had proved disappointing in treasures, but the chambers of a band of wizards . . .

"Forget the library," Elidor said. "This line of inquiry could prove far more profitable."

"I'm sure they can tell us what kind of enchantment there is in this place," Sindri said.

"For now," Elidor replied, "let's just see what they're up to. Questions can wait for later—once we're formally introduced."

Sindri smiled and nodded his agreement.

Keeping a safe distance back, they crept quickly but silently down the corridor after the procession. The passage went down even deeper, into parts of the castle they'd never seen before.

A short time later, the solemn parade stopped outside a large set of iron-bound doors. Two guards stood, unmoving, on either side of the portal. The Scarlet Brethren and their escort opened the doors and passed through. The last wizard in line stopped and lifted the faceplates of the armored sentries.

The elf and the kender stared at the suits of armor.

"They're empty!" Sindri gasped.

The red-garbed wizard began chanting in low, weird tones. As he spoke, he raised his hands up and thrust them inside the empty helmets. He held his hands there for nearly a minute before withdrawing them and shuttering the armored faceplates once more. Then he turned and followed his colleagues through the doors, which swung shut behind him.

"What do you think it means?" Sindri asked.

The elf smiled. "I think it means that the Arngrims are so short of guards that they've set up scarecrows in their place." This was the best news he'd had since coming to the castle. It seemed the watchful eyes of the sentries didn't see everything after all.

"What about the wizard? I thought I saw a red glow around his hands when he opened the helmet."

"I didn't see that," Elidor replied. "You probably just imagined it because of all the red robes and candlelight."

"Why'd he put his hands inside the armor, then?"

"Undoubtedly some kind of ancient ritual," Elidor said. "The Brethren probably open that empty armor every time they pass through the door. You know, invoking the protection of the gods or something. The armor symbolizes protection."

"But there could be some kind of magic connected to it," Sindri said. "Maybe *that's* the magic I've sensed in this place."

"Maybe," Elidor agreed. "Whatever is on the other side of that portal is certainly worth seeing, or they wouldn't be making with all the ritual mumbo jumbo. I'm going to walk over there and through that door. I believe those 'guards' are nothing but empty scarecrows. But if you want, you can use your magic to raise those faceplates and we'll both take another look. If anything funny happens, I won't go."

"I want to see what's behind those doors, too," Sindri said. "But I don't want to be caught by those guards, either. No sense getting thrown in a dungeon just when things are getting interesting. Therefore, I accept your challenge." He rolled up the sleeves of his satin shirt, extended his arms, and concentrated.

Almost immediately, the faceplate on one suit of armor flipped up, revealing the empty space within.

"See?" Elidor said. "No magic. No traps. Nothing but a ruse to fool the gullible." He strode toward the ironbound doors, took the handle, and pulled.

As the door swung open, the sentry on Elidor's left reached out and grabbed his arm.

Elidor fought hard not to scream at the top of his lungs.

Sindri yelped in surprise and ran to help his friend. As he did, the other suit of armor turned to intercept him.

The sentry's grip felt cold as ice on the elf thief's arm. Elidor didn't know what to do. The armor was empty! While he fought down panic, the sentry holding him drew and raised its sword.

Gripped by fear, Elidor watched the weapon descend toward his head.

At the last instant, the sword lurched aside, as if possessed by a will of its own. It slashed sideways, smashing into the back of the second sentry's helmet. The smitten guardsman fell clattering to the floor.

Elidor thrust his hand against the chin of his attacker's helmet and pushed. The silver-and-black helmet flew off. The sentry staggered back and lost his grip on the elf. Hovering where the guardsman's head should have been, was a sickly red mist. For a moment, Elidor imagined he saw the outlines of a face in the eerie fog. Then Sindri yanked him by the arm.

"Come on!" the kender cried, dashing through the portal.

Elidor followed. They slammed the door shut behind them as the sentries regrouped.

Elidor grabbed an unlit torch from a nearby sconce and jammed it under the crack at the bottom of the doors.

"That probably won't hold them long," Sindri said.

"Just as long as it gives us time to run," Elidor replied. He and the kender dashed pell-mell down the dimly lit stone corridor beyond the portal.

"Remind me to thank you for your 'turning the weapon' trick sometime," Elidor said. "You seem to have become quite expert at it."

"You're welcome," Sindri replied. "It hardly even tires me out any more—not on little things anyway. Any idea which way we should be going?" He glanced at narrow passages branching off to the right and left. All the side corridors looked the same.

"Any way will do," Elidor said, "just so long as we stay ahead of those guards."

A resounding crack filled the passage as the torch wedging the door gave way. The two friends glanced at each other then redoubled their efforts, sprinting off into the dark catacombs beneath Castle Arngrim.

20   THE POWER BEHIND THE THRONE

The Scarlet Brethren assembled in a vast, tunnel-ridden cavern deep beneath Castle Arngrim. Stalactites, polished smooth by the passage of years, hung like gigantic icicles from the ceiling far above. The air in the cavern was dank and oppressive, though the red-hooded wizards didn't seem to notice.

Oddvar noticed. He'd grown tired of this cavern in the past few days. Wary of being seen in Arngrim, he'd spent much of his time here, exploring the winding passages, enjoying the underground scenery in ways that only a dwarf could.

The Brethren had been lurking in the maze of tunnels, too, preparing their spells to make ready for the great enchantment to come. Their supposed "pilgrimage" was only a ruse, of course, to keep them hidden while they worked. They'd ventured out only once to trace the sacred spell lines through the dungeons above.

Despite their shared circumstance, Oddvar avoided the red wizards. It was bad enough being more or less trapped in this underground maze. Having to endure the presence of humans as well might have pushed the dark dwarf to violence. Oddvar knew he could not afford violence—not yet.

The Brethren gathered in a circle in the chamber's center, rather than keeping to the shadows, as they had the last time the Theiwar had spoken to them. A flat, round stone, like a giant table, stood in the middle of the gathering. Countless runes, which Oddvar could not decipher, covered the stone's surface. The dwarf assumed the circular stone was probably some type of magical altar.

The red-garbed wizards stood next to each other, arms outstretched, their fingers not quite touching. Their chants filled the cavern, making the rocks vibrate with sonorous tones. The voices set Oddvar's teeth on edge, but he said nothing. A misplaced word in this situation could mean the ruin of his master's plans, or even the dwarf's death.

Finally, Primus—the man Oddvar had come to think of as the leader of the Brethren—spoke.

"The girl warrior has passed the test," he said. "She has proven that she is possessed of the Lionheart. Even now, she makes her way here."

"Can we be sure she is the chosen?" another asked. "A mistake at this time would be costly beyond imagination."

"There's no mistake," Oddvar replied, letting his impatience get the better of him. "My master promised to send you someone to fill your needs—someone who could break the curse that binds your nation. Everything that Maddoc foretold has come to pass. My master has made good on his pledge."

"Not yet, dark one," a red-robed woman said. "The potential is there, but the fulfillment? That is yet to be determined."

"Despite the promising nature of the situation," said a deep voice, "we do not yet put our trust in your master, dwarf." The man who spoke stepped from the shadows. As he did, the wizards fell to their knees.

King Conar Arngrim strode into the cavern, his blue-gray eyes fixed upon the Theiwar. "These people your master 'sent' to us. They arrived with our own son. You failed to mention that the last time we met. Was that also your wizard's doing?" the king asked skeptically.

"My master sees far," Oddvar replied. "Many things are possible."

"Or perhaps your master is merely trying to take advantage of a situation already forming in the webs of fate," the king said. "Despite the encouraging results of our test, we still have only your word that one of these candidates will prove suitable to be the chosen."

Oddvar shrugged. "What would Maddoc gain by leading you astray?"

"What indeed?" the king asked. He crossed the room and stood next to Oddvar, glowering down at the dwarf. "As yet, your master has asked no compensation for the 'service' he does us."

"Winning the king's favor would be payment enough," Oddvar lied. As he smiled at the aging king, the dwarf hoped that the Emergence would lead to the destruction of all Arngrim.

"And what of the others of this group, those not chosen?" Primus, the leader of the Brethren, asked, "Are they part of your master's schemes? Or has he sent them to us on a lark?"

"Yes," the king continued, pacing across the room once more. "What does Maddoc plan for the rest?"

Oddvar shrugged, relishing what he was about to say next. "They are of no import to my master," he said. "Kill them if you like." If the Emergence didn't work, perhaps the Arngrimites would kill all of the foolish teens, even Nearra. Then Oddvar would be free to move on to more worthy pursuits than following a pack of brats around the continent.

"Killing them might simplify things," Secundus, the woman who was the Brethren's second-in-command, said.

"It might indeed," Oddvar replied, suppressing a smile.

Secundus continued, ignoring the dwarf. "The presence of outsiders at this time could interfere with the weaving of the Great Spell."

"No," said King Conar. "We will not kill them. Not yet. We have only Maddoc's word—and our own hopes—that one of these will fulfill the prophecy and break the curse."

"The signs are promising," Primus said. "But, even now, the test notwithstanding, it is impossible to tell which of these five the omen may refer to."

"Exactly," said the king. "Perhaps, against all indications, the chosen is not the one we think. Perhaps that is the game this outsider wizard plays at. Perhaps what he truly desires is that we should squander our chance to end the curse."

"That is untrue, sire," Oddvar said. "My master only wishes the best for your kingdom." Another lie. Maddoc didn't actually care whether the curse on Arngrim was broken or not. He only wanted to encourage the Emergence. Helping the Arngrimites might bring about enough stress to trigger the transformation Maddoc desired. Killing all of Nearra's friends could do the same.

The wizard didn't care whether Nearra's companions lived or died. Oddvar, on the other hand, preferred the bloodletting.

At that moment, one of the king's silent knights entered the room. The sentry said nothing, but merely stared at King Conar and Primus.

"The elf and the kender loose beneath the castle!" the king boomed. "Outrageous!"

Secundus concentrated a moment, then bowed low. "It will be taken care of, Your Highness. Even now our ghost knights are on their trail. We will find them."

"Good," Oddvar said. "And when you catch these interlopers, perhaps you should slay them. After all, these non-humans can't be your chosen. They can only get in the way of your plans."

King Conar stared at the dwarf coldly. "Convey to the sentries that they are to avoid killing if at all possible," he said. "This dwarf is too bloodthirsty for my liking. I see his master's hand in his advice. Those not chosen may, I think, still be of use to us."

The Brethren bowed.

"Yes, Your Majesty," Secundus said. She did not leave the chamber, but stood rigidly for a moment, concentrating. Then her shoulders slumped, and she said, "It is done."

"I will order our sentries to capture the others as well," Primus said. "We do not need outsiders wandering the castle or catacombs at this critical juncture." He paused a moment, as his second-in-command had done.

The king nodded. "Good," he said. "Your order serves us well, as always." He glanced at the knight who had reported to him. The ghost in silver-and-black armor bowed and left the room.

Oddvar silently cursed himself. He had overplayed his hand and made the king suspicious. Though this would not alter the results of Maddoc's schemes, it would deprive the dwarf of the satisfaction of seeing his enemies die.

"I know you distrust my motives, sire," he said, making one last-ditch try, "but if these five were to die, then they couldn't very well be the chosen."

Primus edged close to the king's elbow. "There is some truth to what he says, sire," the leader of the Brethren said. "The prophecy against Asvoria says that the chosen *will* come. It is inevitable."

"Yes," the king replied, "but if we were to kill these children, who is to say that it might not take another thousand years for the prophecy to be fulfilled?" The king's blue-gray eyes gleamed in the dancing light of the cavern's braziers. "I, for one, do not intend to wait that long."

Davyn woke with a start. A piercing scream filled the night air. Nearra!

Maddoc's son bolted from his bed and to the door adjoining Nearra's chamber. She hadn't wanted him to lock it tonight, and he hoped she hadn't locked her side, either. She hadn't. He pushed the latch and dashed through, not bothering even to gather his weapons before he went.

Nearra sat bolt upright in bed. Her eyes darted across the darkened room, as if she didn't know where she was. Looking around, the young ranger saw nothing which might inspire such terror.

"Nearra!" Davyn said. "What's wrong?" He sat down on the bed and put his hands on her shoulders. "Nearra!"

For a moment, she didn't seem to recognize him. Then she blinked, and her scream died away. "Davyn!" she gasped. "Thank the gods!" She collapsed into his arms. He ran his fingers through her soaked hair, hoping to comfort her.

"There's nothing wrong," he said. "I'm here. Nothing can hurt you."

"I'm glad you're here," Nearra said, gently laying her hand on his chest. "But you're mistaken. Something *is* wrong. Very wrong."

"What is it?" he asked.

"Death is coming to this kingdom," she said. "I've seen it."

"Seen it how?" Davyn asked. A chill ran down his spine. "You must have been dreaming. It was only a nightmare."

She sat up and shook her head. "No," she said. "It was no nightmare. I saw that woman, that Asvoria, and she was coming to Arngrim. She was coming to kill everyone and take what she wanted."

"But that happened a long time ago," Davyn said. "You read about it in that history book we saw. You're just dreaming about what you read."

"That's not all," Nearra said. "Our friends are in danger, too. I saw them being chased by, well, I'm not sure what. At first, I thought they were the Arngrims's sentries, and then I thought they were ghosts, and then I thought they were monsters. Oh, Davyn, I think they're going to kill Sindri and Elidor!"

"The guardsmen may be creepy," Davyn said, "but I don't think they qualify as monsters. And I'm sure that Sindri and Elidor are fine. They're both asleep in their beds."

"What about Catriona? Has she returned yet?" Nearra asked.

"I don't think so. But she's certain to be with Alric. I'm sure she's okay." Davyn was, in fact, worried about Catriona. But he was more worried about Nearra. He didn't want the girl to work herself up any further. "What could happen to Catriona when she's with the prince?"

"I don't know," Nearra said. "But I'm sure that something's wrong with Elidor and Sindri."

"Look, if it'll make you feel better, I'll go next door and check on them," Davyn said.

She nodded.

"Are you sure you'll be all right alone?" he asked.

"Yes. I'll be fine."

"Okay, then. Be right back." He left through the main door and went into the corridor which joined all the rooms. He knocked on both Sindri and Elidor's chambers, silently cursing his father all the while.

This trouble was Maddoc's doing. The young ranger felt like he'd led his friends straight into a trap.

He swore. No one had answered at either door. Finding the latches unlocked, Davyn went into first one chamber and then the other. No Elidor. No Sindri.

Where could they be? It was too late for the pair to be prowling around the castle—though Davyn wouldn't have put it past the thief. Would Elidor take Sindri with him? No. That would be crazy. Sindri might have nimble hands and a kender's light fingers, but Davyn couldn't imagine the little wizard being part of one of Elidor's scams.

So, where were they?

He went back to Nearra's chambers.

She looked hopefully at him. "Well . . . ?" she asked.

He shook his head. "They're not there. Neither one."

"I told you," she said. Nearra stood and he saw that she'd changed into her traveling clothes.

"Grab your things," she said. "We need to find them. We need to find them now, before something terrible happens."

Davyn didn't see any point in arguing. He went to his room, quickly changed, and gathered his weapons. Upon returning, he found Nearra fastening her dagger to her belt.

"We can ask the king and queen," he suggested. "Maybe they can tell us where Elidor and Sindri are."

"No!" she blurted, dashing out the door. "There's no time!"

Davyn grabbed a burning candlestick and followed her.

She led them down darkened corridors, taking turns that Davyn didn't even see before they rounded them.

"Where are we going?" he asked.

"Down," she said. "Down to the lowest levels of the castle."

"How do you know where you're going? How can you be sure?"

"I remember," she said. "I remember this place."

"From the books we read?"

"No."

Davyn knew not to push any further. Buried somewhere within Nearra lay the Emergence—something Davyn felt increasingly sure he did not want to happen. He kept running, following Nearra down into the darkness.

FLIGHT FOR LIFE

Catriona rode as quickly as she could. She clutched Alric to her chest, trying not to jar him too much, trying to make sure the manticore's spine didn't sink any deeper into his flesh.

The young prince looked deathly pale, and felt nearly cold as ice. The weather wasn't helping any. Catriona had gotten them lost in the fog once, and they'd wasted precious time. Now that it was dark, she wondered whether she would be able to find their way home at all.

Despite the hardship, a slight smile creased Alric's sickly face. He drifted in and out of consciousness, babbling things that made no sense to Catriona. Fear clung to her heart. Not fear of the perils they still might face, but fear that she would lose him—fear that he would die.

He felt shockingly light in her arms, as if he might transform directly from man into spirit and waft out of her grasp into the mist. She held onto him as tightly as she dared.

Alric's eyes flickered open once again. He grinned weakly at her. "Not home yet?" he asked.

"Soon," she whispered. "Very soon."

"It's all right," he said.

Catriona bit her lip to keep from crying.

"I'm not fading," he said blearily. "Not yet."

"Hush," she said. "Save your energy. You're badly wounded."

He coughed and a thin trickle of pale blood leaked from his mouth. "I don't mind the pain," he said. "I've been . . . numb for so long. My life has been so hollow."

"You have much to live for," Catriona said. She felt as though any minute her brave face would slip and she would burst into tears. She had to stay courageous—for him. It was her fault he was like this. If only she'd been a better knight! If only she'd been stronger or smarter.

"The pain almost feels good," Alric said. "Being with you, even now . . ." His eyes grew hazy and he almost passed out again. Then he rallied. "Even now, I feel so alive."

She held the reins in one hand and put a finger to his lips. "No more talking," she said. "There's nothing you need to say. Nothing that I don't already know. You're going to be all right."

He nodded. "We're all going to be saved." Then he passed out.

Catriona let the tears flow down her cheeks. How much longer could the prince last?

What would she do if he died along the way? What would she tell his parents? What would she do without him?

A pale glow suffused the mist ahead of the riders. As they rounded a bend in the hills, Catriona realized what the glow meant: the city!

It was Arngrim!

They were nearly home!

The maze of rough-hewn tunnels beneath Arngrim echoed with rapid footfalls and the sound of labored breathing.

"Where are we going?" asked Sindri.

"How should I know?" Elidor said.

"Will we get there soon?"

"What did I just say?"

"Do you think those sentries are still following us?"

"Why don't you stop running and find out?"

Sindri glanced behind them but didn't stop. "No thanks," he said. "I'll keep running if it's all the same to you."

Elidor dashed toward the bend in front of them. He'd been getting steadily farther ahead as they went—longer legs, Sindri supposed. Before Sindri could reach the corner, though, Elidor stopped dead. The kender nearly plowed into him. The elf peeked cautiously around the turn.

"Not that way," he gasped. "There are ghost knights that way."

"Really?" Sindri said, stepping forward to take a look.

Elidor grabbed him by the collar and dragged him back. "You little fool!" he said. "You may want to spend the rest of a very short lifetime locked in an Arngrim dungeon, but I don't."

Without bothering to ask permission, he pulled Sindri down the corridor in the opposite direction. Something fell from Elidor's tunic in the commotion—a cricket trinket. Sindri tried to mention this but the elf didn't listen. He just kept running, hauling Sindri along with him.

They ducked down three side passageways, then came to another sudden halt.

"Do you have any idea how to get out of here?" Sindri asked. "Not that I mind being lost. It's just that I didn't bring much of anything to eat, and—"

"Why don't you materialize something and keep your mouth quiet," Elidor hissed. "There are sentries ahead of us, again, in case you didn't notice."

Sindri hadn't noticed. He'd spent so much time enjoying the scenery and the sudden, unexpected "ride" that he'd completely forgotten to listen for the people they were trying to escape.

"Must be down here somewhere," an irritated voice ahead of them said.

"If we didn't need to conserve magic, we could track them down more easily," added another.

"I thought the ghost knights didn't talk," Sindri whispered.

"Shh!" Elidor hissed.

"The sentries will round up the kender and elf," the first voice said, "along with the rest of their worthless friends."

"Why Alric brought outsiders to the castle in the first place, I'll never know."

"Primus is convinced that the chosen is among them," the first said. "That's all we need to know. We'll soon have what we want, and the rest of those interloping children will be safely out of the way. Once the curse is broken, we can safely dispose of them."

Sindri and Elidor pressed themselves up against the wall as two Scarlet Brethren passed within ten feet of them. A ghost knight followed behind. The kender and the elf held their breaths until all three had vanished down the tunnel.

Elidor grinned once the searchers had gone. "I hope they're better wizards than they are bloodhounds," he whispered.

"Did you hear what they were talking about?" Sindri asked.

"I was kind of busy trying not to get caught," Elidor replied.

"They said that they were going to round everybody up. That means Catriona, Nearra, and Davyn!"

"Let's not forget *us* as well," the elf said. "We're the ones I'm most concerned about at the moment."

"We should warn the others," Sindri said. Though he didn't mind being captured himself, the thought of his friends at the mercy of the ghost knights bothered him.

"Warn them how?"

"We should go back to our rooms. Davyn and Nearra are probably still sleeping."

"Don't you think that's the first place the sentries will look?" Elidor asked. "Besides, we don't even know where we are."

Sindri closed his eyes and spun around in a circle, feeling for the magical emanations that would lead him back to their rooms.

"It's that way," he announced when he finally stopped.

"That's the way the red wizards went," Elidor said.

"So?"

The elf sighed. "I know I'm going to regret this," he said, "but I'd hate to see Nearra walk into whatever trap these goons have planned. Let's go. But if I think we're headed in the wrong direction, we follow *my* lead. Understand?"

"Sure," Sindri said.

They headed off in the direction the kender had chosen, moving quickly but cautiously through the natural stone corridors. Sindri watched their surroundings as they went. The rock formations were really interesting. Sindri supposed that these tunnels must have been carved out by water over a very long period of time. The walls were nearly smooth, though not at all regular.

Occasionally, they passed by marks carved into the walls or floor. Sindri recognized these as magical symbols of some type, though Elidor never let him stop long enough to actually read any.

After twisting and turning through what seemed like several miles of tunnels, they came to a crossroads. The left tunnel was dark and filled with cobwebs. The right tunnel appeared to glow with a dim light and the ground seemed to lead up a slight slope.

Sindri headed for the dark tunnel. Elidor grabbed him by the cape.

"Hang on. That doesn't look right," he said.

"But my magic tells me this is the way back to the castle," Sindri said.

"I've had about enough of your magic. My turn to lead." Elidor began walking up the right tunnel. He looked back at Sindri. "Well, come on."

Sindri shrugged. "Have it your way."

STEPHEN D. SULLIVAN

They climbed for a few feet and then the tunnel took a sharp dip downward. They seemed, to Sindri, to be moving deeper into the catacombs, rather than back into the castle.

"I think we're going the wrong way," Sindri said.

Elidor grunted. "I know what I'm doing."

At last, the passage opened into a vast underground space. Elidor stopped, and put his hand out to halt the kender as well.

"I better creep up and check that cavern before we continue," Elidor said, dropping to his knees.

"Why don't you let me?" Sindri suggested, but the elf wasn't listening to him again.

Elidor crawled on his belly up to the cavern opening, with Sindri following a respectable distance behind.

The passage they were in opened into a huge cave. The tunnel's course continued into the vast space, winding along the left-hand wall of the cave, like a trail hugging a cliff face. Sindri guessed the tunnel entered about halfway up the cliff, though he couldn't see either the cavern ceiling, or its bottom .

Ahead and to their left, a sheer wall continued up out of sight, to the hidden ceiling far above; to their right, the path's edge ended abruptly, falling off steeply into the darkness. Sindri couldn't see where the trail they were following exited the cavern; it simply vanished into the blackness ahead of them.

Elidor took this all in, then turned to tell Sindri what he'd found. He seemed a little annoyed to discover the kender at his elbow. "I hear noises down below," the elf whispered. "Someone must be in the cavern. They'll spot us if we stand up, but I think we can make it across if we keep low and creep across the ledge."

"Make it to where?" Sindri whispered. "I can't see the far side of the cave."

"I can," Elidor replied. "The path winds along the cave wall and leaves by a tunnel on the other side.

"How far?"

"About a hundred yards," the elf said. "Let's go."

He crept out into the cavern, moving as quickly as he dared. Sindri followed right behind.

The two of them crawled with their bellies pressed against the stone ledge, keeping as low as they possibly could. Sindri glanced to their right, over the edge of the trail, and saw a steep, sloping cavern wall below them. At the bottom, he could just make out the tops of wide stalagmites poking up from the cave floor, like stone fingers reaching up to grab passing travelers.

The sight was both beautiful and eerie. Before he could tell Elidor about it, though, the ledge beneath the elf suddenly gave way. Sindri grabbed onto his friend's boots and gripped them tightly, trying to keep Elidor from falling to the cavern floor. But the elf was too heavy, and his weight dragged the kender over the precipice as well.

Together they skidded down the slope like rocks down a mountainside, dislodging huge quantities of earth and stone as they slid. A cloud of gray, choking dust built up around them as they fell. Sindri lost count of how many times he tumbled head over heels. Finally, they stopped.

Sindri looked up and saw they had come to rest on the banks of an underground river. Behind them, a huge pile of rocks and rubble sloped up to where the path had collapsed, thirty feet above. They had ridden the landslide all the way to the cave floor.

Sindri's head was swimming but, overall, he'd enjoyed the experience.

"Are you okay?" Sindri asked.

"I've been better," Elidor said.

Sindri followed Elidor's stare and spotted many ghost knights swarming in on them from three sides. With the rockslide making it impossible to climb back to the trail, he and Elidor had no place left to run. They were surrounded.

The Arngrim sentries drew their weapons and closed in.

CHAPTER

22   ALRIC'S FATE

Catriona spurred Alric's horse through the great castle gates and up to the inner keep. "Send the royal physicians!" she called. "The prince is hurt!"

She'd shouted the same thing at the city gate, and again outside the castle walls. She'd wanted to scream all the way through the city, but it occurred to her that the Arngrims might not want word of Alric's wounding to spread through the populace. The royal family might want to keep his illness secret until he either recovered or . . .

Catriona turned her mind away from the bleaker prospects. She guided the horse up the long stone steps leading to the main entryway, and then reined it in.

As she pulled up in front of the great castle doors, they swung open. The king and queen and a great crowd of servants rushed out to meet her. Several of the servants held a litter to carry the wounded prince inside. Catriona lowered Alric from the saddle, holding her breath all the while.

Yes. He still lived. She hadn't had time to check while she galloped the last few leagues. He might still die, but at least she'd delivered him to the castle—to his parents—in time. In this, at least, she had not failed.

"Where are the physicians?" she asked as she climbed off the horse. "He's lost a lot of blood."

"They await in a chamber nearby." The queen motioned to a reception room very close to the front doorway. "The room has been made over as a makeshift infirmary."

The servants carried the unconscious prince into the infirmary and the queen followed them inside.

Catriona tried to run after them, but the king cut her off.

"What happened?" he asked, anger flashing across his blue-gray eyes. "What went wrong? Why do you return to us practically unwounded while my son lies nearly lifeless?"

"We were attacked by a monster," she replied. The deep scratches across her back burned, but that didn't dull the king's accusation. She felt the stab of it like a burning poker. "A manticore Alric called it. One of its spines struck him. It's still in his chest."

"The manticore . . ." the king gasped. His lips drew into a thin line as he held back his fury. Moisture beaded at the corner of his aged eyes. Catriona reached out for him, but King Conar backed away.

"Thank you for bringing him home," he said. "I regret my harsh words. You are not responsible for this terrible turn of events. None of us are. No one could have foreseen this, not even our finest wizards. You have been very brave—all we could hope for. Go now, and rest. A physician will attend you. There is nothing more you can do for my son."

"I want to stay with him," Catriona said. Her eyes misted over as well.

The queen reemerged from the chamber where they'd taken the prince. "Your task is ended now," she said. "We will attend to Alric. Our healers are experienced in these matters. Go to your chambers. We will send word once we know something."

Catriona nodded. She didn't want to leave, but she couldn't refuse the request of Alric's mother. She walked past the room where they'd taken Alric, casting a lingering glance through the doorway. He looked even more pale than before: pale as death. The king and queen brushed past Catriona and entered the room, followed by a slender, red-robed woman. The door swung closed, shutting out Catriona's gaze.

If Alric should die!

The king had been right the first time. This *was* her fault—her fault for letting her guard down at the picnic, her fault for not protecting Alric, her fault for getting lost on the way back to the city. No matter what Alric said, she would make a terrible knight.

She dashed up to the guest quarters and ran to her room. Closing the door behind her, she fell onto the bed and wept—all pretense of strength finally draining away.

Sometime later—Catriona couldn't be sure how long—a knock at the door roused her. At first she hoped it might be news of the prince. Then she feared that it might be her friends, coming to check on her. She couldn't bear to have her companions see her in such a state. So she dried her eyes and carefully composed herself before calling, "Come in."

A servant appeared at the door, holding Catriona's armor and helmet.

Catriona took the armor gratefully. She'd almost forgotten she'd left it behind. Some of the scattered servants must have returned to the valley, rescued it, and then found their way home.

"How is the prince?" she asked. She tried to sound hopeful, but fear for Alric's life still peeked through.

"Don't know, ma'am," the girl replied. "I'm sorry." She was only a few years younger than Catriona. The serving girl curtsied and then left the room.

Moments later, a physician arrived to bandage Catriona's wounds. Once the physician had gone, the young warrior changed into fresh clothing and donned her armor. Armor wasn't particularly appropriate given the circumstances, but wearing the chainmail and helmet made her feel better—more in control.

Catriona suddenly realized that her friends didn't know about what had happened to her and Alric. If the others had heard her crying, they'd been too polite to appear at her doorway. But all of them deserved to know that she had returned and that the prince lay wounded, possibly dying.

She buckled on her sword and girded herself to tell them the bad news. She checked the common room first. She didn't expect to find anyone there at this time of night, but doing so allowed her some extra time to compose herself. She knocked on the doors of all her friends in sequence, going down the hall.

When no one answered. She knocked again. And again.

Could all of them be sleeping so soundly?

Cautiously, she opened the door to Nearra's room. Her friend's bedclothes lay tossed on the floor, with her nightgown beside them. Catriona saw no sign of Nearra in the room.

Cold fear gripped her heart.

She pulled open the adjoining doors, running from room to room. None of them were locked. None of the chambers contained her friends. Davyn's room seemed have been vacated in a hurry, like Nearra's. Elidor and Sindri's rooms, though, looked in perfect order.

The mystery of it all whirled in Catriona's tired brain. Where could they be? Why had two of them left suddenly, while the other two hadn't? Were her friends in trouble? Did they need her help, even now?

She checked again, looking for a note, first in her own room, then the common room, then the chambers of all the rest.

She found nothing. No indication of where they had gone, or when, or why. If they'd had time to tell her what was happening, they'd chosen not to do so.

But why would they do that?

Catriona returned to her own room, flopped down on the bed, and tried to puzzle it out, torn between trying to locate and help her friends and worrying about Alric.

She couldn't leave him. She couldn't go running off blindly trying to find Nearra and the others while Alric lay dying.

If she left, and Alric died, she would never forgive herself. She put her head in her hands and wept again. She wept until Arngrim, and her friends, and the whole world went away.

The door to her room swung open.

Catriona looked up, hastily smearing the tears from her eyes.

Through the portal walked Queen Valaria, gliding in regal strides across the floor.

"Alric," Catriona said, nearly choking, "is he . . .?"

"He stands at death's doorway," the queen replied gravely. "He is fading. His fascination with you has cost him dearly. But you, Catriona, can save him. Do you wish to help Alric, dear girl? Will you save my only son?"

Catriona stood and steeled her jaw. "I will do anything to save him," she said. "Anything."

"I thought so." The queen smiled. "Dry your tears, my child." She swept toward Catriona, reaching out her arms to hug the young warrior. "Everything will be all right now."

Catriona stepped forward, into the queen's embrace. As Valaria's bony arms wrapped around her, a sudden chill shot through Catriona's body. A feeling of overwhelming despair welled up inside her.

Queen Valaria felt cold—as cold as death.

Catriona's knees gave way, but Valaria caught her in a grip like ice. The young warrior gazed up into the queen's gray, unliving eyes. Fear clutched at her heart.

Then darkness claimed her.

CHAPTER

23　　THE DRAGON'S MAW

Why wasn't Davyn running faster? Couldn't he sense it? Didn't he see that their friends— Elidor, Sindri, and now Catriona as well—were all in mortal peril?

Nearra led Davyn through the vast maze of tunnels beneath Castle Arngrim. She glanced back, making sure that he hadn't fallen behind again. Davyn didn't look pleased to be dashing through the semi-darkness with her. The light from the candle he carried waned and flickered as he ran.

"Do you have any idea where you're going?" he asked.

Nearra didn't respond. She could see the picture so clearly in her head—the underground caverns, the stream, the great chasm, the spell room of the Scarlet Brethren. She knew every location in this great underground maze. It was as though her body moved on its own, as if her will was not hers to command.

The tips of her fingers and her toes tingled. The fine hairs on her arms and the back of her neck stood up. Goosebumps covered her pale skin. Her eyeballs burned. Her headache had returned with a vengeance. Nearra ignored it all and pressed on.

Nothing in the world was more important now, not even the return of her memory. She needed to find her friends before they were all killed.

"Nearra!" Davyn said. He grabbed her by the hand and they both jerked to a sudden halt. Deep concern filled his brown eyes. "We can't go on like this. You're burning up with fever. We need to stop, to rest."

She shook her head, which made the pain behind her eyes throb even more. "It's not much farther," she insisted. "You'll see. We need to help them."

"How do you know that?" he asked, both angry and sympathetic. "You're no seer! This is just some fever dream. Come back to your chambers with me."

"No!" she said, yanking away from him.

She turned and ran down the tunnel. For long minutes, he hurried after her.

Then he called, "Nearra, wait! Wait! Stop! I've found something."

She skidded to a stop and turned back to him.

In his hand, Davyn held a small, metal cricket. Its abdomen glowed slightly. "This is Elidor's," the ranger said. "I've seen it before." He stooped and examined the fine grit and dust on the tunnel floor. "They went this way," he said, pointing in a direction other than the one Nearra had been going. "I'm sure of it."

"But the spell chamber is this way," Nearra replied. The words were out of her lips before she even considered them.

A puzzled look washed over Davyn's handsome face. "What spell chamber?"

Nearra thought about it, but doing so made her head hurt. "I . . . I don't know," she said.

"Well, I know that Elidor and Sindri went this way," he replied. "Rushing around blindly won't do us any good. You got us this far. Now let me take over. I'm certain our friends went this way."

"Well, if you're positive."

"I am," he said. "Come on."

Nearra followed, sparing only a brief glance at the way she'd been going. Something was trying to pull her in that direction.

She fought down the impulse. Davyn knew what he was doing; he would lead them to their friends.

Nearra prayed they would be in time.

As she walked, following Davyn now rather than the compulsion of her visions, Nearra felt suddenly very tired. The tingling in her fingers and toes faded. Their entire journey seemed somehow less urgent than it had just moments before.

Could she have been wrong about all of this? Was she going insane? If mad, though, how to explain what she knew about the Arngrims and their castle? Nearra rubbed her eyes to try and ward off the burning headache she felt building.

"This tunnel enters a chamber ahead," Davyn said. "The path winds along one wall, but it looks like it ends in a rockslide."

Nearra nodded. "Let's keep going," she said. She gritted her teeth, trying to quell the pain behind her eye sockets.

"Careful," Davyn said as they entered the cavern and approached the crumbling end of the path. "It doesn't look sturdy."

The broken trail wound along the side of the huge cavern, halfway up the wall. Stalactites, like stone icicles, hung from a ceiling so high it lay hidden in darkness. Wide stalagmites reached their bony fingers up from the floor. The rock formations shimmered with a faint, eerie illumination—as though twinkling stars were trapped on the surface of the stone. On the other side of the large gap in the trail, the path continued hugging the cliff face until it exited through a tunnel in the far wall.

"Look!" Davyn whispered, laying one hand on her shoulder and shielding their candle with the other. Below them, an underground stream snaked through the giant stalagmites lining the cavern floor. The rock slide ended near the stream's bank. Ten yards beyond it lay a massive opening in the cave wall—obviously leading to another, even larger underground space.

Thick points of stone poked from the exit's roof; jagged stalagmites jutted up from its floor. The combination of the two made the opening look like a huge, yawning mouth filled with monstrous fangs. Barely visible in the cavern's natural illumination, four Arngrim sentries moved through the opening. Between them, they carried two limp forms, one man-sized, the other no bigger than a child.

Even from this distance, even in the dim light, Nearra and Davyn easily recognized Elidor and Sindri.

Nearra looked at Davyn. He seemed torn between wanting to get her to safety and wanting to help their friends. "We need to follow them," she said. "How do we get down?"

"I think we can manage that slope," Davyn replied. "It's steep, but we can make it if we're careful. I don't know if we'll be able to climb back up, though."

"We can worry about that later," she said. "After we rescue our friends."

"Okay. Come on."

Carefully, the duo picked their way down the rockfall. They slid several times, but managed to reach the bottom with only a few scrapes and bruises. They crossed the stream, which was very shallow and only a few yards wide, then hiked up to the mouth-like opening.

Nearra stopped. "The Dragon's Maw!" she said, her eyes fixed on the gap.

"What?" Davyn asked.

"This cave opening leads to the Dragon's Maw," she said.

"How do you know?" he asked. Then he added, "A *real* dragon?" He looked even more worried.

"I don't think so," Nearra said. "But I guess we're about to find out."

They squeezed between the sharp stone pillars. A long gentle slope of rock led from the mouth of the cave down to the floor of another huge cavern.

This cave was twice as large as the courtyard of the Temple of the Holy Orders of the Stars; a whole family of dragons could easily have fit inside. The stalactites and stalagmites grew even larger here. Some of them reached down and touched one another, forming towering natural columns of shimmering rock.

The most striking feature of the cave, though, was an immense gorge that divided the cavern nearly in half. The chasm cut through the chamber's floor from one side to the other. Even though it was more than forty yards away, the size and width of the fissure dwarfed Davyn and Nearra. Even a giant would not have been able to step from one side to the other.

Nearra nodded at the fissure. "That," she said reverently, "is the Dragon's Maw."

Numerous black-mouthed smaller tunnels opened into the cavern on either side of the immense crevasse. None of these other exits lay near to the main gap through which the anxious couple entered the cavern, though.

"I don't see Elidor and Sindri," Davyn said. "Where could the sentries could have taken them?" He swallowed hard. "You don't think they threw them into that pit—the Dragon's Maw—do you?"

Cold fear ran up Nearra's spine. "I don't know," she said. "I hope not."

"We'd better check," Davyn said. He edged down the slope toward the dreadful chasm.

They quickly reached the bottom of the slope and began to pick their way toward the fissure. As they did, a sound like metal scraping against stone echoed to their ears. They turned.

Nearly a dozen Arngrim sentries clattered toward them over the rocky cavern floor. Some emerged from openings in the cave wall. Others had apparently lain waiting behind the titanic natural pillars.

"Run!" Davyn said.

"We're cut off!" Nearra replied.

The black-and-silver armored knights had surrounded them on every side save one—and in that direction lay the awful fissure of the Dragon's Maw.

"Back off!" Davyn commanded the sentries. He quickly drew his bow and nocked an arrow to the string. "We don't want to hurt you."

Nearra looked nervously from one armored guard to the next. "I'm not sure they feel the same way about us," she said.

"We're friends of the royal family," Davyn said, "guests of Prince Alric himself." He shifted his aim from one guardsman to the next as they advanced.

Nearra drew the dagger from her hip, feeling completely useless despite the weapon. Her head pounded and she concentrated on her breathing, trying to keep the world from spinning. Her fingers and toes began to tingle.

"We're just looking for our friends," Davyn explained. His voice sounded more desperate with each passing second. "Tell us where they are, and we'll go on our way. This doesn't have to turn violent."

Kill them! whispered the voice in Nearra's head. Before she could stop herself, her lips repeated the thought. "Kill them!"

Davyn grimaced and let fly his arrow.

The shot glanced off the shoulder of the nearest guardsman, scuffing the black-and-silver armor only slightly. Davyn drew another arrow, took a deep breath to steady his aim, and fired again.

This time, the ranger's shot flew straight into the eye slit in the guard's visor. Davyn and Nearra gasped as the shaft clanked on the back of the sentry's helmet.

There was no blood, no cry of surprise and pain. The guardsman kept coming, the arrow sticking out of his steel helmet.

Sweat beaded on Davyn's forehead. He drew and fired again, choosing a different target. This time, his arrow hit the sentry's head full on. The helmet rang loudly and flew from the guardsman's shoulders.

The man had no head. A pale, red fog hovered over his metal neck. In the mist, Nearra imagined the outline of a ghostly face. The headless knight did not slow down.

Nearra screamed. "They're dead! They're already dead!" Her heart pounded loudly in her chest.

Davyn slung his bow and drew his hunting knife. He positioned himself in front of Nearra. "Stay behind me," he said. "I'll protect you for as long as I can." The two of them backed slowly toward the Dragon's Maw.

Nearra's brain burned and her eyes watered. Her head swam with images, but she couldn't be sure if they were thoughts, or memories, or dreams. What madness had gripped Castle Arngrim? How could the faithful guards be spirits? Why were the sentries pursuing them? A feeling grew in the back of Nearra's mind that she knew the answers, but she couldn't force the thoughts to the surface.

Did she even want the thoughts to surface? The tingling in her limbs grew stronger and spread throughout her body. She fought down panic, trying to examine the situation calmly.

None of the sentries had drawn their swords yet. Perhaps they didn't intend to harm her or Davyn. But where had they taken Elidor and Sindri? And what did the sentries intend to do with them—with all of them?

She stuck her knife back into her belt and clutched her temples. Spots danced before her eyes and the pain in her head throbbed. The ghost knights kept advancing. She and Davyn retreated farther and farther, with every step moving closer to the edge of the Dragon's Maw.

Davyn stabbed his hunting knife at one of the sentries. The knight walked right onto the point, but his armor turned the blade aside. He grabbed Davyn's knife arm with one hand and reached for the ranger's throat with the other. Davyn kicked hard into the sentry's knee.

The armor crunched and the ghost knight released his grip. Davyn lurched back, almost stumbling.

Nearra caught him and he leaned against her for a moment. Only a few yards and a couple of stalagmites separated them from the terrible chasm now. They stepped backward and found themselves pinned against one of the stone pillars jutting up from the floor.

Davyn took a deep breath. He charged forward, a cry of frustration bursting from his lips.

Nearra tried to shout, "Davyn, no!" but no words came from her lips. Fighting the spectral sentries seemed useless. The sounds of the brawl echoed within the cavern, adding to the cacophony in her mind.

Davyn put his head down and aimed his shoulder for the sentry's armored waist. The young ranger winced with the impact, but the guardsman went down, clattering as his hollow armor hit the stony floor.

The sentry grabbed for Davyn. The ranger struck the thing's helmet with the pommel of his knife. The helmet flew off the guardsman's shoulders, skidded across the rocks, ricocheted off a stalagmite, and fell into the Dragon's Maw.

The loss of its head didn't slow the knight down at all. It seized Davyn by the arms, but he twisted away. Davyn regained his feet just as another sentry tried to grab him from behind.

The stalagmite felt cold against Nearra's back. It was the only feeling she could sort from the sensations rampaging through her sweat-drenched body.

Davyn kicked backward, catching the sentry behind him full in the chest. The armored figure staggered and Davyn turned on it. The ranger put his hands onto the knight's breastplate and pushed with all his might.

The guardsman lurched toward the edge of the Dragon's Maw. The ghost knight tried to regain its balance, but failed. It toppled into the yawning chasm and vanished from sight. The sentry neither cried out nor made any sound as it fell.

Before Davyn regained his footing, two more sentries grabbed him. He struggled mightily, slashing with his knife and bruising his fists against the guards' steel armor. His attacks had little effect, but he managed to keep the ghost knights away from Nearra. As the ranger fought, more sentries converged on them.

Panic filled Nearra's mind. They had no way out. She would surely be captured or killed. Davyn would probably be killed trying to protect her. If only her head would stop hurting, perhaps she could think of a way to help him.

Davyn knocked another knight down, but two more came to take their comrade's place. The specters seemed to be concentrating on the ranger, now, forcing him away from Nearra, trying to either drag him down or push him into the pit. Davyn slipped and his foot nearly went over the precipice. Tiny stones sprayed out from under his boot and clattered down the side of the chasm.

As he tottered on the edge, another knight surged forward, its arms outstretched to push him over.

The tingling sensation in Nearra's body blazed into white hot fire. The world twisted and darkness closed in around her. She screamed

"Noooooooooo!"

Blazing blue-white energy flashed from her fingertips and burst against the steel armor of the undead knights. The sentries surrounding Davyn reeled. One exploded into shards of empty armor. Another crashed into a stalagmite and vanished in a puff of dust. A third fell into the Dragon's Maw.

Yessss! screamed the voice in Nearra's mind.

Davyn stared at her, shock etched across his face. As he stood dumbstruck, one of the remaining Arngrim knights seized him.

The sentry lifted the ranger off the ground as though he were a rag doll.

Davyn flailed desperately and managed to kick his attacker in the chest. The knight lurched wildly and dropped its prey.

Davyn toppled backward, over the edge of the cliff and into the Dragon's Maw.

CHAPTER

24   POWER AND CORRUPTION

Nearra wailed in agony.

Images of death and devastation flashed through her mind. She saw herself destroying all the knights of Arngrim, killing the royal family, and reducing their castle to rubble. She laid waste to both the city and the surrounding countryside. When she finished, only ash and smoke remained.

Something hard hit the side of her head. Nearra blinked, realizing that one of the knights had struck her. She staggered toward the precipice, just as Davyn had done.

The knight swung at her again. She blasted it, and the silent sentry melted away into nothing.

Hatred blazed from Nearra's eyes.

These hollow specters would pay for killing her friend! By the gods, how they'd pay!

Raw magic poured from her: sparkling, terrible energy. She blew some of the ghost knights to smithereens, while reducing others to lumps of twisted metal. She ripped off armored legs and arms, leaving only reddish mist behind. Using the power felt wonderful—and at the same time, terrifying.

Nearra felt her soul shrinking even as the magic within her grew ever stronger. *I must not lose control!* she thought.

188

But she wanted to lose control. She wanted to make her dream to ravage Arngrim a reality. She had the power to do it. She would make every man, woman, and child in the kingdom pay for what they'd done.

The magic blazed through her, coruscating waves of energy destroying anything they touched. She shattered stalagmites that had stood for millennia and rained stalactites down on her enemies like gigantic stone daggers. There seemed no limit to what she could do.

She screamed with joy and anger and fear—destroying the ghost knights in droves.

A small worry crept from the back of her mind and coiled snake-like around her consciousness.

How long could she continue?

How long before all semblance of control washed away?

How long before the power destroyed her as well?

Alric moaned and his eyes flickered open. The prince tried to sit up, but his wasted body wouldn't obey. He found himself lying on a cot in a makeshift infirmary near the castle entrance. The weary prince glanced down at the bandage covering the wound in his chest. "Is that all my blood?" he whispered. "There doesn't seem to be enough."

"You've come a long way," the king replied, "but you're not well yet."

"Lie peacefully, Son," Valaria said. "You've had a terribly close call. Primus and the Brethren were able to revive you, but you are still not well."

Alric laughed, then winced from the ache in his chest. "I'd almost forgotten how pain felt," he said.

"Soon there will be time for plenty of things long forgotten," his father replied. "Joy, love, revenge." The king and his wife shared a wicked smile.

"Yes," Alric said. "I suppose there will be. How did you—?" He stopped, noticing a serving maid lying on another cot close beside him. His hand brushed hers and he felt the coldness of her body—a coldness he was all too familiar with. He pulled his hand away from the corpse.

"You used this girl to bring me back?" he said. "You stole her life to prolong my existence?"

"Yes," the queen replied.

"What about Catriona?"

"She is safe in our dungeons, awaiting the proper moment," the queen said. She laughed, a coarse, dry cackle. "You were right, Son. She *is* the chosen."

Alric looked confused. "No, I . . ."

King Conar's eyes went wide and he held up his hand. "Wait!" he said.

"Yes," said Valaria. "I sense it, too."

She and her husband stared into the distance for a few long moments.

Alric struggled hard and sat up. "What is it?" he asked.

"We sense power!" his mother replied. She and the king looked at one of the sentries, stationed near the door to the chamber. The sentry stared back blankly.

"The guards have found the chosen's companions," the king said, "and one of them—"

"We must go," Queen Valaria hissed.

"I'll go with you," said Alric, trying to rise from his bed.

"No," the king replied. "You will remain here until you feel better. The sentries will see to your needs." He glanced at the dead girl. "And dispose of the remains."

Alric looked as though he might say something, but stopped. He nodded slowly.

The king and queen swirled their gray-and-silver robes around themselves and vanished from the room.

I won't! Nearra thought. I won't let the power destroy me. I must control it. I must! She struggled, trying to fight down the blazing heat consuming her slender body.

Only a half-dozen of the ghost knights remained now; she had slain all the rest—if the undead could truly be said to perish.

Concentrating, she fired a short burst of lightning into the chest of the nearest guard. The knight flew back across the cavern and crashed into a stalagmite—incapacitated, but not slain.

I did it! Nearra thought. I don't have to kill! Joy at the accomplishment welled up within her. She could control this terrible energy; she would not be consumed by it. But just as she thought it, she felt the power waning within her. Had she used the all magic up, or—

Use it! screamed the voice within her.

She lashed out, flinging a semicircle of blazing energy from her fingertips.

The conflagration burst against the armor of the remaining guards, pounding against them like waves crashing upon the shore. The sentries flew through the air and fell down, only to rise once more.

No!

Stabbing pain shot through Nearra's head. The tingling in her body cooled and began to subside.

Not now!

She blinked the sweat out of her aching eyes, trying to muster the force to repel the advancing knights once more.

All at once, the sentries stopped dead in their tracks.

Nearra sensed a presence behind her. She turned and her blood ran cold. King Conar and Queen Valaria swooped down on her like giant bats. Nearra could see the cavern walls and ceiling through their transparent flesh.

They reached for her, grasping with their claw-like hands, preying upon her life energy. Their semi-corporeal talons pierced Nearra's flesh. Her body went cold and she slipped into the darkness.

Davyn's whole body ached.

He pulled himself away from the edge of the pit, grateful he had landed on a stony ledge rather than falling headlong into the abyss. He could dimly see the rim of the crevasse above him. The sounds of fighting drifted down to his ears. Intermittently, bright blue-white light—like distant lightning on a summer night—blazed across the cavern's ceiling.

He knew it was Nearra causing the lightning. Was this what his father had wanted, to turn the girl into an unstoppable killing machine? How could Maddoc hope to control such power?

Davyn found his hunting knife near the precipice of the ledge and went to retrieve it. His bruised fingers fumbled with the handle and he nearly knocked it into the pit. He tucked the knife back into its sheath, then rose carefully to his feet. Though he felt terrible, nothing seemed to be broken. Quickly and deliberately, he climbed up the sheer side of the chasm.

Blood caked the ranger's fingertips by the time he reached the top. His body felt as though it were made of lead. His lungs ached so badly that he feared they might burst. He paused at the precipice, trying to catch his breath.

Nearra stood a dozen yards away, white hot power blazing from her slender form. She didn't see Davyn hanging onto the top edge of the fissure; she was concentrating all of her energy on slaying the undead sentries. The ghost knights swarmed in on her, paying no heed as their companions fell in droves.

Davyn wanted to crawl up and help her, but his strength failed him. He lost his grip on the edge and nearly slid back into the chasm. Scrabbling with his bloody fingers, he caught hold of the rough stone rim just in time.

With a mighty effort, Davyn heaved himself up over the edge and rolled to his feet. He staggered forward and leaned against a stalagmite, trying to regain the strength to continue.

Then he saw something that made his blood run cold.

As Nearra faltered, the king and queen of Arngrim swooped down upon the girl. They were hideous, ghostlike wraiths, their faces full of hatred and unliving hunger.

Davyn tried to move, tried to go to Nearra's aid, but his body wouldn't respond. The royal couple seized the girl in their transparent arms. Nearra went very pale and collapsed to the cavern floor.

The monstrous specters hovered above her, their steely eyes gleaming. The king turned to the remaining sentries and hissed, "Take her to the spell chamber."

The ghost knights nodded their compliance and dragged Nearra's body away. The queen paused, then turned in Davyn's direction.

Davyn stepped back, pressing himself against the stalagmite, his heart pounding in his chest. Had she seen him?

The queen's voice echoed through the cavern. "The sentries say that her companion fell into the Dragon's Maw."

"No need to worry about him, then," the king replied. "Come. The time is nearly upon us. We have much to do."

The queen floated over to the chasm and glanced in briefly. Davyn pressed himself further into the rock, held his breath, and squeezed his eyes shut.

When he opened them again, Queen Valaria had gone.

Peering around the stalagmite, Davyn saw the ghost knights carrying Nearra out of the room on their shoulders.

Davyn's mind raced. He was badly outnumbered and his weapons had no effect on the undead sentries. It seemed that the king and queen were ghosts, too—and they were powerful enough to overcome Nearra. What could he do? Fear and despair clutched at his heart.

Then, an awful thought occurred to him: was this all part of Maddoc's plan?

Davyn collapsed to the cave floor, fighting the urge to either weep or retch. How had he let his friends get into this terrible situation?

All the others might be dead by now. The sentries might be taking Nearra to her death even as Davyn sat here, feeling sorry for himself.

The thought of Nearra perishing steeled the resolve within him. The ranger rose to his feet and wiped the sweat from his face.

Davyn drew his bow and nocked an arrow. Then he dashed across the cavern in the direction he'd seen the sentries take Nearra.

Though fear still wrenched at his guts, he would *not* fail his friends again. He would not fail Nearra. Not this time.

CHAPTER

25 THE CURSE

The world was made of gray mist and numbing cold. Catriona lay in the center of it, aware only of the lethargy suffusing through her whole body. Where was she? How long had she slept?

She cracked her eyes open and gazed at the stone castle ceiling above her head.

In a flash, she remembered: Alric's wounding, the long ride back to the city, the red-robed figure that came to attend him as she left, and . . .

Alric's mother! The queen had said she would save her son, and Catriona had promised to help. But then the queen had done something to Catriona—something awful.

The warrior sat up. Her head throbbed. Her limbs ached and felt very weak. She had no energy. It was as though she hadn't eaten or moved for days. Had she fallen ill?

She rubbed her eyes and, gradually, the room came into focus. She wasn't in her chamber in Castle Arngrim. She looked around. Three stone walls surrounded her and, on the fourth side stood a grate of iron bars an inch thick. She rested on a straw-covered cot. She was in a dungeon cell!

Catriona rose on rubbery legs and walked to the bars. A door, also made of iron bars, was set into their middle. A heavy lock and stout hinges secured the portal. Catriona grabbed the bars and shook them with all the might she could muster. They hardly rattled; there seemed no chance of bending or breaking them.

"I'm sorry," said a voice from outside the cell.

Catriona jumped back from the bars; she hadn't realized that anyone was watching her.

Alric Arngrim, dressed in a clean gray-and-silver tunic, stepped out of the shadows on the other side of the dungeon corridor. Beyond him, she now noticed, stood more rows of iron-barred cells, similar to hers. "Oh, Alric," she said, "you're alive!" A burst of joy flared within her chest.

He laughed bitterly. "This isn't the way I meant it to be," he said.

"What isn't the way you meant it to be?" Catriona asked. "What's happening? Why am I in this cell?" A mixture of fear and panic quickly replaced her joy.

Alric moved toward the cell and wrapped his fingers around the bars. He looked sick; his gray eyes lacked their usual sparkle. He turned his face away from her, as if ashamed.

Catriona reached out and touched his hand. Immediately she felt as though a cold dagger had plunged into her gut. She gasped as her body grew weaker and her knees buckled. Alric felt cold and insubstantial, like the fog that suffused his kingdom. She stared at him.

Alric pulled his hand away. "I'm sorry," he said again. "You shouldn't have done that. It might have killed you—though you couldn't have known, of course. Touching me is dangerous now. I have no control over it. There's not much left of me—less every moment, I'm afraid."

"What do you mean?" she asked. Fear clenched a fist in the bottom of her stomach. Every fiber of her being felt cold.

"The injury I sustained from the manticore," he said, "it weakened me severely. My life force is draining away . . . again."

"You mean you're dying?"

"Not exactly." He sighed, and paced to the other side of the corridor and back. "It's rather a long story."

Catriona clenched her fist around the bars and pulled herself upright again. "I don't seem to be going anywhere," she said. Anger and fear fought for supremacy within her. How dare he do this to her? What had he done with her friends? Were Nearra and the others all right?

"A very long time ago," he began, "before the Cataclysm, Arngrim was a great kingdom. We were a center of trade in this part of the world. Our location in this mountain valley made us an ideal rest stop for people using the Vingaard passes—for visitors from all over Ansalon.

"People of wealth and learning flocked to our city from every part of Krynn. These were great times." He paused, caught up in his memories, then continued. "Undoubtedly it was that prosperity and fame which drew the sorceress to us.

"The Scarlet Brethren were a force to be reckoned with in those days. Asvoria heard of their skills and tracked them to our home. She claimed that she came to Arngrim to learn, but almost from the beginning, we knew that wasn't the truth.

"We resisted as best we could, but even the Brethren proved no match for her power. She took what she wanted from them and then smashed them like kindling. Only one, his body broken by her magic, managed to escape. The rest of us were not so lucky."

Again, icy fear gripped Catriona's heart. "What do you mean?"

"For daring to resist her, Asvoria placed a terrible curse upon Arngrim and its rulers," Alric said. "She didn't want to kill my family outright. She wanted us to suffer—suffer endlessly. So she turned our kingdom into a land of the dead.

"She slew all our knights, then raised them as the hollow, ghostly sentries you've seen. They are undead automatons, compelled to serve, but unable to supply us with what we want most."

"Which is what?"

"Our kingdom," he replied, "the way it once was. The way it was meant to be."

"But you talk of all this as if you had been there," Catriona said. "If this happened before the Cataclysm—"

"Oh, Catriona . . . sweet, loyal Catriona. Haven't you guessed yet?" He paused and took a long, slow breath. "I, too, am dead."

Catriona gasped.

"So are my parents—so, very nearly, is the kingdom itself. Without life force to sustain us, we are no more substantial than ghosts."

"But the peasants . . . the servants . . ." she said desperately, "they're not ghosts. They toil and suffer the same as anyone." For an instant she hoped that he might be mad, that this was all some delirious nightmare rather than the truth.

"Oh, our people are real enough—as is Arngrim's suffering. Generations upon generations have lived and died in Arngrim, serving our undying reign. They both fear and love us. The curse clouds their minds. Though we have reigned for their entire lives—the lives of nearly countless generations—they do not question that our royal family never changes, that our reign never ends. They are merely grain before a scythe, while we are eternal."

"How could you do this?" she cried. "You're a good man. I've seen it! You don't want your subjects to suffer. Why didn't you flee this place and leave your people in peace?"

"We cannot," he replied. "Asvoria's curse chains us to Arngrim just as surely as it binds us to this horrible un-life. Until recently, we were little more than shadows, ruling our kingdom through the power of our sentries. Our suffering has been unfathomable. Now, though, it may, at last, cease.

"The War of the Lance changed the world. Over the centuries, the Scarlet Brethren had replenished their numbers. There are nearly as many now as there were when Asvoria destroyed our kingdom. The chaos and death that the great war brought freed energies which our wizards can shape. They've used that magic to give me substance, after a fashion. Additionally, they've discovered a way to make Arngrim whole again."

Catriona felt as though she were caught in a nightmare. Almost against her will, her lips asked, "How?"

"They will break Asvoria's curse, and return us to the land of the living. The Brethren have discovered that the life force of others can make us, make *me*, whole for a time. A small life brings only a brief span, but a powerful life force—like that possessed by a pure-hearted warrior—could revive us for good. This force—the Lionheart—if strong enough and harvested correctly can shatter Asvoria's spell. Then, as prophesied, Arngrim will return to greatness and be a power in northern Ansalon once more.

"Unfortunately, years of isolation have sapped such life force from our populace. What remains is barely enough to sustain my corporeal form. Recently, though, a strange dwarf came to the Scarlet Brethren. He knew of the prophecies regarding the resurgence of Arngrim. He knew of the chosen—whose Lionheart would destroy the curse and end Asvoria's blight. He told us that a group of travelers, young but strong of will and courage, would soon pass through our city.

"I was not here, when the dwarf told this to our wizards and my father," Alric said. "I was in the mountains, fighting against Kokar's raiders, and trying to bring those few remaining serfs who lived in the mountains to safety. Unfortunately, I was too late. Several times, Kokar nearly slew me—though I do not know whether I can truly die or not. I thought I might never return to Arngrim. And then . . . then I met you."

"I thought you wanted us to help you fight against your enemies," Catriona said, stunned.

"Force of arms is not enough to sustain Arngrim," Alric replied. "It's force of spirit we lack. That force burns brightly within you, Catriona."

Catriona looked at him, her heart pounding. "You want my life force," she said. The cold realization seeped through her mind. "I won't be the first whose life you've stolen," she said. "Will I."

"Sadly," he said, "no. The spell the Brethren used to restore me is not perfect. I need to renew my life force form time to time. Because of that, I have preyed upon those who would destroy our kingdom."

"You sucked the life from Kokar's raiders! That's why they hated you so!"

Alric turned, anger flaring in his gray eyes. "What would you have had me do, let them ravage my country? No. Far better that they should die and sustain me at the same time. Every life I've taken has been for the greater good. The kingdom must survive. My people must survive."

"So," she said quietly, "I am to be your next victim."

He drew closer to the bars, though not within her reach. "At first, that was the plan, yes. But now. . . I will not kill you, or cause you to be killed, no matter what my parents wish. I will find someone else. Even now, there is another who might be suitable."

"Who? Is it one of my friends? Alric, you can't kill any of my friends! Promise me!"

He avoided her eyes, and took something from around his neck. He held out his hand. From it, a silver pendant dangled on the end of a heavy silver chain. The medallion was a lion's head, carved in profile, with a deep blue gemstone for its eye. Catriona had seen it once before, on the day of their picnic when he'd stripped off his armor.

"Take it," he said, thrusting the medallion into her palm. "It will protect you during the coming trials." Instinctively, she closed her hand around it.

Alric turned and walked toward a stairway at the far end of the corridor. "It's not much, my love," he said, "but it's all I can offer."

Catriona took the medallion and threw it at him.

The amulet sailed through the dark, dungeon air. It struck Alric squarely in the back, and passed right through. The pendant hit the dungeon wall and clattered to the floor near his feet.

Alric glanced at it forlornly. "When I return," he said, "I will make you my queen." Then he walked away.

"Come back, you bastard!" Catriona cried. "You can't just leave me here to rot!" Her words echoed off the empty hallway. She tried to rattle the bars again, but received only a faint creaking noise in response.

Then she slumped to the floor of her cell and wept.

The Ancient Evil

As the tears streamed down Catriona's face, a familiar voice echoed in her ears.

"I hope you're not going to spend all your time crying. We really need to get out of here."

Catriona jumped to her feet, her hope returning. "Elidor! Are the others here as well?"

"I'm here," called Sindri. "We're just a couple of cells down from you—just like in the guest quarters."

"What about Davyn and Nearra?"

"We haven't seen them," Elidor replied. "The ghost knights captured us after we discovered the Scarlet Brethren had been lurking under the castle the whole time."

"You know," Sindri said, "I'm beginning to wonder if Alric and his people ever intended to help Nearra at all."

Catriona could almost see Elidor rolling his eyes at the remark. She shook the bars once more. "These cells are solid," she said. "There's no way we can break out."

"Not by brute force, perhaps," Elidor replied. "Fortunately, some of us have other alternatives."

"We were thinking about breaking out earlier," Sindri said, "but there were too many guards hanging around. Now they're all gone."

"To where, I wonder?" Catriona asked.

"Never question your blessings, as my grandfather used to say," Elidor replied. "I think, between the kender and I, we can escape from these cells in no time. But before we release you, Catriona, there's one thing I need to know."

"Yes?"

"When you get out, which side will you be on—Alric's, or ours?"

Sindri huffed. "Even I know the answer to that question."

"He's right," Catriona said. "Whatever feelings I may have had for Alric are dead now. I know who my true friends are. I vow to free Nearra and Davyn, or avenge them if necessary. I will liberate us from the evil grip of Arngrim, or I will die trying."

Davyn watched helplessly as the undead knights carried Nearra through the catacombs beneath Castle Arngrim. The caves were dank and dimly lit, making it easier for Davyn to hide. The constant clanking of the undeads' armor disguised the sound of his footsteps as well.

The young ranger walked carefully, weaving through the stalagmites, hardly daring to draw a breath. Despite the echoing clamor, he kept back a safe distance, hoping he might have an opportunity to pick off one of the rearmost sentries.

No opportunity came. Though the king and queen shot off into the darkness ahead of them, the ghost knights stayed together, marching as one. Though they numbered only six, Davyn knew he stood no chance against them. Neither his knife nor his bow could kill the monsters. Only two things had been effective against them: Nearra's magic, and toppling them into the Dragon's Maw. Perhaps three things, as he'd seen several sentries crushed under fallen pillars as well. With its armor shattered, even a ghost knight could not rise again.

With no sun or moon to tell the time, it seemed like the young ranger wandered underground for ages. Eventually, the twisting passages opened up into another huge cavern.

The cave stood taller than a four-story building, and could easily have fit three monstrous warships inside. Titanic stalactites and stalagmites crowded the cavern's fringes, but not the room's center. Filling that space was something that looked like a monstrous spider web.

Huge strands of gossamer silk stretched between the floor, the ceiling, and the glittering natural columns on either side. The fibers of the web glowed faintly with an ever-changing iridescence. Pale rainbow patterns flashed across the web, like lightning in a storm-tossed sky.

In front of the web, in an arc devoid of silken strands, lay a carved stone table. Nine red-robed wizards—the Scarlet Brethren—stood in a circle around the altar, waiting. King Conar and Queen Valaria hovered nearby, like huge vampire bats.

The undead procession crossed the chamber and gently laid Nearra on the altar. The sentries then retreated to the fringes of the chamber. As they did, Alric Arngrim entered through a side passage. He was wearing his leonine armor. He looked as proud and fierce as the day the companions had first met him, though his face seemed paler now and his gray eyes colder.

Davyn had hoped that, somehow, Alric might be an innocent pawn caught in his parents' subterfuge. Now those hopes were dashed. Clearly, the young prince was as deeply involved in this plot as the rest of his monstrous family.

King Conar grinned at his son. "Just in time," he said. "But where's the girl Catriona? Why haven't you brought her with you?"

"Catriona remains in her cell," Alric said. "She won't be taking part in this ceremony."

"Won't?" the queen asked, raising one iron-gray eyebrow.

"That's right," Alric replied. "She is no longer necessary to the rejuvenation of Arngrim. I share the psychic bond with our knights,

STEPHEN D. SULLIVAN

I know what you know." He pointed at Nearra. "That woman, there, is just as suitable for the ritual as Catriona."

"But the red-haired girl is the chosen," the king said. "She passed the test we set for her. She slew the manticore, then brought you home to us. She clearly possesses the Lionheart."

"We don't need to sacrifice her, though," Alric said. "This one will do just as well. Catriona may have passed your test by standing up to the Brethren's manticore, but this one stood up to a legion of our undead knights. She even slew many of them."

"Your personal feelings cannot enter into this, Son," Queen Valaria said. "What is the worth of one girl's life compared to the value of our kingdom?"

"You shall have your sacrifice," Alric said. "But it must be Nearra, not Catriona."

"Son," the king replied, "it is too late to change things. Preparations have already begun. Our wizards have worked long and hard for this day. They've been making our caverns ready since these strangers first entered our land."

"Who's in charge here," Alric asked, "us, or the Scarlet Brethren?"

Primus of the Brethren bowed to the prince. "You are, highness," he said. "Everything we have done, all the long centuries of waiting and planning, we have done for you."

"Then changing the ceremony should be no great difficulty," Alric said. "You've had time to study both girls?"

"Yes, my prince," the red-robed Secundus replied.

"Then make the switch."

"Alric, son," the king said, "this girl Nearra may be powerful, that's true, but when she came to our country she was wounded and weak as a newborn kitten."

"I am wounded, too," Alric said. "Would you judge my power by how I appear to you now, or by what you know to be within me? It is *because* Nearra was wounded that none of us sensed her potential. The dwarf was right when he said that the chosen could be among this group of young travelers—doubly right, it seems. His master has provided us with both a sacrifice and a future queen."

Oddvar stepped from the shadows. Davyn hadn't noticed him before. The Theiwar looked nervous.

"If I might say," Oddvar began. His voice was low, subtle, and persuasive. "It seems to me that the original course might be the best."

"You've said in the past that it didn't matter to your master who among these teenagers lived, and who died," King Conar said.

"That is true," Oddvar replied. "But working for a wizard has taught me the value of preparation. To switch subjects at a time like this, well, it could be detrimental to the success of your plan. You've worked toward this day for so long, it would be a shame to ruin it because of a boy's love for a girl. Drain the life from the young knight, as you had planned. Put her in the great web. Leave the others for later."

Queen Valaria's eyes narrowed. "I begin to wonder if this 'advice' is not some trick of our enemies."

"Enemies?" Oddvar said. "I have come here expressly as a friend. I have told you how the prophecy might be fulfilled and the curse lifted from Arngrim. Surely, you don't accuse me—"

The queen cut him off. "This girl Nearra—it may be that her amnesia was a ploy. Perhaps she was sent here by the wizard Maddoc to test us—or even to destroy us. It's plain now that she is not what she seems."

Oddvar stepped forward impulsively. "Kill the one you know will work!" he said. "Kill the girl Catriona!"

"And deprive the kingdom of a future queen?" Alric asked angrily. In an instant, he crossed the cavern and lifted the dwarf into the air.

Oddvar's eyes bugged out and his face went ashen before Alric threw him across the room. The Theiwar landed in a heap and lay motionless against one of the titanic natural pillars.

Hiding in the shadows, Davyn felt his heart grow even colder. From the way Oddvar reacted, it seemed that even Maddoc's plans had gone awry. If the lives of Nearra and all Davyn's friends hadn't been in jeopardy, he might have been pleased. As it was, the fear within him grew stronger by the moment. If the wizard Maddoc had not anticipated this outcome, what chance did he, Davyn, have to stop it?

"Perhaps our son is right," the queen said. "This dwarf and his master seem far too interested in the girl Nearra. If she is his pawn, it is better that we dispose of her. Fortunately, that suits our own purposes as well. Drain the life from this creature, whatever she may be. Then, once we are material again, Alric can marry the lady knight and begin a new dynasty in Arngrim."

"Yes," the king agreed. "Our son may have a point. Perhaps Nearra *is* the chosen. True, Catriona slew the manticore—but, against our plans, it nearly cost Alric everything. Nearra, on the other hand, destroyed an army which has survived unscathed for hundreds of years."

"In time," Primus said, "we will be able to reconstitute the knights who were dissipated. They will again enforce your rule in Arngrim, as they have done since before the curse."

The thought of these monsters escaping Castle Arngrim and founding a new dynasty shot chills up Davyn's spine. He wanted to yell, to scream that they were all mad and that no good would come from their scheme—no matter how well intentioned.

Then he realized that he might have said the same thing to his father. Maddoc's plan for the Emergence might be brilliant, it might benefit the world as a whole, but it was heartless and cruel—just like the plans conceived by the rulers of Arngrim.

The nine red-garbed wizards moved forward and lifted Nearra off the table. Carefully and deliberately, they began attaching her into the web. Their droning chants echoed through the cavern.

Only Davyn noticed when Oddvar got up and sneaked out of the room. Though he didn't want the dwarf to get away, Davyn knew he would only call attention to himself by alerting them to the Theiwar's escape.

Davyn needed a plan, but both his brain and legs seemed frozen. All he could do was watch helplessly as the wizards entangled Nearra in their silken netting. The web glowed more brightly as the Brethren wrapped the sticky strands around the girl.

What could Davyn do? If he tried to fight his way to Nearra, he would surely be killed. He doubted that he could slay the Arngrims any more than he could destroy their remaining ghost knights.

As the Brethren's spell progressed, more of the silent warriors streamed into the chamber. Davyn wondered if every knight in the castle now stood assembled around the edges of the cavern.

Suddenly, Alric moved across the room toward Davyn's position.

The ranger flattened himself against the wall, trying to blend into the shadows as much as possible. For a brief moment, he considered fleeing. No one knew he was alive. He could quit the castle and run into the mountains, never looking back. Why risk his life for nothing? He couldn't help his friends anyway.

Then his resolve firmed. That was Maddoc talking. Years of training with the wizard had left its mark on Davyn. The teenager vowed not to give in, not to take the easy way out. He rested his hand on his knife, ready to give Alric whatever wounds he could before he died.

But the young prince passed by him, oblivious. Alric continued his circuit of the chamber, apparently inspecting the ghost knights. The prince's handsome face appeared deep in thought.

Davyn let out a long, relieved breath. He stepped farther back into the shadows, but not to retreat. There was only one possible way to save Nearra. He needed to go back into the castle and find his friends.

Davyn doubted that they could win the day. But, together, they might make a death that would be worthy of a song.

ESCAPE INTO THE UNDERWORLD

T hat's it . . . easy," Catriona said, encouraging Sindri as he levitated the bits of metal
over to Elidor. The guards had stripped the elf and the kender of
anything they thought might help the companions escape. Sindri's cloak full of useful objects was gone, as were Elidor's knives
and lock picks. Catriona assumed these confiscated items—along
with her sword and helmet—occupied the cabinet she saw at the
end of the hallway.

Sindri might have used his powers to open the cabinet, but
he couldn't see it. Though his magic seemed to grow stronger
every day, he could only move things telekinetically that he
could see. That left them with few options until Elidor hit
upon an idea.

Fortunately, the guards hadn't removed Catriona's chainmail.
Perhaps Alric didn't want the ghost knights manhandling his
future bride, or perhaps the specters didn't see the need; she
and the rest would soon be dead anyway. Whatever the reason,
Catriona thanked the gods for the oversight.

Elidor wanted to take the mail apart and use the metal links to
fashion a new set of lock picks. Catriona had agreed, but she'd been
210 unwilling to surrender the whole suit to the elf. The armor had

belonged to her late aunt, and was a powerful symbol of Catriona's quest to redeem herself.

She willingly removed some links from the hem and passed them through the bars, so Sindri could levitate them to Elidor. This proved more difficult than expected. The kender levitated fairly large objects with ease now, but the wire links were difficult to see, and thus manipulate. It was like picking up needles from a straw-covered floor.

After several failures, Catriona had torn a strip of cloth from the edge of her tunic. She then bundled the remaining wires into the cloth, and Sindri quickly moved the package to the elf.

Catriona prayed that their plan would work. They'd already been imprisoned far too long. She feared that Nearra and Davyn might have been killed in the interim. She didn't know if she could forgive herself for failing to save her friends. Her burden of guilt was heavy enough already.

A lock clicked, shattering Catriona's thoughts. She smiled as Elidor appeared across the corridor. He winked at her, quickly manipulated the lock of Sindri's cell, then freed her, too. As the knight and the kender exited their cells, Elidor retrieved their belongings from the cabinet at the end of the corridor.

"They gathered all our possessions there," he said, "even our traveling packs and the extra clothing they made for us. They probably planned to dispose of them—along with our bodies."

"That's a stroke of luck," Catriona said, buckling on her short sword. "We'll need those packs. I won't stay in this accursed place a moment longer than I have to." She noticed Sindri examining a section of floor nearby. "What are you doing?"

The kender stood. "Hmm? Oh, nothing. I was just trying to figure out which way we need to go to find Davyn and Nearra."

"They might be back the way we came," Elidor said thoughtfully. "If the Scarlet Brethren are planning something, I'm betting they'll be working in the cave complex beneath the castle."

"There are catacombs beneath the castle?" Catriona asked.

Sindri nodded. "Come on. This way." He headed toward a descending passage nearby.

Elidor gazed between that stairway and the stairway up into the castle proper. "Perhaps we should split up and check the castle, too," he suggested.

"No," Catriona said. "Your first impulse was right. We should go where the wizards are. And we should stick together; there's strength in numbers."

"Sticking together could just get us all captured again, too," the elf said.

Catriona understood his conflict. Elidor was torn between helping his friends and a very sensible desire to escape.

"It took all three of us working together to get out of these cells," she said. "We're stronger as a group than separately. There's no time to argue. Every minute we spend here is another minute the guards may return."

Elidor nodded grudgingly and the two of them followed Sindri into the cave complex beneath Castle Arngrim.

They ran through narrow rock corridors and caverns filled with towering natural pillars. Looking up, Catriona saw stalactites easily large enough to crush the manticore she'd defeated. She hoped they would find no such beasts in the underground. The caverns gave her goosebumps; she couldn't imagine living in such a place.

The elf and the kender seemed unaffected by the eerie atmosphere and dim, glowing natural light. They moved cautiously but quickly. Every so often, Elidor had to remind Sindri not to talk. Catriona didn't share the kender's enthusiasm for new sights and situations. They had a mission and the young warrior stayed constantly on her guard.

As they walked, Catriona began to feel more like her old self. The lethargy and coldness from Alric's touch slipped away. She forced herself to think about the quest ahead—to find and save their friends—rather than dwelling on the failures that brought them to this juncture.

They paused in a wide cavern with several exits. "This way, I think," Sindri said, pointing to one.

"No," Elidor said. "I hear something down this one." He indicated a passage on the left.

"But this is the way we came," Sindri replied.

"The wizards weren't meeting in the cavern where we were caught," Elidor reminded him. "Their hideout lay farther ahead. This is the way, I feel cer—"

Elidor's sentence ended abruptly when a steel-armored glove clouted him in the jaw. The elf reeled backward and hit his head on a fat stalagmite behind him.

A lone Arngrim sentry lurched out of the tunnel they'd been about to enter. The ghost knight looked deformed, its armor scorched and partially melted. It wobbled slightly as it walked.

Sindri tried to trip the sentry, but it kicked him aside and drew its sword. Catriona drew her own.

The sound of their swords clashing echoed through the cavern. Though damaged, the sentry attacked tirelessly: slashing, then chopping, then lunging—low, high, and middle—trying to pierce Catriona's guard. Catriona parried each assault, though the last skidded across her chainmail-covered side. The guardsman's barrage was so furious, she found no chance to counterattack. She backed into the center of the cavern, seeking maneuvering room amid the rock formations.

A stray stone under her boot tripped her. She landed hard against a stalagmite. The sentry raised its sword for a killing blow.

Suddenly, the sword flew out of the dead knight's hand and sailed across the cavern. Sindri cheered and mopped his sweating forehead with a purple handkerchief. Elidor got to his feet once more.

Catriona thrust at the eyehole in the guard's visor. Her sword passed through the slit and clanked against the back of the helmet.

The blow carried the helmet off the guard's shoulders. The empty headpiece rattled to the floor.

Catriona gasped, staring at the vacant space where a man's head should have been. The ghost knight grabbed for her.

"We forgot to tell you," Sindri said, "there's no one inside the armor." He picked up a stone and threw it toward the back of the sentry's knees.

The rock struck hard, and the guardsman's legs buckled before it could seize Catriona in its dead embrace. She ducked aside and slashed at its weaponless arm.

The sentry proved too quick. It caught her arm in its iron glove and twisted, hurling Catriona through the air. She crashed into Elidor and Sindri, knocking them over.

The elf and the kender moaned as Catriona scrambled to her feet once more. The scorched knight charged her.

Before she could raise her guard, the undead sentry seized her, pinning her arms to her sides. He lifted her off the floor and squeezed, crushing the life out of her.

United Against the Darkness

Catriona gasped for breath. Spots danced in front of her eyes. She kicked at the knight, trying to break its grip—but the undead thing proved too strong.

Then, without warning, the sentry lurched forward and they both toppled toward the floor.

Catriona landed on the knight with a crash. The fall broke the monster's grasp and Catriona rolled away. Elidor, half-conscious, lay at the sentry's feet, his nimble fingers entwined around the guard's metal toes. The elf had tripped the monster.

The Arngrimite scrambled backward, like a wounded crab, and tried to rise. Catriona got to her feet first and kicked it in the chest plate. The sentry staggered back and crashed into a stalagmite pillar. The column cracked, raining several small rocks onto the dead knight's burnished armor. The broken pillar smacked into a large stalactite next to it, which shuddered and cracked as well. Stone dust filtered down onto the guardsman's undead form. The eerie red mist hovering above the sentry's shoulders sparked and crackled.

"Catriona, look out!" someone yelled.

A sharp cracking sound shook the cavern.

Catriona looked up and saw a gap at the base of the stalactite above the undead knight. A shattered arrow tumbled through the air and clattered to the floor beneath the sentry.

Davyn nodded to her from one of the cavern's other entryways. He aimed a second shot at the dangling rock formation.

"Sindri! The stalactite!" the ranger shouted. "Help me!" He nocked another arrow and fired again.

The kender nodded groggily and pointed his hands toward the hanging stone that Davyn had struck previously. He concentrated, and sweat beaded on his brow. As the ranger's second shot hit the stalactite's base, Sindri's telekinesis shook the stone loose from the ceiling.

The headless sentry pushed itself away from the wall, lumbering toward Catriona once more.

The huge stalactite crashed down on top of it, crushing the guardsman like an empty barrel. The red mist inside the armor popped and hissed, then quickly dissipated.

Elidor rose to his feet. "That, I guess, is how you kill a ghost knight," he said.

Sindri dusted himself off and beamed at Davyn. "Boy, am I glad to see you."

"The feeling is mutual," Davyn replied. He crossed the room and clapped Catriona on the shoulder. "Are you all right?"

"I'm fine," she said. "All things considered."

"We don't have much time," Davyn explained. "They've put Nearra in some kind of web-like spell. They're planning to suck the life force out of her."

"A fate they'd previously intended for me," Catriona said. She pushed aside the guilt springing up in her mind. If she wanted to stop Nearra being sacrificed in her stead, she needed to concentrate on the task at hand. "Do you know the way to the spell chamber?"

"Yes," Davyn replied. "Follow me."

216

He led the others back the way he'd come, winding through the twisting passages, darting across adjoining caverns. Fortunately, they encountered no more ghost sentries. "The knights share some kind of psychic bond," Davyn explained. "I heard the royal family talking about it. Maybe it has a range limit, though. Or maybe when Nea—maybe that one got damaged somehow and its link got broken."

"It looked kind of melted," Sindri said.

"Either way, I'll be grateful if we don't run into any more," Catriona said.

"Unfortunately, there are plenty of them left in the spell chamber," Davyn said. He seemed nervous to Catriona, but that was only natural, considering.

As they ran, a low, throbbing chant built and echoed around them.

"We're getting close now," Davyn said. "They'll have us badly outnumbered, I'm afraid."

"Let me worry about the fighting," Catriona said. "You concentrate on freeing Nearra."

The others nodded silently. She saw in their eyes that they feared for her safety. Catriona felt frightened, too, but she wasn't about to let it keep her from doing her job. Not this time.

They approached the cavern cautiously, moving in single file and pressing themselves against the wall. Catriona took the lead, with Davyn right behind. They paused at the entrance to the spell chamber.

"Free Nearra then escape, all of you," Catriona whispered. "I'll handle Alric and the rest of the undead."

"But that one knight nearly killed you," Sindri whispered back. "You're no match for all of them."

"Nevertheless," Catriona replied. "I've vowed to protect Nearra—and the rest of you, as well. It's my duty. Please, do as I say. I have a score to settle with the Arngrims."

The others nodded. "This is no time for foolish heroics," Elidor said. "Don't get killed if you can help it."

A grim smile crept over Catriona's face. "Don't worry," she said. "If I am to die, I'll take as many of them with me as I can."

The Arngrims and their lackeys stood gathered in the center of the room. The spell web formed an eerie backdrop, like a great glowing tapestry suspended in midair. Nearra dangled from the web's bottom edge. Her head hung limply from her neck and she seemed to be unconscious. Around her, the gossamer strands glowed and scintillated with pale colors.

In front of the girl, the stone altar shone with a dim, red radiance. King Conar, Queen Valaria, and Alric stood next to it, their hands outstretched over their heads as though beseeching the gods—or some darker force.

The Scarlet Brethren gathered in a semicircle. Standing side-by-side, they stretched out their arms, nearly touching fingers. Small sparks of reddish energy began to dance between their fingertips as they continued their droning chant.

A rank of ghost knights, each clasping a sword, kept watch just beyond the edge of the wizards' semicircle. The eyes of everyone in the room focused on the web—the center of the enchantment to restore the kingdom. The cavern shook from the noise of the incantation and the escalating power of the spell.

"Flank out along either side," Catriona whispered. "Keep hidden behind the stalagmites as long as you can. When I distract them, cut Nearra free."

"How are you going to distract them?" Sindri asked.

Catriona smiled. "By attacking."

Davyn looked from Catriona to Nearra. He seemed torn between helping Catriona and freeing his friend. Finally, he nodded and said. "Okay. Let's go."

The ranger went left while the kender and the elf sneaked to the right. Catriona waited in the entryway, keeping as much out of sight as she could. She planned to wait until her friends were halfway around the room's circumference—close to the edges of the web.

At the center of the web, Nearra's eyes flicked open. Her pupils went pure white. Her mouth gaped in a voiceless scream. Then her slender body jerked and trembled in convulsions.

Catriona knew she couldn't wait any longer.

She charged the back row of the ghost knights' formation, plowing into her enemies like an enraged bull. Two sentries lurched forward, falling into members of the Scarlet Brethren. The wizards collapsed under the weight of the ghosts' heavy-armor.

Catriona swung her sword, severing the weapon arm of one guardsman. She knocked the helmet from another with her pommel on the backswing. The sentries turned, confused, and the chant within the chamber wavered.

"Keep up the spell!" the king shouted. "The guards will deal with this interloper."

Nearra's body writhed. A piercing wail escaped her lips.

Catriona pushed past the startled guardsmen and ran her sword through Primus's back. The leader of the Scarlet Brethren col-lapsed, bleeding, onto the cavern floor.

The young warrior smirked. The wizards, at least, seemed mortal. She turned to strike another, but a sentry stepped between Catriona and the wizard. The guard swung at her head, while a second ghost knight lunged for her back.

Catriona dodged aside just in time. The second guardsman impaled the first and the first sunk his sword into the second's helmet. As the two tried to extricate themselves, Catriona lopped off their legs at the knees. The two knights fell and flailed on the stone like pinioned bugs.

Catriona smiled, but paid for it when Secundus's dagger stabbed at her spine. Catriona's mail turned the blow aside, saving her life, but the attack left a painful bruise. Catriona spun and smashed the sorceress across the face. Secundus fell into the king, and both of them went down.

With their circle broken, the Scarlet Brethren edged away from Catriona to regroup. The Arngrim sentries surged forward, protecting their masters. Catriona slashed at one ghost knight and then another. From the corner of her eye, she noticed her friends creeping toward Nearra. None of the Arngrimites had yet noticed her companions.

An undead knight charged at Catriona, swinging its sword wildly. She ducked under the blow, stepped forward, and flipped the thing over her back. The knight sailed into the edge of the great web and stuck there.

Sparks shot from its armor and a sickly green steam leaked into the air. The knight trembled for a long moment, then its scorched shell clattered to the floor. Catriona's heart leaped. She'd found another way to kill them!

She pushed a second into a corner of the web, making sure to keep the sentry far away from where her friends were trying to free Nearra. The second guardsman died sizzling like the first. More charged at her, seeking to avenge their destroyed comrades.

Beyond the melee Catriona spotted her friends working on Nearra's bonds. The companions didn't seem to be doing very well; many sticky strands of netting wound around the girl's body.

Catriona needed to buy Davyn and the others more time. She backed up, putting stalagmites between her and the sentries, playing cat and mouse with the ghosts, striking fast and quickly retreating.

Alric and the queen helped the king to his feet. The remaining Scarlet Brethren stood close together, chanting. As one, they raised their hands and pointed at Catriona. She ducked behind a pillar just as their spell struck.

Red light exploded in her eyes as the top of the stalagmite

shattered. Shards of stone pelted her armor and helmet. The remains of a ghost knight staggered past, its body missing from the waist up. Apparently, it had been caught in the crossfire. The bisected guardsman fell to a clattering halt next to Catriona's feet.

The Scarlet Brethren aimed another spell in her direction. Catriona seized a rock and threw it at the circle of wizards, striking one in the head. The group's new spell disintegrated in a hiss of black smoke and sparks.

"Kill her, Alric! Kill her!" the king urged, pushing his son forward. "Is this the woman you would make queen?"

Alric stopped, glancing from his parents to the young warrior.

His eyes caught Catriona's and she paused a moment. In that instant, the sentries descended upon her. She batted aside their swords, disarming many. Even weaponless, they kept coming, like a swarm of monstrous insects.

They grabbed her arms and legs, ignoring the cuts she inflicted upon them.

"Don't kill her!" the queen hissed. "We can use her life force for Alric." Valaria's aged face pulled into a wicked smile.

The sentries grappled with Catriona. She held tight to her sword, but they pinned her arms, and latched onto her legs. She screamed with frustration as they lifted her up and dragged her toward the altar.

Secundus, having recovered from her fall, drew a curved dagger and approached the captured knight. "Your life will flow directly into the prince," she said, preparing a fatal cut. "Your death will make him strong."

Catriona glanced at Alric. His face looked torn, but the king maintained a tight grip on the prince's arm. One of the guardsman pulled Catriona's head back, baring her neck for the knife.

Just as the dagger descended, Secundus's hand went limp and the knife clattered to the floor. One of Elidor's throwing knives had pierced her throat. She burbled incoherently and fell to the floor.

Catriona wanted to both cheer and cry as Sindri and Elidor stepped from the shadows. Her friends were brave, but now all of them—save perhaps Davyn and Nearra—were doomed.

Elidor threw a knife at the king, but Conar saw it coming and became incorporeal. The blade passed through him and stabbed a nearby member of the Scarlet Brethren.

At that moment, the queen noticed Davyn trying to cut Nearra free from the web. "Get them!" Valaria roared. "Get them all and kill them!"

Two of the wizards turned and pointed toward Davyn—but they didn't catch the ranger unprepared. At the queen's bellow, he had stopped cutting the web and grabbed his bow. He aimed at the wizards facing him, then spotted another taking aim on Catriona.

The warrior had struggled free in the confusion and was again chopping at knights, trying to fight her way to her friends. A wizard pointed a sparkling finger at her, but an arrow from Davyn hit the man's arm, spoiling the spell.

The ranger paid a high price for helping his friend. A volley of crimson magical darts streaked from the Brethren into his body. Davyn gasped and collapsed at the base of the web, just below where Nearra dangled.

"Davyn!" Catriona screamed. From this distance, she couldn't tell how badly he'd been wounded.

The companions' sudden attack had taken the ghost knights and their masters by surprise. Now, though, the Arngrimites regrouped. The undead sentries closed ranks and advanced on the tiring companions. The remaining wizards turned their backs to the conflict. The Brethren resumed chanting, funneling the power of their dead and wounded into the Great Spell surrounding Nearra.

Catriona pushed past the undead, dodging around stone pillars, toward Sindri and Elidor. The sentries swarmed in from all sides, pressing the three embattled companions back toward the wall of the cave.

"Show them no mercy!" the king hissed. "Their interloping nearly ruined the Great Spell!"

Catriona, Elidor, and Sindri, their backs to the wall, exchanged glances. Each knew they'd reached the end.

29   BENEATH THE MASK

Catriona batted a ghost knight's blade aside and lopped off the creature's sword arm. Two more rushed in to take the injured wraith's place.

Sindri fell, bleeding from a cut across his forehead. Catriona stepped forward, protecting the kender's body, knowing it would leave her back exposed. Elidor shifted to cover her, but paid for it with a stab in his left thigh. He yelped and his knives flashed. The sentry's iron-gloved weapon hand fell, severed at the wrist. Another ghost knight replaced the disarmed one.

"Nice knowing you, Catriona," Elidor said through clenched teeth.

Despite his tone, Catriona knew he meant it. "You, too, Elidor," she replied. "Too bad we couldn't free Nearra."

The elf didn't reply, but their backs were pressed together, and she felt him nod.

Sorrow mingled with pride welled up inside Catriona. She felt sad that she hadn't been able to protect her friends as she'd promised to. She'd tried, but it hadn't been enough. On the other hand, she had done her best. In the end, that was all any knight, even a full-fledged one, could do. This time, at least, she hadn't run. Perhaps that made up for deserting her aunt.

Dying to prove her loyalty was cold comfort though. The undead knights closed in for the coup-de-grace. Catriona steeled herself. At least she would be dying among friends.

A sword flashed out of the mob at her. It struck her helmet, but didn't penetrate. The blow made Catriona's skull ring and her eyes blur. She winced and fought back, slashing with all her might.

To her astonishment, the crowd of knights parted before her.

The next instant, she saw the reason why.

"Alric!" Catriona cried.

Prince Alric Arngrim waded into the undead knights, his rune-carved sword flashing. Grim determination filled his gray eyes.

"Alric! What are you doing?" his mother screamed.

Alric beheaded one of the Arngrim sentries. Sparks flashed where the prince's royal blade met undead enchantment. The creature toppled into its comrades, dead.

"I'm protecting the woman I love," Alric replied. "I won't save this nation at the cost of my soul!"

"Fool!" the king shouted. "Even if you slay all our undead subjects, your soul was forfeit the moment we opposed Asvoria! The best any of us can hope for is survival—and to regain the kingdom we lost so long ago. Your duty is to your family and to Arngrim! Kill that girl!"

Alric ignored his father. He and Catriona fought side by side. Her sword could not slay the knights, but his apparently could—perhaps an effect of the curse that bound them together. So she defended his back, and set up their opponents for Alric's killing blows. With Catriona and the prince pressing the fight, Elidor helped Sindri to his feet.

"Go!" Catriona whispered to the elf. "Take Sindri and try to free Nearra. Then get out of here as quickly as you can. Alric and I will hold them."

Elidor nodded.

"I'm okay," Sindri said woozily. He pushed himself away from the elf. "I can help."

"Help, *me* then," Elidor said, "and be quick about it!" He pulled the kender by the collar and, together, they skirted the edge of the cavern to where Davyn had fallen.

Catriona knocked down another ghost knight and Alric ran it through.

"If the slaughter of innocents is the price for saving our kingdom," Alric called to his parents, "then Arngrim does not deserve to be saved."

"Son!" the queen replied. "Think of all we've done so far, all the sacrifices we've made! We've waited centuries for just this moment!"

"I am thinking of what we've done," Alric replied, "and it sickens me." He chopped at another knight, but a sword thrust got under his guard. The weapon pierced the chainmail beneath the prince's arm.

Catriona spun and chopped the attacker's sword in half. Alric grunted and staggered. Seeing their opportunity, the king and queen closed in.

"I won't allow you to ruin our plans," Conar said. A glance from the king's feral eyes caused the remaining Scarlet Brethren to turn toward the combatants once more.

"I'm sorry we have to do this, Son," the queen said.

"In the end," the king added, "you'll see it's for the best."

Glowing red bolts flashed toward Alric from the Brethren's outstretched hands. Catriona stepped between the prince and the wizards, taking the enchanted missiles in her chest.

She gasped and the cavern spun around her. She heard Alric scream—very dimly, as though he was far away. The prince thrust Catriona aside and slashed at his parents. His rune-carved sword had no effect on the king and queen. They grabbed him by the arms and pulled him away, their undead eyes gleaming.

Catriona toppled back, leaning against a stalagmite, fighting to remain conscious. Around her, half a dozen ghost knights lay slain, their empty armor strewn across the floor. Beyond them, the king and queen tugged Alric aside, clearing the way for more sentries to finish what the red wizards had begun. The Brethren watched calmly, their hooded eyes shining with bloodlust.

Only Catriona noticed Davyn getting to his feet.

The world slowed to a crawl.

The evil knights closed in on her.

Alric fought in vain against his parents.

Elidor and Sindri joined Davyn in cutting Nearra from the web.

Everything seemed so remote—so unreal—as if Catriona were living in a dream.

She tried to raise her sword, but her arm wouldn't obey.

Alric screamed something. "Catriona!" she thought, but she couldn't hear through the blood pounding in her ears.

The ghost knights raised their weapons. Catriona knew her life was about to end, but she could do nothing to stop it.

King Conar and Queen Valaria smiled victoriously.

CHAPTER

30 THE DOOM OF ARNGRIM

KHOOM!
A deafening roar filled the vast cavern.

Davyn and the others severed the last strands binding Nearra to the monstrous spell web. They pulled the girl down, and hurried toward the nearest tunnel exit.

Catriona smiled weakly and a horrible burden lifted from her heart. Her friends were escaping! She'd bought them the time they needed. She'd won!

Her senses stopped reeling as the spell chamber erupted into chaos.

The dead knights coming at her froze in midstride. Their blades hung in the air, poised mere inches from her flesh. Catriona quickly backed away and ducked around a pillar.

Alric's parents and the Scarlet Brethren howled as the spell holding the web together shattered. Uncontrolled magic swirled through the cavern. Bolts of purple lightning flashed everywhere, striking down both wizards and undead knights.

"What have you done?" the queen wailed at the prince. "What have you done?!"

Alric pushed himself away from his parents. He fought through
the last of the sentries surrounding Catriona.

The remaining red wizards ran frantically around the cave, seemingly unable to escape.

The shimmering web twisted loose from its moorings. It wavered and twitched, wafting through the dank air like a monstrous floating jellyfish. Its gossamer tendrils flailed, unleashing bursts of deadly magic. Three more of the Brethren and two knights disappeared in puffs of oily black smoke.

The king and queen stood petrified with horror. They screamed like wounded banshees, their eyes glued to the berserk magical web. At the center of the broken spell, a swirling darkness formed.

Alric shoved the last of the undead guards aside. Catriona raced into his arms. They embraced, but only for the briefest instant. Catriona felt the chill of his touch and shuddered.

"We have to get out of here!" he said, shouting to be heard above the wailing of the magic gone wild. She nodded and they staggered around the edge of the room, toward where she'd last seen Davyn and the rest.

A howling wind built inside the cavern as the darkness within the web grew. Biting gusts lashed the couple as they forged their way through the stalagmites. Catriona spotted the exit ahead of them and pointed.

The cyclone clawed at the warrior and the prince, trying to pull them into the growing darkness in the center of the room. Catriona gritted her teeth and fought on. They would not give up! They would make it out of this nightmare alive!

The blackness that had been the spell web swirled faster with every moment, sucking everything nearby into its greedy maw. The empty armor of the ghost knights and the bodies of the Scarlet Brethren flew through the air and vanished into the void.

Howling hurricane winds and ear-splitting thunder shook the cavern. Catriona and Alric clung to the stalagmite pillars, trying to cross the last few yards to the exit tunnel. Step by painful step they crept forward.

Roaring like wounded lions, the king and queen of Arngrim descended upon the couple. Murderous hatred gleamed in the royal parents' red eyes; their fingers had transformed into hideous talons; they bared their fang-like teeth and ripped at the youngsters with their claws.

The queen's long fingernails tore into Catriona's left calf.

Catriona screamed and lost her footing. The wind pulled her toward the swirling darkness.

"No!" Alric cried. He grabbed Catriona's hand and cold agony shot through her. He yanked her to her feet and thrust her toward the exit with all his might.

Catriona lurched forward into the escape tunnel, out of the spell's grasp. She turned and extended her hand to the young prince. His parents ripped at him, trying to claw their way to Catriona, tearing the leonine armor from Alric's pale body.

Sorrow filled Alric's gray eyes. "I'm sorry, Catriona," he said. "It just wasn't meant to be."

He seized his parents in his arms. They shrieked like demons, slashing his face, gouging long lines down his handsome cheeks. He sprang toward the center of the cavern, thrusting them all toward the maelstrom.

The black cyclone caught them and sucked them in.

Catriona screamed. "Nooooo!"

The swirling darkness expanded as the last of the Arngrims vanished into its depths.

Tears burst from the young warrior's eyes. She felt the tug of the growing whirlwind, but it didn't matter. Nothing mattered any more.

"Catriona!" a voice called. A familiar hand grabbed her sleeve.

"Elidor?"

The elf nodded. "Davyn and the others went ahead," he said. "We thought you might still make it. I'm the quickest, so naturally I was elected to stay behind. Come on!"

She nodded weakly and he put his arm around her, guiding her up the passage as, behind them, the dark maelstrom grew.

They ran as fast as their legs would carry them, up through the catacombs to the castle entrance far above. As they went, the walls of the castle crumbled. Rotting beams fell from the ceiling and cracked stones crashed down close to their heads.

They caught up with Davyn, Sindri, and Nearra at the castle gate. Outside the palace, chaos filled the city streets. Peasants ran pell-mell, seeking shelter as the city disintegrated around them.

"Get out, you fools! Get out!" Catriona cried. She couldn't tell if anyone heard her.

The companions kept going. They raced through the city and out the gates into the foggy countryside beyond.

Arngrimites fled around them. Some paused long enough to curse at the companions. Most, though, were too busy saving their own lives.

Catriona and the rest climbed up the bluff overlooking the city. As they reached the hill's crest, the earth shook. A shudder ran beneath their feet, and all five companions toppled to the ground. They looked back toward the city.

A nightmarish black vortex had formed in the center of Arngrim. Around it, the buildings crumbled and faded. Winds howled like a legion of damned souls. The spinning, web-like spell reached its tendrils into every part of the city, pulling Arngrim down, sucking it in.

The furious cacophony of destruction built until the hills quaked and the mountains trembled.

Just as it seemed the world could survive no longer, the devouring blackness halted.

In an instant, the dark spell turned back upon itself and vanished.

Silence reigned.

The companions looked down where Arngrim had once been, but saw no trace of the city.

It was as if Alric, the palace, and his whole accursed kingdom had never existed.

Only the fog remained.

31   RUINS

Davyn picked himself up and peered into the fading mist. He shook his head in disbelief. If not for the wounds he and his friends had suffered, he might have thought the whole experience nothing more than a terrible dream.

Catriona buried her head in her hands.

Davyn kneeled down next to Nearra. He pulled some strips of cloth from his pack and bandaged her wounds, then dabbed some water across her pale face. The web had left terrible purplish marks all across the girl's body. Davyn couldn't help but feel that this—all of it—was somehow his fault.

He rubbed the bruises on his chest where the Scarlet Brethren's spell had struck him. His muscles ached and throbbed. Probably, he deserved worse.

Sindri smiled and dusted himself off. "Well, that wasn't as bad as it could have been," he said.

"Not as bad, how?" Elidor asked.

"Well, we all made it out alive, didn't we?" the kender replied.

"You little fool!" Davyn snapped. "We're no closer to helping Nearra now than when we started! We're battered and bruised, and homeless, and without provisions . . . We were lucky to get out with our packs and belongings!"

He stared daggers at the kender.

"Sindri's right," Catriona said quietly. She stood and wiped the tears from her face. "We're alive. We should be grateful." She looked back toward where the city had been and her eyes misted over again. "Not everyone was so lucky."

"Not everyone was *alive* to begin with," Elidor said.

Catriona rounded on him, anger flaring in her emerald green eyes, but she held her tongue and, finally, turned away instead. "How's Nearra?" she asked.

"I think she'll be okay," Davyn replied. "She's pretty beat up, of course, and the gods only know what that magical web did to her. Fortunately, I think we got her out in time."

"I . . . I'll be okay," Nearra said. Her blue eyes flickered open and she stared up at her companions. "What happened?"

"The Arngrimites tried to kill us," Elidor said, "and you especially."

"Me?" Nearra said. "Why?" She looked hopefully at Davyn.

"They seemed to think you were chosen to free them from some kind of curse," the ranger replied. He hoped that she wouldn't press the question.

"What kind of curse?" she asked.

"They were all dead," Sindri said, cheerfully. "At least, that's what I figure, having heard what Alric told Catriona. It was pretty awful."

"Dead?"

"Yeah, the whole bunch of them," the kender replied. "The kingdom, too, as near as I can guess. They put you in some kind of big magical spell. Then we broke you free and the whole city just up and vanished. It was one of the most amazing things I've ever seen."

Nearra chuckled. "I'm almost sorry I missed it." Davyn gave her another drink of water.

She sat up and then struggled to her feet. "I guess the Scarlet Brethren didn't work out, then," she said, forcing a smile.

"Nope," Sindri said. "They were part of the whole evil plan."

Nearra rubbed her brow gingerly. "At least my headache is gone."

Davyn nodded, suspecting that this was merely the calm before the next storm. And with Maddoc watching their every move . . .

The young ranger froze. Off to their left, a dark shape moved across the snow-dappled hills. The figure skirted between the rocks, trying hard to stay out of sight. Oddvar!

Davyn quickly nocked an arrow to his bow and fired it in the direction of the dwarf.

Catriona sprang to his side, her sword in hand. "What?" she asked. "What's wrong? What are you shooting at?"

Davyn shook his head. "Nothing," he replied. "I thought I saw something, but it was only a shadow."

Elidor nodded. "We've all been seeing shadows lately," he said. He looked meaningfully from Davyn to Catriona, but they both turned away. "So," the elf continued, "what are we going to do now?"

"Oh! I know!" Sindri chimed. "We could go to Tezrat Junction. I heard about it in the Arngrim marketplace."

"No!" Davyn barked. "I know that place. Going there will just take us into more peril." Actually, he didn't know anything about Tezrat Junction. He suspected, though, that the location might have been planted for Sindri to find—just as Maddoc had planted the map that led them to Arngrim in the first place. Davyn swore to himself that he would *not* lead his friends into another of his father's traps.

"But I'm sure . . ." Sindri began.

"So am I," Davyn replied. "Going to Tezrat Junction is a dangerous way to pass through the mountains. I know a quicker, safer way."

"Does this way have a name?" Elidor asked skeptically. "Or are we just going to blunder our way through the Vingaard peaks?"

"Oh, so you've become a *real* guide now?" Davyn shot back caustically. He wouldn't give Maddoc another chance to betray the group. He would take matters into his own hands and foil his father's wicked schemes. He would protect his friends—even if they never had any idea that he was doing so. "Anything Sindri found out in Arngrim is suspect," he said. "Alric was an evil man. The whole kingdom was evil."

As he said it, Davyn felt the gut-wrench of hypocrisy. He was the one who had really led them into Arngrim. He was the one who hadn't had the guts to truly disobey his father or even to tell his friends the truth. This time would be different.

"Alric *wasn't* evil," Catriona said, glaring angrily at Davyn. "In the end, he saved me—he saved us all. It cost him his life. You can't ask for any more than that."

Sindri tugged at her sleeve. "I nearly forgot. . . I have something for you," the kender said. "It materialized in my pocket after we'd left the dungeon. I'm sure it must be a sign . . . from Alric, I mean. I'm sure he meant you to have it, even though you threw it away."

The kender reached into his cloak and pulled out the lion's head medallion that Alric had given to Catriona in her cell. Sunlight peeked through the iron gray clouds overhead. The lion's silver face glistened and the stone of its blue eye twinkled.

Catriona bit her lower lip to keep it from trembling. She took the pendant from the kender and hung it around her neck. It felt cold—like Alric—but it gave her comfort.

As Davyn and the others made ready to leave, Catriona collected stones and built a small cairn in memory of her Arngrim prince. She knelt to place the final rock on Alric's memorial and noticed a tiny flower, poking up nearby.

Catriona gazed at the delicate bloom: bright yellow, like sunshine, symmetrical, perfect. It blazed amid the gray, dead foliage—a tiny ray of hope in the bleak landscape. Perhaps summer had, at long last, returned to Arngrim.

Catriona shuddered and a long sigh escaped her parched lips.

"Come on. Let's go," Davyn said. "Follow me." He hiked upslope into the jagged peaks once more. Nearra, Sindri, and Elidor fell into line behind him.

With a final, longing glance, Catriona turned away from the empty space where the great city had once stood.

She clasped the Lion of Arngrim close to her chest, then walked into the snow-capped mountains alongside her friends.

The adventure continues in

THE DRAGON WELL

by Dan Willis

Determined to escape from Maddoc, Davyn leads his friends deep into the Vingaard Mountains. Fending off goblins and armed raiders, it seems Nearra and her friends will never find the truth about Nearra, or a safe place to hide. But then they meet a mysterious woman, a seer who's had a vision of Nearra's destiny—and a vision that could destroy them all.

The clairvoyant predicts the friends will defeat the bandit king terrorizing her village home. When they return victorious, she will reveal how Nearra can recover her identity, once and for all. Desperate to help Nearra, the group strides into battle. But soon the mission turns to disaster. Ancient powers rise before them. Secrets long buried come to light. And none of them will ever be the same.

Available September 2004

ACKNOWLEDGMENTS

Like most of my books, this one would never have been written without the love and support of my family, especially my wife Kiff, and my children, Julie & Kendall.

Thanks also to Tracy Hickman & Margaret Weis, for imagining such a great world and—once again—allowing me to play in it.

WANT TO KNOW HOW IT ALL BEGAN?

WANT TO KNOW MORE ABOUT THE **DRAGONLANCE®** WORLD?

FIND OUT IN THIS NEW BOXED SET OF THE FIRST **DRAGONLANCE** TITLES!

A RUMOR OF DRAGONS
Volume 1

NIGHT OF THE DRAGONS
Volume 2

THE NIGHTMARE LANDS
Volume 3

TO THE GATES OF PALANTHAS
Volume 4

HOPE'S FLAME
Volume 5

A DAWN OF DRAGONS
Volume 6

Gift Set available September 2004
By Margaret Weis & Tracy Hickman
For ages 10 and up

ENTER A WORLD OF ADVENTURE

Do you want to learn more about the world of Krynn?
Look for these and other **Dragonlance®** books in the fantasy section
of your local bookstore or library.

TITLES BY MARGARET WEIS AND TRACY HICKMAN

Legends Trilogy
TIME OF THE TWINS, WAR OF THE TWINS,
AND TEST OF THE TWINS
A wizard weaves a plan to conquer darkness—
and bring it under his control.

THE SECOND GENERATION
The sword passes to a new generation of heroes—
the children of the Heroes of the Lance.

DRAGONS OF SUMMER FLAME
A young mage seeks to enter the Abyss in search of his lost uncle,
the infamous Raistlin.

The War of Souls Trilogy
DRAGONS OF A FALLEN STAR, DRAGONS OF A LOST STAR,
DRAGONS OF A VANISHED MOON
A new war begins, one more terrible than any in Krynn have ever known.